The Ghost
of
Golden Joe

K.T. McGivens

Cover Design by Regina Madlem

Copyright © 2020 Lillian Finn

ISBN: 979-8-61-619152-6

CONTENTS

AUTHOR'S NOTE

For some time, scientists have been aware that the seasonal flu virus mutates each year, and that even without the creation of a new vaccine, ones used in previous years do provide some protection. However, the flu epidemic of 1947 is notable for the complete failure of a vaccine effectively used in the 1943-44 and 1944-45 flu seasons. Although there was not a significant increase in deaths that year caused by the flu, it did highlight the need for scientists to continuously monitor and characterize each seasonal flu virus and evaluate each vaccine created to combat it.

CHAPTER 1
THE LEGEND

"You need glasses, Katie! That ball was definitely out!" exclaimed the voice from the other side of the net.

"Not so, Ruthie. It was most definitely in," replied Katie Porter, brushing a strand of light brown hair from her face. "But since I'm so far ahead and this is match point, I don't mind playing it over."

Ruth White, her best friend since childhood, spun her tennis racket in her hand several times before bending her knees and rocking up on her toes in preparation for Katie's serve.

Katie's execution was superb and the ball came flying past Ruth with such great speed that it caused her to swing and miss. Katie's Yorkie, Nugget, retrieved the tennis ball and, trotting past Ruth, dropped it at his mistress's feet.

"Ace!" That's the game," shouted Katie, bending over to pat the little dog and pick up the ball. She walked over to the side of the tennis court to wipe the sweat from her brow with a hand towel and take a drink of water. The two friends were practicing for the annual tennis tournament hosted by the Fairfield Country Club.

"Either you're playing remarkably well or I'm playing remarkably poorly because I usually give you more of a challenge," sighed Ruth, mopping her face with her towel.

"You are a little off your game," replied Katie with a nod. "But I think I'm also having a really good day. I'm feeling very energetic this afternoon!"

"Yes," agreed Ruth, smiling. She looked at her friend intently.

"But it's more than that. You're happy, Katie. Happier than I've seen you in a very long time. Must be love."

"Don't be daft Ruthie!" chuckled Katie, blushing. "I'm usually in a good mood."

"There's being in a good mood, Katie dear," teased Ruth, her eyes twinkling. "And then there's being euphoric!"

"Well, I suppose it's because things are going very well lately," remarked Katie in mock defensiveness. "Gran is recovering nicely from her bad cold, I've been assigned a very interesting story concerning our local bank robberies, and you and I are going to win the doubles category in the Country Club Tennis Tournament."

"You're also going to win singles," Ruth pointed out. "And I think we have a very good chance of placing in mixed doubles for the very first time. But I believe your mood has more to do with Jim Fielding than anything else. And speaking of love," she added, picking up her racket and glancing around. "Where are the fellas?"

As if right on cue, their tennis partners came around the corner of the Rosegate mansion and jogged toward the courts.

"Sorry I'm late," said Ruth's fiancé, Robert Reed. "Surgery took a little longer than I anticipated. Hello darling!" He scooped Ruth up in his arms and swung her around.

"Put me down you crazy man," scolded Ruth, but she was laughing. "I'm hot and sweaty."

"My apologies as well," added Jim, stepping forward. "I was held up on the phone trying to nail down an interview for an article I'm writing."

"We've already been playing for over an hour, so we'll take a break while you warm up," remarked Katie, receiving a kiss on the cheek from him.

"Any excuse to sit and admire our athletic prowess," said Robert, grinning at the two women and flexing his biceps.

"Yeah, sure. That's it," replied Katie sarcastically as she walked over and sat down on the bench next to the tennis court.

Ruth just shook her head and gave him a smack on his backside with her tennis racket.

"Ouch!" Robert exclaimed, chuckling. "Hey, aren't you going to back me up, Jim?"

"No," replied Jim, pulling off his sweater. "I know better than to contradict my tennis partner," he added, giving Katie a wink.

The two men batted the ball back and forth across the net for several minutes and, truth be told, Ruth and Katie did enjoy watching them. Both men were excellent tennis players with Jim being the slightly better of the two. At twenty-four, he was a year younger than Robert and a bit more muscular in build. He was also much lighter on his feet and his body flowed gracefully over the court seemingly without much effort.

"Much like he dances," thought Katie to herself, reflecting on the few times she had danced in his arms. She dropped her head and pretended to examine her racket to hide the fact that she was blushing. A few weeks ago, she had finally given up trying to convince herself that she had no interest in Jim Fielding and had accepted his invitations to go dancing twice, to the movies twice, and once to dinner. They also met nearly every day for lunch at Polly's Coffee Shop. It had become their favorite place to eat and was conveniently located between the two newspaper headquarters where they each worked as reporters; Katie at the *Fairfield Gazette* and Jim at the *Middleton Times*.

"Dining with the enemy," E.M. Butler, her newspaper colleague and friend, had teased her. "But I really can't blame you. You make such a handsome couple."

"Occasionally eating lunch together doesn't make us a couple, E.M.," Katie had replied.

"More like every day," he had countered. "But stay in denial if it pleases you, Katie Porter. You'll come to your senses sooner or later."

Watching Jim now on the Rosegate tennis courts made Katie's heart flutter and she had to admit that E.M. was right. She was definitely attracted to Jim Fielding and, if she was completely honest with herself, probably had been from the moment they had met.

"OK, I think we're ready," Jim said to the waiting women. "Katie, how about you play the net and I'll cover back court."

"Right you are, chief," Katie replied, getting up from the bench and walking onto the court. "But try not to hit me in the back with the ball today. I still have a bruise from the last time we played."

"I've apologized at least a million times for that!" Jim huffed, placing his hands on his hips. "But in my defense, how was I to know that you would step right into the path of the ball?"

"Hey now!" scolded Ruth, taking her position on the other side of the net. "Less talk and more tennis! Or are you two afraid that Robert and I will beat you again?"

"Indeed not, Ruthie!" replied Katie, bending her knees and rocking up on her toes. "Prepare for defeat!"

The competition was fierce but, in the end, Katie and Jim pulled out a narrow victory. After several hours of play, the thirsty couples retired to the sunporch for lemonade.

"Katie's covering the local bank robberies, Jim," remarked Ruth, filling her glass. "What are you working on?"

"Well, now," replied Jim, looking over at Katie. "That's quite a coincidence as I've been assigned the robberies as well! Looks like we're going to be competing for the same story, Porter."

"Then you might as well admit defeat now, Fielding," chuckled Katie. "Because I've managed to obtain an exclusive interview with Mr. Martin of the First National Bank. I'm meeting him first thing in the morning."

"Isn't he the bank president?" asked Robert, sliding his hand over Ruth's.

"One and the same," grinned Katie, nodding. "And the First National was the first bank robbed here in Fairfield."

"Very good," said Jim, smiling. "But I'm not about to concede because I also have an exclusive interview scheduled. And it's not with a banker. It's with the police sergeant assigned to the case. I'm meeting her for drinks later."

Ruth and Robert exchanged looks before glancing over at Katie, their eyebrows raised. Katie, herself, paused for a moment before saying to Jim, "Her? For drinks?"

"Jim, you devil," remarked Robert, chuckling. "Using the old Fielding charm to get the officer to spill the beans," he added, and then winced as Ruth nudged him with her elbow.

"No, it's nothing like that," Jim replied, shaking his head seriously. "Sergeant Smith can only give me a few minutes to answer questions and told me that it would have to be while she stops for dinner on her way home."

"Dinner and drinks?" replied Ruth, cocking her head to one side. "That's sounds like an awfully strange way to interview someone over something so serious."

"Just drinks," said Jim, shaking his head. "Katie and I already have dinner plans for this evening. I'm having a quick glass of wine while the sergeant waits for her meal. That will give me just enough time to ask her some questions before I pick up Katie." He reached over and took her hand. "That is, if we're still on?"

Katie relaxed and smiled. "Yes, of course," she replied, giving his hand a squeeze. "I'm looking forward to it. I can pump you for the information you got from Sergeant Smith while we eat."

"Just as I suspected," Jim replied, chuckling. "Always working an angle, huh, Katie Porter." He reluctantly released her hand as Gertie entered the room carrying a tray of finger sandwiches.

"I thought you might be hungry for a little snack," said the housekeeper, setting the tray on the table in front of them. "Since you've been playing so hard all afternoon."

"How delightful," said Katie, reaching for the nearest one. "Thank you Gertie. I believe we've all worked up quite an appetite and it's still a few hours before dinner."

"Better eat it before Golden Joe snatches it!" teased Gertie as she turned and left the room.

"Golden Joe?" asked Jim, glancing from Katie to Ruth as the two women chuckled.

"Gosh, I haven't heard that name in years," remarked Ruth, taking a bite of her sandwich.

"The threat of a visit from Golden Joe was used by the grown-ups here in Fairfield to get us kids to behave," explained Katie. "When I refused to eat my dinner, Gran or Gertie would warn me that Golden Joe might sneak into the house and snatch my plate away. The threat often worked because I preferred to eat rather than risk seeing him," she added.

"My parents told us that Golden Joe would visit children at night who were still awake after nine o'clock," added Ruth. "Tom used to try and stay awake just to see if he would really appear but he always fell asleep well before that."

"How about you, Robert?" Jim asked, smiling over at the doctor. "Any Golden Joe threats?"

"Nope," replied Robert, shaking his head. "I was a well-behaved child unlike these two here," he added, nodding to Ruth and Katie.

Ruth gave him a wink. "That's not what your mother says, Robert dear."

"How does a tale like Golden Joe get started, I wonder?" asked Jim, smiling at the engaged couple.

"I don't actually know," replied Ruth.

"I asked Gran once and she told me that Golden Joe was rumored to have been a real person about a century ago. He was a hermit who spent all his time prowling around the hills of Rosegate in search of gold. Hence the nickname Golden Joe," Katie responded. "It was a fruitless effort, of course, because there is absolutely no gold around here, which probably led him to break into shops and houses for food and supplies."

"I wonder if there is any information about him in our newspaper archives." Jim mused. "I suppose no one remembers his real name."

"You could ask his ghost," chuckled Ruth. "He's supposed to haunt the hills on occasion."

"Really?" asked Jim, curiously.

"Well, I've never seen him," smiled Katie. "But several folks in Fairfield say they have. Of course, they've usually been intoxicated at the time or kids playing in the woods and scaring each other. Why this interest in an old hermit and his ghost?"

"Oh, no particular reason really," Jim replied, shrugging. "I suppose I've always been interested in childhood tall tales, especially ghost stories. In East Haddam, where I grew up, we have several old buildings and an old Opera House that used to be a theater for stage plays. Unfortunately, it closed decades ago and is in much disrepair. Very sad because it's a beautiful building. Rumor has it that it's haunted and the town's kids used to sneak in at night in search of ghosts."

"Did you ever see one?" Katie asked, smiling.

"No, not a one," sighed Jim. Glancing down at his watch, he added, "gosh, I'd better be going! I need to shower and change clothes before my meeting. Pick you up at seven, Katie?"

"Yes, sounds good," she responded, tilting her face up as he bent down to kiss her cheek. "See you then."

"We must be leaving as well," said Ruth, slipping on her tennis sweater. "Robert has promised to look in on mother. She hasn't been feeling very well lately. Probably has the cold that's been going around."

"Gran is just getting over it herself," replied Katie. "I hope you can help her, Robert, because it's a pretty severe one."

"I'll do what I can," he replied. "But usually these things just need to run their course."

* * *

"You look very lovely, dear," smiled Gran as Katie entered the library later that evening. "Is that a new dress?"

"Thank you, Gran," replied Katie, laying her fur coat across the back of a nearby chair and twirling so that her grandmother could get a good look. "Yes, I bought it yesterday. Jim and I are going to try out that new restaurant on Willow Avenue. Camilles, I believe it's called. It's supposed to be very chic and it's their grand opening tonight."

"Sounds exciting," nodded Mrs. Porter, looking intently at her twenty-one-year-old granddaughter. "And expensive. Are you sure Jim Fielding can afford it?"

Katie paused thoughtfully for a moment before answering. "I really don't know and have wondered about that myself. I know he makes more than I do as a reporter for the *Times* but not a significant amount more. I also know that he sends money home to his mother and sister. I wouldn't mind picking up the tab once and awhile, of course. Especially at a place like Camilles. But I also don't want to insult him."

"Do you think he would be insulted?" asked Gran. "After all, it's not as though he doesn't know that you're wealthy."

"But that's just it, Gran. I don't want to flaunt that fact either. I don't know how Jim might react to being reminded of it."

She remembered a lunch meeting with him months earlier when she had barely known him. She had been following a lead concerning a story at Sunset Hill and, ironically, had been the one who had been insulted when he had offered to pay the check. In the end, he had treated the situation with respect and humor.

"Jim Fielding seems to me to be a reasonable man," remarked Gran. "If you wish to continue to go out with him, you should probably discuss this."

"You're right of course," admitted Katie, leaning over and patting her grandmother's arm. "Perhaps I'll have an opportunity to do so tonight. Now, are you going to be all right? Are you feeling better? I can always cancel my date and stay home with you."

"Don't be silly," replied Mrs. Porter, waving a hand at Katie. "Go and have a good time. Gertie and Andrews are perfectly capable of looking after me. In fact, they've been driving me crazy with their ministrations."

Katie chuckled and was just leaning over to give her grandmother a kiss when Andrews entered the room and announced Jim's arrival. The young man was on his heels and quickly stepped around the butler.

Jim Fielding was a very handsome man and often turned heads wherever he went. Katie wondered if he realized women were admiring him because he never seemed to notice. At least not when he was with her.

Although the fashions for men had begun to include more color these past two years, perhaps due to the drabness in clothing during the war, Jim tended to keep to simple classic cuts and dark colors. This evening he was wearing a black single-breasted suit with matching vest, a crisp white shirt, and a simple grey and black striped tie. Katie could just detect the familiar scent of the aftershave he wore as he came to stand near her. He held a bouquet of roses in each arm.

"Hello!" he said, a warm smile spreading across his face. He leaned toward Mrs. Porter, and with his blue eyes twinkling, handed one of the bouquets to her. "I hope you don't mind but I brought these for you. They're from my own garden. I heard that you haven't been feeling well. Of course, these roses are not as grand as your own."

Mrs. Porter was impressed. "Thank you, Jim. These are lovely. New Dawn?" she asked, recognizing their wonderful pink color and deep fragrance.

"Yes," he replied. "I've been very lucky. I've several bushes this year that have produced some beautiful blossoms."

"Indeed," replied Gran, cradling them in her arms. "Very nice."

"And these are for you, Katie," said Jim, turning to his date and handing her the second bouquet.

"Oh Jim! They're beautiful!" replied Katie, looking down at the dozen bright red roses. "I'm afraid I'm not as much of an expert as you and Gran so may I ask if these have a name?"

"They're called General Jacqueminot," smiled Jim. "Or General Jack to us simple folk."

"Well, they're simply gorgeous no matter what they're called! Thank you, Jim," said Katie, blushing slightly. "I'll ring for Andrews so that both these bouquets can be placed in water immediately.

Before she could summon the butler, however, he appeared at the doorway.

"Excuse me Miss Katie but you have a phone call," Andrews announced.

"Please take a message," she replied, glancing down at her wristwatch. "I'm on my way out to dinner." She handed him the flowers as Jim reach over to pick up her coat.

"It's Mr. Conner," replied Andrews solemnly. "He says it's urgent."

Tom Connor was the *Gazette's* editor and Katie's boss.

"Oh dear," sighed Katie, glancing up at Jim. "I'd better answer it. I'll just be a minute."

"Porter!" shouted the editor in her ear when she picked up the phone. "The Fairfield Banking and Trust has just been robbed!"

CHAPTER 2
THE BANKING AND TRUST

"I'm terribly sorry about this, Jim," said Katie as they sped down the road toward town. She glanced over and saw his slight frown and knitted eyebrows as he concentrated on the road ahead, his hands tight on the steering wheel.

"No need to apologize," he replied, shaking his head. "I'm covering the same story, remember? I suppose it's the curse of being a reporter. I bet my own editor has left me a million messages on my answering machine by now."

"True," she sighed. "Still, I was looking forward to a nice evening out."

"Were you?" he asked, turning his head briefly to give her a smile. "Well, that's one consolation at least."

They pulled up in front of the Fairfield Banking and Trust building and found it swarming with uniformed police officers from the local department. Katie noticed a very attractive well-dressed woman standing by the bank's front door apparently in deep conversation with one of the officers. She had never seen the woman before and wondered if she might be from out of town. The woman glanced in their direction as Jim moved around the car to open the passenger side door for Katie.

"There's Sergeant Smith," Jim whispered to her, tilting his head in the sergeant's direction. "Lucky break. Maybe we can get some answers from her before other members of the press arrive."

"Hello Jim," said the sergeant, nodding to him as they

approached. "I'm surprised to see you here after you told me that you had an important dinner date with your wife." She turned her gaze to Katie, her dark eyes swiftly taking note of Katie's fur coat and fashionable high heels. "But I guess she's used to having her dinner plans interrupted and being dragged along when you've got a story breaking."

"Er…no…," Jim stammered, his face turning red. "Katie and I…"

"Are working the same story," interrupted Katie, sliding her arm through Jim's. "But for competing newspapers. Imagine that! Jim works for the *Middleton Times* and I work for the *Fairfield Gazette*. But we try not to let that interfere with our daily lives, do we darling?" she added, smiling sweetly up at Jim.

"That must be challenging," remarked Sergeant Smith with a shrug as she turned back toward the bank.

"You have no idea," replied Jim, giving Katie's arm a slight squeeze.

They followed the sergeant over to the front of the bank. "There's no sign of forced entry," said the officer. "We're examining the windows now. The really interesting thing is that the thief was able to bypass the alarm system."

"Really?" asked Jim. "It wasn't tripped when they broke in?"

"No," she replied, shaking her head.

"Perhaps someone forgot to turn it on," prompted Katie, looking up at the windows that lined the building's façade.

"No, it was on," said the sergeant. "We know because we accidently set it off when we entered."

"Inside job?" asked Katie, taking out her reporter's notepad.

"Perhaps," replied Sergeant Smith. "We'll be questioning all of the bank personnel shortly."

"Exactly what time did the break-in occur?" asked Jim.

"Not more than half an hour ago," replied the sergeant. "So the clues are still fresh."

"If the alarm wasn't set off," continued Katie. "How did you know the bank was robbed?"

"A passerby thought they saw the shadow of a figure through the second story windows and called us," said Sergeant Smith.

"Hey Sarge!" shouted an officer coming around the corner. "We've got something to show you."

Jim and Katie followed Sergeant Smith around the building and stopped to look where the police officer was pointing. On the ground under an open upstairs window were two prints. They were not those of shoe prints or holes made from a ladder, but of parallel circles resembling disks.

"Unusual design," said Jim, kneeling to get a better look.

"And not very deep," added Katie, quickly sketching a picture of the prints in her notepad.

"Evans take a mold of these and get them down to the lab," Sergeant Smith commanded.

An officer peeked his head out of the open window above. "No prints on the window, Sergeant," he said, looking down at them. "I've dusted it thoroughly and nothing comes up."

"Gloves," said Jim and Katie in unison.

Just then Mr. Watkins, President of the Fairfield Banking and Trust, drove up and came to a stop in front of the building. He quickly stepped out of his vehicle as Sergeant Smith, Jim, and Katie walked back around to meet him.

"I got here as soon as I could," he said, reaching into his pocket for the keys to the bank. "I was eating at the new restaurant on Willow and it was so crowded that I had difficulty getting out."

"Camilles?" asked Katie wistfully.

"Yes, that's the one," he replied absently, his head bobbing up and down. "My word, officer, but it appears that I've forgotten my keys."

"No need to trouble yourself, Mr. Watkins," replied Sergeant Smith calmly. She pointed to the door. "We used the bank's master key that you and the other bank presidents provide us."

"Oh, yes, I see," stammered the bank president. "Well then, shall we go in?"

"So that means that the thief, or thieves, did not leave by the front door," Katie remarked to the sergeant as they entered the bank.

"Looks like that, Mrs. Fielding," replied the officer, casting a gaze around the lobby.

Katie blushed but fortunately the sergeant failed to notice. Avoiding making eye contact with Jim, Katie continued. "It seems rather awkward for them to make their escape back out the window, don't you think? Difficult to balance a bag of money while descending a ladder."

"And then there's the ladder itself to contend with," added Jim.

"The thief has to carry the money and the ladder away. Most likely he tossed the ladder in some bushes nearby before getting into a getaway car."

"Most likely, which is why my men are searching the surrounding area," replied Sergeant Smith. "It could also indicate that there were at least two thieves. One to carry the money and one to take care of the ladder."

"Of course," agreed Katie, nodding. She looked over at Jim. "One thief could have remained on the ground holding the ladder while a second man made his way up and into the bank. He returned to the window, dropped the money bag down to his accomplice, climbed back down the ladder and then carried it off."

"Sounds plausible but doesn't explain the prints or how they got past the alarm," replied Jim.

"That's true," shrugged Katie, stepping beside him as they followed Sergeant Smith through the lobby and up to the 2nd floor. Mr. Watkins had proceeded to a back room in the direction of the bank's large safe. No one was surprised to find it open.

"Anything?" said Sergeant Smith to a young officer who was dusting the safe's door for fingerprints.

"No, ma'am," he said, straightening. "Clean as a whistle."

"And no damage to the door or the lock," said another police officer, stepping forward. "This safe's been cracked."

"Interesting," muttered the sergeant, leaning over to examine the safe's combination dial.

"I still say it's an inside job," Jim whispered in Katie's ear.

Mr. Watkins stepped around the officers and entered the safe followed by Jim and Katie. There were empty bank bags and a few bills strewn across the floor but the shelves themselves were completely empty.

"I don't understand," the bank president muttered, shaking his head forlornly. "This is an *American Sentry* top of the line safe. The company assured us that this lock is nearly impossible to crack."

"Nearly impossible, perhaps," remarked Jim, glancing around and making a note in his reporter's pad. "But no matter how difficult the lock, someone's going to come up with a way to crack it."

"Where there's a will, there's a way," quoted Katie softly.

"Exactly," replied Jim. "These culprits would have blown it up with dynamite if they'd been unable to crack the combination."

"How very odd," Katie whispered under her breath. She looked intently down at the floor of the safe and then moved out into the room.

"What's that?" asked Mr. Watkins, as he and Jim followed her.

"No footprints," began Katie. "There are no footprints anywhere to be found although the ground underneath the window was soft enough to make those strange rounded marks."

They slowly made their way over to the open window carefully studying the floor as they went.

"You're right, Katie," Jim agreed, stooping occasionally to take a closer look. "Perhaps that area directly under the window is usually soft due to water runoff from the building's roof. The thief could have remained on solid ground and then stepped over and onto the ladder without ever touching the soft dirt."

"Possibly," nodded Katie. "But it's worth investigating once we're finished in here."

"So, has the husband and wife team of competing reporters solved this little mystery yet?" Sergeant Smith asked sarcastically as she walked over to them.

"No," replied Jim, giving her a charming smile. "But we're just lowly reporters, not officers of the law who have experience in such matters. Perhaps you could enlighten us?"

The police sergeant smiled back. "You mean answer more questions, don't you? Well, OK. Shoot."

"Do you have any suspects?" asked Jim.

"No," replied Sergeant Smith.

"Is this burglary connected to the one at the First National Bank?" asked Katie.

"Yes."

"What makes you think so?" asked Jim, his eyebrows raised.

"Same type of prints found under a window," said the sergeant.

"Interesting," remarked Katie thoughtfully.

"Yes, indeed," agreed Sergeant Smith, giving her a nod.

"Front door locked?" asked Katie.

"Yes."

"Thieves entered and left by a window?" asked Jim.

"Yes."

"And didn't set off the alarm?" Katie asked.

"Yes, the alarm was not tripped," answered the sergeant.

"Safe cracked?" asked Jim.

"Yes."

"Sergeant Smith!" an officer called out. "There's a call from headquarters for you."

"Sorry folks," said the sergeant turning away. "Duty calls."

"One last question, Sergeant," Katie called over to the officer, "was the window used at the First National on the second floor as well?"

"No," replied Sergeant Smith. "The third."

"Why go through the trouble of climbing in and out of windows when our safe cracking culprits could most likely easily pick the front door lock and let themselves in?" Katie asked Jim as they made their way back to the lobby.

"Too visible?" replied Jim.

Suddenly they were besieged by a crowd of press waiting in the lobby just inside the doors. Both Katie and Jim were fairly well known as reporters for their respective newspapers and this drew the immediate attention of their competitors.

"Hey, how did you two get here so quickly?" yelled a reporter from a nearby out of town newspaper. "Did you do it?"

"You'll never prove it if we did!" countered Jim smiling, as they made their way through to the front door.

"Mind if I take your picture?" shouted a photographer from a local magazine. "You're both so dolled up that it'd be a shame to miss a great photo for our society page!"

"You do and you'll be buying a new camera," Katie joked back at him, putting up her hand.

They quickly stepped outside and onto the sidewalk only to run into E.M. Butler who let out a whistle.

"My, my," he teased. "Don't you both look stunning! Is this the way you usually dress to investigate a story?"

"We were on our way out to dinner when I got the call from Mr. Connor," replied Katie, somewhat embarrassed. "What are you doing here?"

"Mr. Connor wanted some pictures to go along with your article and I happened to be available," E.M. explained, holding up the camera bag he had slung over one shoulder.

"Oh, I see," Katie remarked. "You answered your phone like I did."

"Exactly," sighed E.M. "So, what do we have?"

"Thieves entered through a second story window and cracked open the safe," said Jim, pointing to the side of the building. "Used a ladder that left very strange prints."

"Really?" remarked E.M. turning to make his way around the corner of the building.

"Yes. Katie and I are going to prowl around the area to see if we can find it," replied Jim, and then added gruffly, "and I'll give you ten bucks for some of those pictures since I see that the *Times* failed to send over one of our photographers."

"Deal," chuckled E.M., taking his camera out of the bag. "If Katie can help out a competitor, I don't see why I can't."

"Thanks, pal," Jim replied, reaching into his pocket and pulling out his wallet.

"On second thought," said E.M. with a wave of his hand. "Keep your money. I'll give you the pictures for free. Buy something nice for my dear friend here. Afterall, she's missed dinner."

Katie winced but Jim replied calmly, "it will be my pleasure." Then taking Katie by the arm, he added, "we're going to look around over there. We'll let you know if we find anything."

"Yell something like 'it sure is getting cold' or some such thing like that," E.M. suggested. "We don't want to tip off the rest of the bloodhounds."

They needn't have worried because, after searching for over half an hour, they found no trace of a ladder or any more prints. It appeared that the culprits had made a clean getaway. Eventually, E.M. left to turn in his film at the newspaper office to be developed and the rest of the swarm of press soon followed suit.

"This is very disappointing," sighed Katie, sliding into the passenger seat of Jim's sedan. "Now what?"

"Hungry?" Jim asked.

"Starving," she admitted. "But I'm not sure we can get into Camilles at this late hour."

"I know a great place just around the block," replied Jim, starting the car and pulling away from the curb. "We're a bit overdressed but it won't matter."

He turned onto Oak Avenue, took an immediate right onto 2nd Street, and then pulled into the driveway of a nice looking, single-story brick home. Well-tended rose bushes lined the way to the front porch, filling the air with a seductive scent.

"Jim Fielding," Katie said, her eyebrows lifting. "This is your house. What on earth are we doing here?"

"Eating dinner," Jim replied chuckling. "I owe you a meal and that's exactly what you're going to get. Unless you're afraid to eat my cooking?"

"I'm so hungry I'll take my chances," she answered, accompanying him up the walkway.

"May I take your coat?" he asked once they were inside. "I never got a chance to say it, but you look lovely this evening, Katie."

"Thank you," she replied, a bit embarrassed. "And I really am very sorry about Camille's."

"No need to be," Jim assured her. "I happen to know the chef here and can vouch for the food being excellent."

Katie chuckled as she slid out of her fur coat and then glanced up into his soft blue eyes. His good looks still startled her a little and she wondered if she'd ever get used to looking at him.

"What can I do to help?" she asked, following him down the short hallway and into the kitchen.

"You could pour us some wine," he answered, taking off his jacket and slinging it over the back of a chair. "Glasses are over in that cabinet and there are several bottles of wine to choose from in the pantry."

"Red or white?" she asked through the pantry door.

"Hm, let's see," said Jim, looking through the refrigerator. "Are you up for Italian?"

"I'm up for shoe leather at this point," replied Katie, popping her head around the door.

"Well, that's not very discriminating," he laughed. "But fortunately, you won't have to settle for that. I happen to have some of my famous homemade Fielding tomato sauce left so Italian it is. Red wine, I think."

"Sweet or dry?" she asked, smiling as she watched him put on an apron and tie it around his waist.

"I prefer moderately sweet, but you can have dry if you wish," he replied, placing several pots on the stove.

"Moderately sweet is my preference as well and I see a tempting Cabernet that looks promising," Katie said, disappearing back into the pantry and returning with the bottle.

Thirty minutes later they were seated comfortably around Jim's small kitchen table enjoying heaping plates of spaghetti adorned with Jim's homemade sauce. He had also added toasted bread and a large salad. They had both kicked off their shoes and Jim had loosened his tie.

"This is wonderful, Jim!" exclaimed Katie, swallowing a mouthful of spaghetti. She had a warm glow on her face, likely due to the wine, but also from the light of the small candle that Jim had placed in the middle of the table. The reflection of its flickering flame highlighted her soft brown hair and danced within her twinkling blue eyes.

She's so beautiful, Jim thought to himself. He was in high spirits and couldn't remember a time in his life when he had been this happy.

"Where did you learn to cook, Jim?" Katie asked, interrupting his thoughts. "Did your mother teach you?"

"Well, she got me started," he admitted. "She taught me just enough to get by so that I wouldn't starve to death when I left home. But, for the most part, I taught myself. I love to experiment with recipes and different types of food. I find it relaxing."

"In addition to growing roses," added Katie, smiling warmly.

"Yes, in addition to growing roses," he nodded, reaching over and refilling her wine glass before filling his own. "It's important to have things in one's life that are relaxing. Something we do just for ourselves. So, what do you do to relax, Katie Porter?"

"Well, let's see," Katie replied thoughtfully. "I love to ride my horse through the pastures at Rosegate. I love to read, and I also cook. But most of all, I love music. All kinds."

"Yes, I'm a music lover myself," Jim nodded, turning in his chair and stretching his long legs out in front of him.

"Can I admit something to you?" she asked sheepishly.

"Yes, of course," he replied, looking curiously at her.

"I absolutely love hearing you sing," Katie admitted, resting her chin in her hand as she looked across the table at him. "You have the most beautiful voice I've ever heard."

He smiled at her. "Really, Katie? Or are you just teasing me?"

"I'm being perfectly honest with you," she replied, blushing slightly.

"Well then," he responded. "I'll sing to you whenever you wish."

Suddenly there was a loud knock on the door that made them jump. They looked at each other for a moment before Jim got up and went to answer it.

"Excuse me, Jim," Katie heard a familiar female voice say. She got up and walked down the hallway to stand behind him.

"Hello Mrs. Fielding," said Sergeant Smith, giving her a nod. "Sorry to bother you at this late hour, but I thought you might like to know that a money bag from the Fairfield Banking and Trust has just been found."

"Where?" asked Katie, stepping around Jim. "Did it still contain the money?"

"No money," replied the sergeant evenly. "The bag was found along the edge of the woods on the Rosegate Estate. I believe that's your grandmother's property, is it not, Miss Katie Porter? You're coming with me down to the police station for questioning."

CHAPTER 3
KATIE IS QUESTIONED

"So, where were you between the hours of 5:00 and 7:00 this evening?" asked Sergeant Smith rather aggressively. She sat on the other side of a small table in a tiny room used to interrogate suspects and glared at Katie.

"I was getting ready for a dinner date," Katie replied, looking directly into the dark green eyes of Sergeant Smith. The police officer's questioning resembled a scene from a B-rated movie and, if the situation hadn't been so embarrassing, Katie would have found it amusing.

"With Jim Fielding," continued the sergeant.

"Yes."

"Who is not your husband."

"That is correct," replied Katie.

"Then why did you tell me you were married?"

"I didn't, Sergeant," Katie responded sweetly. "You assumed we were married."

Sergeant Smith paused for a moment, trying to recall her previous conversation with the couple.

"But when I met Jim at the bar...I mean the restaurant...er...at dinner, he said that he had an important dinner date with his wife and then the two of you showed up at the bank dressed to the nines," said the sergeant, chagrined.

"Oh, that's just Jim's way of warning women off who are flirting with him," replied Katie, smiling innocently. "He finds it less offensive than telling them that he's just not interested."

"Listen here…" began Sergeant Smith angrily.

A male police detective, whom Katie knew well, had been sitting in the corner chewing nervously on a toothpick. About a year ago, Charlie Grant had taken Katie to the movies on two occasions but they found that they didn't have much in common and had amicably gone their separate ways. It unnerved him to see her subjected to the rather harsh treatment of this new police sergeant who didn't have any idea how important the Porters were in Fairfield.

He now felt that the interrogation was getting out of hand and got up from his chair.

"Katie," he said gently, stepping over and placing his hands on the table. "We don't really suspect you of robbing the bank, but it would be helpful if you could give us any information as to how the money bag ended up at Rosegate."

"I honestly don't have any idea, Charlie," replied Katie, looking up at him with relief. "I plan to ask Gran as soon as I'm allowed to return home, but I doubt that she'll know." Directing her gaze back to Sergeant Smith, she explained, "the property is quite large and it's not surprising to find people hiking through our woods or enjoying a picnic there. We're not thrilled about it, of course, but the estate is very pretty so we understand the attraction. Until it becomes a problem, we're not inclined to chase folks off."

"Unfortunately, it may now be a problem," explained Charlie. "Our culprits may be hiding out in your woods and may have accidently dropped the bag during their escape. Do we have your permission to search the area?"

"We could get a warrant," interjected Sergeant Smith, still miffed.

"That won't be necessary," replied Katie, looking at Sergeant Smith and then back up at Detective Grant. "You have my permission, of course. Please search wherever and whenever you wish. I will also ask Andrews, Mr. McKinney, and Robert to pitch in and help if that would be useful. They've been with us for many years and know the woods well."

"And who are they?" asked Sergeant Smith.

"Our butler, groundskeeper, and stable hand," answered Katie, trying her best to sound matter of fact.

"Nope. No thanks," replied Sergeant Smith, shaking her head and glancing at Detective Grant. "No one from the household. How do we know that they're not all in cahoots?"

"Suit yourself," shrugged Katie. "I'm just trying to be helpful. May I go now?"

"Yes, of course," smiled Charlie Grant, backing away from the table and opening the door. "We'll contact you if we need you. Isn't that right, Sergeant?"

Sergeant Smith looked as though she wanted to say something but then thought better of it.

"Certainly," was her only reply.

"So, you and this Fielding fella are dating?" Charlie whispered to Katie as she passed by him.

"Yes, 'fraid so," Katie replied, smiling up at him.

"Lucky man," Charlie nodded and pointed her in the direction of the front lobby.

She found Jim twirling his hat in his hand and nervously pacing the floor. His tie was hanging loose around his neck and his suit jacket was unbuttoned. He looked as exhausted as she felt.

"Are you all right?" he asked, quickly coming over to her.

"Yes, I'm fine, Jim," she assured him. "Just tired. What time is it?"

"Just after one," he replied, glancing down at his wristwatch. He placed his hand gently on the small of her back and guided her out of the police station.

"Oh dear! Gran is going to be worried," said Katie. "I wish I had thought to call her when we were at your place."

"This whole thing is completely ridiculous," said Jim, scowling as he started the car and drove out of the parking lot. "I can't imagine why the police think that you have anything to do with the break in."

"In general, the Fairfield police don't," replied Katie, yawning. "But their new sergeant is convinced that I'm guilty."

"She is? I wonder why?" Jim mused. "She seemed unbiased enough when I spoke with her earlier this evening."

"That was before she met your wife," replied Katie, giving him a sideward glance.

Jim winced. "Oh, about that Katie," he began. "You know I…"

"You don't have to explain anything to me, Jim," she interjected with a wave of her hand. "And you were right to warn her off. She's quite smitten with you, you know."

"Really? I was hoping I was just imagining things," he replied, reducing the speed of the car and carefully negotiating the hairpin curve in the road that led to Rosegate. "Thanks for going along with it, by the way. I hadn't had time to tell you and thought you might blow my cover. Do you honestly think that's why she's after you?"

"Well, it doesn't help but there's also the fact that the money bag was found at Rosegate."

Jim turned off the country road and through the entrance of the estate, continuing up the long winding drive.

"Oh dear," said Katie, seeing that a few lights were still on in the mansion as Jim pulled up near the front steps and stopped the car. "Gran must have waited up."

"I'll walk you to the door," said Jim, stepping out and starting around the front of the car.

"No, that's all right," replied Katie, stepping out on her own. "It's very late and we both have articles to write. And I have an appointment to interview a bank president first thing after breakfast."

She started to walk away and then stopped and turned to look back at him as he stood in front of his sedan. "Thank you for the lovely dinner, Jim," she said. "I really enjoyed it."

"Katie," he started to say. "I…"

But she was through her front door before he could finish.

Katie crept quietly into the house, closing and locking the door behind her. She noticed that a light was on in the library and, removing her hat and coat and laying both on the hallway table, walked to the library door and peered in. Sound asleep in her chair was her grandmother, the newspaper crossword spread across her lap and Nugget curled up at her feet. The little Yorkie lifted his head and gave a sharp yelp when he saw her, jumping to his feet and scampering over to his mistress.

"Hush, Nugget," said Katie, picking him up and curling her arms around his wiggling body. "You'll wake Gran."

"Too late," said Gran, slowly opening her eyes and looking around. "I guess I nodded off. What time is it, Katie?"

"It's nearly 1:30, Gran," her granddaughter replied. "I'm sorry I'm so late but you needn't have waited up for me."

"Normally I wouldn't have, dear," replied Gran, slowly getting to her feet. "But when the police came looking for you and I realized that I had no idea where you were, I became worried."

"Oh Gran," said Katie, mortified to know that she had worried the elderly woman. "I am terribly sorry. Let's get to bed and I'll explain everything in the morning."

* * *

Katie was a little heavy eyed from lack of sleep when she made her way down to breakfast. Gran was already at the table reading the newspaper when Katie entered the dining room.

"Good morning, Gran," said Katie, bending to give her grandmother a kiss on the cheek before moving to the sidebar to pour herself a cup of coffee.

"Good morning, Katie," replied Mrs. Porter, looking up from the article she was reading. "Did you sleep well?"

"Well enough? Yes. Long enough? No," exclaimed Katie, sliding into her chair and glancing down at the two soft boiled eggs propped up in their little cups on the plate in front of her. She took a breath and then looked back at her grandmother. "Gran, about last night. I should have called you to let you know where I was when it got to be so late."

Gran did not reply and sat gazing calmly at her granddaughter.

"As you know, I got a call from Mr. Connor just as Jim and I were leaving to go to Camilles."

Mrs. Porter nodded.

"Mr. Connor told me to go to the Fairfield Banking and Trust because it had just been robbed. You will remember that I'm doing a story on the robberies after City Bank was hit over in Wakefield, the Union in Cumberland, and the First National here. The police in all three towns suspect that the crimes may be connected and the sergeant on the scene last night admitted that there is a connection between the Banking and Trust burglary and the one at the First National."

Gran raised her eyebrows but continued to say nothing.

"This means that the stakes have been raised for newspaper coverage here because Fairfield has been hit twice now, whereas the other towns had only one burglary each."

Katie paused and looked at her grandmother. Mrs. Porter waited for a moment before saying, "I understand the importance of your job, Katie, but fail to understand why the police would be looking for you unless they suspected you as being one of the bank robbers."

"No, of course I'm not, Gran," Katie replied, knowing that her grandmother didn't really believe that either. "But a money bag from the Banking and Trust was found in our woods and the police believe that it may have been dropped accidently while the thieves were making their escape."

"So there is a possibility that they may be hiding in our woods," said Gran, shaking her head thoughtfully.

"Yes," Katie acknowledged. "The police obviously wanted to talk to me about it in case I could shed some light on the situation which, of course, I couldn't. I told them you wouldn't know anything about it either."

"Yes, that's true," replied Gran, looking down at her breakfast plate.

"Having missed our reservations at Camille's, Jim and I went to his place to have dinner. I should have called you from there but, honestly, I forgot. I'm truly sorry about that, Gran. I don't ever want to cause you any worry. It was around 11:00 o'clock, and we had just finished eating, when the police came banging at the door. The sergeant in charge of the case insisted I come down to the police station for questioning. They held me for hours!"

"Outrageous!" exclaimed Mrs. Porter, looking up sharply. "You should have called Judge White. He would have had you home in a minute."

"The whole thing was silly, really," replied Katie, tapping open her eggs. "I decided it best to go along with them and answer their questions. Besides, Jim was in the lobby waiting for me and most likely would have called in reinforcements should things have gotten ugly."

Gran suddenly lifted an envelope from her lap and placed it on the table beside her plate. Katie saw her pause in thought for several minutes, her hand resting on it.

"Katie, dear," Gran finally began. "You know that I trust you, don't you?"

Katie nodded, her eyes glancing at the envelope.

"I have done my best to raise you to be a gracious, caring, and honest young woman and I am very proud of you."

Katie couldn't fathom what on earth her grandmother was talking about, but it must be serious because Mrs. Porter seldom spoke in such somber tones.

"I realize," continued Gran. "that the war changed quite a lot of things. Young women are much more independent these days and social behavior is more relaxed. Besides, you are twenty-one and a grown woman. You could stay out all night if you wanted and I really couldn't say a thing about it. Fortunately, I do like Jim Fielding quite a lot and believe him to be a gentleman, although you have a right to date anyone you please, of course."

"Gran," said Katie, putting down her spoon and turning completely in her chair to fully face her grandmother.

"However," continued Mrs. Porter. "Old families such as ours have reputations to protect, which I've always thought completely ridiculous because…well, why should we care what other people think? But there it is." Gran shrugged her shoulders and pushed the envelope over to Katie. "Folks in Fairfield need to believe that we're above reproach, no matter how innocent our actions may be."

Bewildered, Katie opened the envelope and gasped. Inside was a photograph showing her being led out of Jim's house by the police, obviously very late at night. Sergeant Smith, wearing plain clothes, was walking down the steps in front of her and no one would have known what was happening had two uniformed officers not been walking on either side of Katie. Just over her shoulder Jim could be seen following behind, a frown on his face and his hands jammed in his pockets.

"Oh!" exclaimed Katie, turning red. She was mortified. Who could have taken this picture and how? She remembered that the headlights on the patrol car were very bright. Perhaps this had been enough to cover a camera's flashbulb.

"Gran," began Katie, but she was so shocked that she couldn't continue.

Mrs. Porter pointed to the envelope. "There's a note included. The envelope was addressed only to "Rosegate," so I assumed it was for me and opened it. I read the note. I believe it explains everything."

Katie put down the photograph and pulled the note from the envelope. Glancing down at the signature, she saw that it was from the same photographer who had teased her and Jim in the lobby of the Fairfield Banking and Trust.

"Dear Miss Porter,

I was given a tip that the police would be picking you up at Jim Fielding's place and that it might be worth my while to be there to take this photograph, which I did. One could say that it's quite a scoop. But, as I was developing it, I got to thinking that maybe this wasn't right. I don't know you but I happen to know and like Jim a lot. He's a standup guy who's helped me out from time to time when I've really needed it. He's also an Army Vet and purple heart recipient like myself.

So, I called him early this morning to ask him what it was all about. He said that you and he had been working the bank burglary story and had stopped by his house to grab a bite to eat. The cops came by before he could take you home. They wanted to ask you a bunch of questions and thought it best that they do it at headquarters. Jim was really put out about it.

He vouched for your character, Miss Porter. He says you're a close friend and admires you quite a lot. So, I say, any friend of Jim's is a friend of mine and I'm turning over the photograph to you. There are no copies and this will not appear in any papers.

Besides, I don't like dirty cops.

Signed,

Harry Smith."

Katie put down the note and, looking over at her grandmother, was relieved to see her smiling.

"Katie, dear," said Gran, reaching over and patting her hand. "The next time you wish to enjoy a private romantic dinner with Jim, please invite him here. He is always welcome as long as you want him to be." And with that, she returned to her newspaper and nothing more was said about it.

* * *

Katie was rushing to get dressed for her appointment with Mr. Martin, the bank president of the First National Bank in Fairfield, when the telephone rang.

"Hello," said Katie, picking up the receiver from her nightstand as she plopped down on the edge of her bed to slip on her shoes.

"Katie? It's me," said Ruth from the other end of the line. "Listen, would it be all right if I came over and stayed with you for a couple of days? Mother is very sick and now Boots has it. Robert thinks it's influenza, although we all got our shots. It doesn't appear to be working this year. Robert says that there are several people already hospitalized with it and that Mother and Boots are highly contagious. He wants me to leave the house immediately and I'm most likely safest at Rosegate. Your grandmother may have already had it when we thought it was just a bad cold. And hopefully you have built up some immunity caring for her."

"Sure, Ruthie," replied Katie, switching the receiver to her other ear so that she could put on an earring. "You know you don't need to ask. Just come over. Your room is always ready and waiting for you. But what about Tom and Poppy?"

"Tom is going over to the Stewarts," replied Ruth. "But Poppy is refusing to leave Mother. I didn't want to leave her either as she's extremely ill but Poppy and Robert don't want anyone else in the house to come down with it. We've hired a nurse to help out around the clock so there's not much I could do anyway."

"Well we're delighted to have you," Katie assured her. "In fact, your timing is perfect as I'm going to be tied up at the *Gazette* all day and Gran will be needing a bridge partner this afternoon. Mrs. Galloway's companion usually takes my place when I'm unavailable, but Gran prefers you because you're a much better player."

She heard Ruth chuckle. "Wonderful. I look forward to it. Please let your grandmother know that I'll be over shortly. I'll see you this evening when you get home from work." And, with that, she hung up the phone.

Katie collected her reporter's notepad and, dropping it into her purse, quickly left her room and descended the staircase. She met Gran in the hallway on her way out to her rose garden.

"I've got to go, Gran," Katie said, giving Mrs. Porter a quick kiss and then turning towards the front door. "And Ruthie is on her way over. She's going to be staying with us for a few days while her Mother and Boots struggle with the flu."

"Oh, that's nice," replied Gran, pulling out a drawer from a hallway side table and reaching in to retrieve her rose pruners.

"She's also available to be your bridge partner this afternoon," added Katie as she stepped out of the door and closed it behind her.

Mrs. Porter's expression brightened. "Wonderful!" she murmured under her breath. "Now I have a chance to beat Eloise Dempsey for a change."

As Katie drove her MG roadster down Rosegate's drive, she encountered several police cars driving up toward the mansion.

"Darn it!" she muttered, coming to a stop. "If they delay me now, I'll be late." But the police turned onto one of the drive's offshoots that led past the stables and to the woods at the back of the property. Detective Grant gave her a wave but did not stop.

Katie proceeded on her way and managed to reach the First National Bank right on time.

"Ah Miss Porter!" Mr. Martin said, greeting Katie with an extended hand. "So nice to see you again. How's your grandmother?"

"Just fine, thank you," she replied, taking a seat across from him in his office. "And thank you so much for agreeing to see me. As I mentioned over the telephone, I'm writing a newspaper article on the recent bank robberies and knew you would have a different perspective on the situation seeing that yours was the first Fairfield bank to be hit."

"A distinction that I'm not very pleased to have," remarked the bank president, frowning.

"No, I would assume not," replied Katie, giving him a sweet smile. "I imagine that you've heard that the Banking and Trust got robbed last night."

"Yes, I've heard," replied Mr. Martin, nodding. "I just got off the phone with Henry Watkins an hour ago. He's understandably very distressed. The thieves got away with several bags full. You see, the Brinks truck wasn't due until today."

"Brinks truck?" said Katie, puzzled.

Mr. Martin smiled. "The banks in Fairfield are branches of main banks located elsewhere. Three days a week, Brink's takes a large portion of the money we have in this location and delivers it to our main bank. That way, if something happens, such as being robbed or the building burning down, we don't lose a huge sum at one time."

"Unless you're robbed between pick-ups," replied Katie, absently tapping her pen on her notepad.

"Yes. Which is what, unfortunately, happened with the Banking and Trust," Mr. Martin added, nodding his head.

"Did Mr. Watkins happen to mention how much the thieves got away with?" asked Katie.

"No. You'd have to ask him," answered Mr. Martin.

"About your burglary," said Katie, shifting tactics. "The police tell me that the culprits broke in through a third story window."

"Yes, at around midnight," Mr. Martin confirmed.

"Did they set off an alarm?" she asked, recording the time of the crime in her notepad.

"No. And that's very strange," replied the banker. "You see, it's impossible to enter the bank without setting off the alarm if you don't know the code."

"My apologies for having to ask, but could one of your employees be in league with the thieves and have shut off the alarm for them?"

"Absolutely not!"

"You sound sure about that. Why?" questioned Katie.

"Because I'm the only one, besides our vice president, who knows the code that disarms the system and Andrews currently out of the country visiting his parents in London."

Katie pondered the situation for a moment. "Are you certain that the alarm was working that night? Perhaps it malfunctioned."

"It was working because the police accidently set it off when they came to investigate," explained the bank president. "You see, there had been a late meeting at City Hall, which you know is just a few doors down, and the councilmen were just leaving when several of them noticed that one of our windows was open. They called me right away and I called the police before making my way over. When I arrived, the police had already entered the building and had set off the alarm. It's quite shrill and they were very relieved to see me. Unfortunately, it took me several minutes to find my way through the lobby in the dark and finally shut it off."

"You didn't think it safe to switch on the lights?" Katie asked, intrigued. "Was it possible that the thieves might still be in the building?"

"No, they were long gone by that time," replied Mr. Martin. "I'm sorry but I guess I failed to mention that the electricity was off in the building. The police believe that the thieves cut the power before they entered."

"Wouldn't that have shut off the alarm system as well?" suggested Katie.

"No, Miss Porter," smiled Mr. Martin. "That certainly wouldn't make for a good alarm system if all a thief had to do was turn off our power. No, our system has a backup battery in case we lose electricity due to a storm or fire. So, you see, it's quite a mystery."

"Indeed," replied Katie, looking down at her notes. "I have one more question, Mr. Martin. Did the culprits use a ladder that left very strange looking prints? Something like these?" She turned to the drawing in her notepad that she had made the night before and showed them to the banker.

"Yes," he exclaimed a bit surprised. "Exactly like those. Don't tell me that the police found these same prints at the Banking and Trust?"

"Yes," confirmed Katie, snapping her pad shut and dropping it into her bag. "It appears that this bank burglary thing is becoming quite a habit for someone!"

She thanked Mr. Martin for his time and drove to the *Fairfield Gazette* newspaper building. Waving to Miss Applegate, the receptionist, she proceeded directly to E.M.'s desk in pursuit of the pictures he took.

"Hello, E.M.," she said in greeting. "Do you have the photographs of last night's fiasco? I need to write that bank article before I get canned."

"Yes, here you go," he said, handing her a folder and then breaking out into a coughing fit. Katie waited a few moments until he stopped and took a good look at him. He looked terrible.

"E.M. Butler!" she exclaimed. "You look like death warmed over. You're sick!" She reached over and placed her hand on his forehead.

"I'm fine, truly," he replied, starting to cough again. He pulled his handkerchief out of his breast pocket and held it over his mouth. When he was finally able to speak again, he added, "It's just a little cough. Probably allergies."

"I think you have a fever," she announced. "Come on. I'm taking you over to see Robert right now."

E.M. started to protest but he was cut short by another coughing fit.

Robert's office was in a wing of the hospital located just across the city park from the *Gazette* newspaper building so Katie had him there in a matter of minutes. "I think it's influenza," she said, hovering over Robert as he listened to E.M.'s lungs with his stethoscope. E.M. was sitting on the exam table with his shirt open and a thermometer stuck in his mouth. He was sickly pale and looked as though he might collapse at any moment.

"You may be right, Dr. Porter," replied Robert, a bit tersely.

Katie looked up at him with raised eyebrows and then said, "I'm sorry, Robert. I shouldn't be diagnosing patients for you. It's just that E.M.'s my friend and I'm rather worried about him."

Robert returned her glance. "I'm sorry, Katie. I didn't mean to sound so harsh. I suppose I'm just tired. I'm in over my head with flu cases. As you may have noticed, my waiting room is standing room only and the hospital is full. We've just discovered that the flu shot that we've used in the past is not working this year." He paused as he removed the thermometer from E.M.'s mouth and read it. "We're not sure *why* it's not working but now we have an unexpected epidemic on our hands."

"I appreciate you seeing us, Robert, and so quickly" replied Katie gratefully, and she reached over and patted his arm. "Is he going to be all right?" she added as E.M. burst out coughing again.

"I don't know," replied Robert grimly. "You were right. He's got the flu. He's got a temperature of 102. So far, he's not bad enough to be hospitalized, not that we'd have a bed available anyway, but he needs to go home and straight to bed."

"I'll take him now," said Katie, helping E.M. off the exam table and buttoning up his shirt for him. "We'll keep your tie off, Mr. Butler, but let's put on your jacket."

Robert wrote out instructions for his care and handed the note to Katie.

"Plenty of fluids. Plain tap water will do. Aspirin twice a day to keep the fever down and help with aches and pain. Please swing by and check on him often, Katie, and take his temperature once in the morning and once in the evening. If it reaches 104, call me immediately," he instructed as he walked them through his crowded waiting room and out into the hallway. "I'll drop by and check on you tonight, E.M., on my way over to the Whites."

"Oh yes," said Katie, just before the doctor stepped back into his office. "How are they doing?"

"Not good," Robert replied softly, and he closed the door gently behind him.

Katie drove E.M. to his apartment and had him tucked in bed within half an hour.

"I'm fine, I'm fine, I tell you," he muttered, as she fluffed up his pillows and pulled the covers to his chin. She placed a glass of water and a box of tissues on the nightstand next to him and saw that he had already fallen asleep.

"Sleep well, dear friend," she whispered, as she backed out of his room, leaving his bedroom door slightly ajar. "I'll check on you again very soon."

She then drove back to the *Gazette* to start work on the article. The pictures that E.M. had taken were very good and she was glad that he had so skillfully captured the strange prints left by the ladder and the open second story window above. She had just finished typing the first page when the phone on her desk rang.

"Porter," she said abruptly into the receiver, cradling it on her shoulder as she rolled a fresh piece of paper into her typewriter.

"Porter. Fielding," Jim teased, responding just as abruptly. "How about lunch?"

"Oh gosh," replied Katie, her voice softening. "Is it that time already?" She glanced over at the large clock hanging on the wall of the press room and saw that it was just past noon. "I'm sorry but I can't today. I've got to finish this article by 2:00 so it will be ready to go to press in time for the evening edition. Looks like I'll be skipping lunch altogether."

"How about I swing by the deli and pick us up some sandwiches? We can eat at your desk. That way you can continue to work and I can sit and gaze into that beautiful face of yours."

"A workable solution for me," she replied, chuckling. "But a boring one for you, I imagine."

"Not at all," he responded softly. "A face and a thousand ships, you know." And he hung up before she had time to recall the meaning behind the famous quote.

He arrived half an hour later carrying their lunch in one hand and a single red rose in the other.

"So, this is where you work," he joked, glancing around the newsroom. There was the usual chaos of clacking typewriters and the loud voices of reporters shouting into telephones.

"Much like the *Times,* I bet," replied Katie, smiling up at him from her typewriter. "Here, pull up that chair," she added, pointing to the one behind the empty desk of her neighbor. "Fred was fired last week for fraternizing with a reporter from a competing newspaper."

"Really?" Jim exclaimed, an expression of shock spreading across his face. He handed her the rose and then grabbed the chair, rolling it beside her desk. "Gosh, Katie," he began as he sat down and removed his hat. "If I thought for one minute…"

"I'm joking, Jim," she interrupted, grinning. "Fred's out with the flu, which seems to be spreading like wildfire around here, I might add. E.M. woke up with it this morning. Now, let's eat. I'm starving!"

As Jim lifted the sandwiches from the bag, Katie took a quick sniff of the beautiful rose before placing it in her water glass at the corner of her desk.

"I finished writing my article this morning," Jim remarked. "I was hoping to see E.M. to thank him for the pictures. He dropped them off at my desk very early and they really added to the story. I'm sorry that he's got the flu."

"Well you'll get a chance to thank him later," replied Katie, turning back to her typewriter. "I'm taking care of him and you can help."

"Of course," Jim responded, searching among the wrappers for the pickle that usually came with his sandwich.

They ate in silence, with Katie taking bites between paragraphs. Jim, having no other distractions than to bask in her presence, finished his lunch quickly and spent his time glancing over a copy of the *Gazette*, which Katie kept on the corner of her desk, and watching her as she worked. He marveled at the fact that, unlike other women he had dated, he didn't have to entertain her or find ways to impress her. He felt immense contentment in just being in her company and he believed, or rather hoped, that she felt the same way. It was wonderful to find someone who didn't mind being quiet together.

"Thank you for lunch, Jim. And for the lovely rose," she said finally, pulling the last page of her article from her typewriter and looking around for the copy boy. "You're spoiling me, you know," she added, gazing fondly at him. She racked her brain for the words to gently ask him if he could really continue to afford it, but her thoughts were interrupted when her telephone rang.

"Miss Porter? This is Officer Jameson of the Fairfield Police. Detective Grant asked me to call you and request that you come home immediately."

"What is it, officer?" asked Katie anxiously. She looked at Jim who leaned closer. "Is my grandmother all right?"

"Yes, ma'am," the officer replied. "It's nothing like that. Your dog has discovered a policeman's uniform half buried in your woods and he won't let us near it. We'll have to shoot him if you don't come quickly."

CHAPTER 4
NUGGET'S DISCOVERY

"Nugget!" yelled Katie, as she and Jim approached the ring of police officers surrounding the little dog, their service revolvers drawn.

The Yorkshire Terrier was sitting smugly on a dirty blue uniform shirt in the middle of the circle. A few feet away from him stood Sergeant Smith. Every time she made a move toward him, Nugget growled and bared his teeth.

"Shoot it, shoot it!" Katie heard the sergeant screaming.

"Don't you dare!" shouted Katie, pushing through the circle and strolling up to her pet. "What do we have here, Nugget?" she said gently, bending down to pick him up. She grabbed the shirt and raised it in the air. "Yours, Sergeant?" she exclaimed, turning to the angry woman coming toward her.

"No, it's evidence!" snarled Sergeant Smith, reaching out to snatch it from Katie's grasp. Nugget, however, growled and snapped at the woman, preventing her from getting any closer to Katie.

"My mistake," replied Katie calmly. She turned and handed the item to Charlie Grant who was also standing nearby. "I thought the strips on the sleeve indicated the rank of sergeant," she explained.

Detective Grant's eyes twinkled as he took the policeman's shirt from Katie, but he said nothing.

"That dog is vicious and should be put down!" exclaimed Sergeant Smith, pointing at Nugget.

"It's interesting that the dog doesn't snap at you, Detective," said Jim, coming up and gently taking the Yorkie from Katie's arms. "Or me either." He stroked the little dog between the ears as Nugget happily plastered his face with wet kisses.

The muffled sound of laughter could be heard coming from the circle of officers causing Sergeant Smith to swing around and glare.

"Get to the squad cars, all of you!" she barked. "It's time to leave!"

Returning their revolvers to their holsters and chatting among themselves, the officers slowly walked toward the police cars parked several yards away.

"It would serve you well to stay out of my way, Miss Katie Porter," warned Sergeant Smith. "Or else!"

"Surely you're not threatening me, Sergeant," replied Katie evenly. "And while on my property."

Sergeant Smith took a step forward and then stopped. She paused for a moment before turning abruptly and stomping off in the direction of the police cars. Stepping around them to follow her, Detective Grant tipped his hat and said, "see you in the funny papers," and then he too was gone.

"Nugget, you rascal," chuckled Katie as Jim put the little dog down. "You were not very nice to the police sergeant, but I can hardly blame you!"

Nugget responded by running wide circles around them, jumping and barking for joy.

Katie and Jim were just about to turn and walk back to the mansion when they heard rustling in woods behind them.

"Who's in there!" Jim demanded loudly, gently pulling Katie behind him. "Come out now or I'm coming in after you!"

There was more rustling and then a young voice called out. "Hold your horses, Uncle Jim! "It's just us!" And suddenly out of the bushes and trees crept a half dozen boys ranging in age from 6 to 10. They were dressed in feathers and moccasins with war paint adorning their young faces. Two had small wooden knives strapped to their hips.

"Ah," said Jim, nodding. He held up his hand and opened and closed his palm twice in a kind of a salute. One of the older boys, wearing a full feathered head dress, stepped forward and made the same salute in return. "Chief Jumping Deer," Jim continued solemnly. "We didn't realize that these woods were part of your hunting grounds."

"Yes, Uncle Jim...er...I mean, Standing Chief," replied the boy, deepening the tone of his young voice. "We hunt here all the time. This is the land of our tribe."

At that moment some of the boys spotted Katie stepping out from behind Jim and they started whispering to each other.

"Who's that?" the young chief demanded, leaning slightly to the side to get a better look.

"Oh," replied Jim, turning to Katie. "This is Princess *Cariad*. She owns all the land as far as the eye can see." Jim waved his hand dramatically from right to left, illustrating the vastness of Rosegate's back property. "Including these woods, brothers. Her armies are mighty and her power even greater. I would not challenge her right to these hunting grounds if I were you."

The tribe of boys were greatly impressed and they stared up at Katie, their eyes wide. Their chief, however, wasn't convinced.

"Ah, Uncle Jim," he said, after a moment. "She's just a silly girl."

This comment was met with gasps from the younger boys and they were about to run for their lives when Katie, who could not hold back any longer, burst out laughing.

"See I told you so," said their chief, somewhat miffed. "Girls are silly."

"Wait a minute," said a thin redheaded boy, stepping forward. "You're Miss Porter, aren't you?"

"Yes, I am," replied Katie with a nod.

"My name is Thomas and I help Robert clean stalls at your stables every Saturday," he replied proudly, and then turning to the rest of the boys, bragged, "If I work really hard, he lets me exercise one of the horses."

"Why that's wonderful, Thomas," Katie responded, giving him a warm smile. "We are very grateful for the extra help. Thank you."

"Hey, Bobby," said Thomas, turning back to the chief. "Uncle Jim is telling the truth. Miss Porter and her grandmother own the whole lot! I told you we shouldn't be playing in here."

"It's quite all right, really," replied Katie quickly. "In fact, my grandmother and I are glad that your tribe has kept the bears and buffalo away from the house."

"And ghosts," nodded one of the younger boys, kicking at a tree root.

"Hush, Junior," admonished another boy, giving him a little push. "You're not supposed to tell anyone about the ghost. We took a blood oath, remember."

Jim looked over at them, his eyebrows raised. "Ghost?" he asked.

"Look what you've done!" exclaimed Chief Bobby. "Now he won't leave any more messages."

"Who?" asked Katie, growing concerned. She hadn't been entirely convinced before, but could it be possible that the bank thieves *were* hiding in Rosegate's woods? And perhaps the boys had accidently discovered their whereabouts? This could put them all in grave danger.

"Golden Joe," replied Thomas. "We've seen him come out at night and leave messages in the old stump by the creek."

"Show us, boys," said Jim, sternly. "No fooling around now. This could be serious."

"Nugget!" called Katie, looking around for the dog. "Come!"

Nugget scampered out from the woods and bounded towards her. He was covered in dirt and dried leaves. "Come on, stinker," she commanded, waving her arm forward. "We're going to follow the tribe."

The boys lead them to the shallow creek that ran through the Rosegate estate and pointed to a large stump where an enormous oak had once stood. Katie knew it well, having climbed the tree often as a child. Later, after it had fallen, the remaining stump became a quiet place to eat lunch or sit and read while listening to the trickle of the water passing by.

"There's a little space hollowed out on the east side, Jim" said Katie, walking over. Jim followed close behind her and the two of them knelt to exam the hole. There was nothing there.

"That's where Golden Joe's ghost hides the messages," Bobby assured them. "I swear."

"And you saw him put one there?" asked Jim.

"Yes. We even took it out and read it," replied Bobby. "But the ghost caught us and told us to put it back in the stump. He motioned that if we ever came back, he would kill us." And Bobby demonstrated this by sliding his finger across his throat and making a hissing sound.

Katie shuddered. "So, you boys never came back after that?"

"No, we came back," said one of the other boys calmly. "We're not chicken, but we're not dumb either. We hide up there on the hill and watch and don't try to get the messages anymore. Sometimes we see the ghost and sometimes we don't."

Jim and Katie exchanged looks.

"Do you remember what was in the message you read?" Jim asked.

"Yeah. It was really crazy," replied Thomas. "We figured it was some kind of code or something. It had pictures of animals running along one side of it."

"Animals?" asked Katie. "Like cats and dogs?"

"More like wild animals and even birds," replied Thomas. "And next to each picture was a number. You know, like 1, 2, or 3. Crazy huh?"

"Yes, very," said Katie thoughtfully. She absently ran her hand over the top of the old stump.

"Gather round, boys," said Jim, squatting down and resting on his heels. He signaled for the boys to sit down around him. "I am going to ask you to promise that you'll never come here again to spy on Golden Joe. Understand? And never, ever, come here at night for any reason."

"Ah, all right Uncle Jim," replied the group in unison.

"Badger Tribe promise?" said Jim, holding up his hand and opening and closing his palm twice.

The boys groaned but reluctantly committed to the promise by returning the same gesture.

"OK, boys," said Jim, standing. "Let's meet back at Princess *Cariad's* back patio where, if we're lucky, she might honor us with lemonade and cookies from her well stocked panty!"

The boys gave a shout of delight and all, except one, tore off through the woods, running and jumping, with Nugget leading the way.

"Uncle Jim," said young Junior, tugging at Jim's pant leg. "I'm tired. Will you carry me, please?"

"Certainly," replied Jim, scooping the little boy up in his arms. "Even the mightiest of warriors grows weary at times."

They were halfway to the house when Katie, walking beside him, turned and said, "My dear Mr. Fielding, may I ask you two questions?"

"Yes, of course," he replied, shifting the weight of Junior in his arms. The little boy had fallen asleep against Jim's shoulder.

"Uncle Jim?" she asked. "And *Cariad*?"

Jim chuckled. "Can't get anything past you, can I, Ace?"

Katie responded with raised her eyebrows. "No indeed."

"I volunteer at least twice a week at the Boys Club downtown," explained Jim. "The boys started calling me Uncle Jim and I guess it stuck. These boys here are part of that group. They're good kids really. Just need a positive role model since none of them have fathers. Since I lost my own dad at an early age, I know what that's like."

Katie shook her head in amazement. Just when she thought there was nothing more about him that could surprise her, he came up with something like this. It was getting harder for her to deny that she was falling deeply in love with Jim Fielding.

"And the other name?" she asked again.

"That one you'll have to look up," he chuckled. "But I will give you a hint. When I was little, I remember hearing my father often call my Welsh born mother by it."

* * *

"Ruthie, do you believe in ghosts?"

"Hm?" replied her friend, cutting into a slice of ham on her dinner plate.

"Ghosts. Do you believe in them?" asked Katie, looking across the dining table. She had just returned from checking on E.M., who, despite his temperature having returned to nearly normal, was still resting fitfully. She had debated calling Robert but decided against it. The poor doctor had other patients who were in greater danger.

She and Ruth, along with Mrs. Porter, were now enjoying an early dinner.

"No, I can't say that I do, Katie," replied Ruth, shaking her head. "Do you?"

"No, I do not," answered Katie firmly, putting down her wine glass.

"Why do you ask, dear?" said Gran, looking over at her granddaughter.

"Because apparently we have one dancing around our woods leaving messages."

"Is that why the police were here today?" Ruth asked.

"No," said Katie. "One of the money bags from the Banking and

Trust was found along the tree line and they believe that might indicate that the culprits are hiding out there."

"Oh dear. That's quite possible you know," said Ruth.

"Possible, yes. But probable, I don't think so," responded Katie, her fork and knife paused in midair. "Think about it. Why would they? Why come all the way out to Rosegate when there are plenty of more accessible places to hide? An old warehouse, for instance. Fairfield has plenty of them, especially south of town. And there are no caves or other places of shelter in our woods. Plenty of trees and vegetation, yes, but nothing that would provide much protection against the elements."

"The thieves may have a tent or erected some sort of hideaway made from branches and limbs," suggested Ruth.

"Not very pleasant, I would think," murmured Gran, spooning a helping of cream corn onto her plate. "It can get fairly cold out in those woods at night and the bugs will drive one crazy."

"My thoughts exactly, Gran!" replied Katie, nodding at her grandmother. "And we haven't seen any bonfires blazing after dark."

"True," nodded Gran.

"And I suspect our ghost might be a couple of kids playing a prank, though it's not safe for them to be out there until the bank thieves have been caught," Katie said thoughtfully.

"So, what are your plans?" asked Ruth, looking dubiously across at her friend. "I hope we're not spending the night in the woods in order to capture a bunch of thieves or chase away any ghosts."

"No," Katie assured her, smiling. "At least not yet."

"Thank goodness for that!" sighed Ruth, returning to her plate.

"How are your mother and sister Margaret doing?" Gran asked, changing the subject. "I hope they're recovering well?"

"Boots is on the mend," replied Ruth. "But my mother is not doing very well, I'm afraid. She still has a very bad cough and is finding it difficult to breath. We're quite worried about her. Robert is seriously thinking about placing her in the hospital."

"Oh dear!" exclaimed Gran. "I'm sorry to hear that but I'm sure your mother will recover in due time. She's a strong woman, after all. But, until then, we're very relieved to have you here, Ruth, safe with us."

"Thank you," replied Ruth gratefully, although Katie sensed that her friend would have preferred to be home caring for her mother.

"Besides, it's nice to have someone around the house who's not running out the door at a moment's notice and who can play an excellent game of Bridge," Mrs. Porter added.

"Gran!" exclaimed Katie, looking distressed until she saw the twinkle in her grandmother's eye and realized she was being teased. "You know that I had an article to finish today and the police to contend with. And then there's E.M."

"Oh, I almost forgot," said Ruth suddenly. "The evening editions arrived about twenty minutes ago and your article turned out very nicely, Katie. Jim's is good as well, but I believe yours is better."

"I think you're a little biased, Ruthie dear," replied Katie, although she was beaming. "But thank you. I'll look both over after dessert."

An hour later she had to modestly agree with Ruth's assessment. She had had the benefit of the additional interview with Mr. Martin, of course, but her style of writing was also easier to read than Jim's, who tended to be more technical in his technique.

"Very nice work, Katie," he said to her over the telephone later that evening. "I think mine is good, but I have to admit that yours is better. Your article contains information that I didn't have, of course. But even if I had gotten my own interview, I still think you would have come out on top."

"Thank you, kind sir," replied Katie. "Can I get that in writing?" She was teasing him, of course, but she was secretly thrilled at receiving his praise.

Jim chuckled. "Yes, I'll give it to you in triplicate if you like." He paused and Katie heard what sounded like him kicking off his bedroom slippers. "So, now that we've wrapped up our stories concerning break-ins," he began again, "what are your plans other than the tennis tournament?"

"Oh, I'm not finished with the bank break-ins," replied Katie. "Until the police catch the thieves, there's still a story to follow."

"I figured you'd say that, Porter," Jim replied. "So, what do we have? Where do we start?"

"An alarm system that was tripped by the police but not by the thieves, a ladder that makes very strange prints, several money bags carried out through windows instead of doors, top of the line safes that have been cracked, a Banking and Trust money bag found in my back yard along with a policeman's uniform shirt, the electricity cut off at the First National bank," Katie replied breathlessly.

"And a second story window used in one bank and a third story window used in the other," added Jim. "And a ghost who leaves strange messages and may or may not be connected to the bank jobs."

"And, last but not least," continued Katie. "A very angry female police sergeant who would love nothing more than to remove my head from my shoulders and serve it on a platter."

"Yuck! What an unpleasant thought!" exclaimed Jim, and then he yawned.

"Oh, yes, there's one more thing," she added.

"Which is?"

"I have to stop by the library and look up the definition of an old Welsh word."

Jim chuckled again. "Well, it appears we're going to be very busy for the next couple of days."

"We?" asked Katie, intrigued.

"Yes," he replied. "Unless you don't want my help?"

"Yes, of course I do," Katie answered. "With the long list I just mentioned, you don't think I can handle it all by myself, do you?"

"Actually, I'm fairly certain that you *can* handle it all by yourself," he responded. "But I would like to see you occasionally and this seems to be the only way."

"I am sorry about that, Jim," she replied softly. "But I just feel as though we may be on to something."

"Well count me in," he said, yawning again. "But promise me that you'll make time in your busy schedule to go out dancing with me soon. I'll even sing to you if you do."

"A bribe, huh?" Katie chuckled. Just the thought of it made her blush. "OK, you've got a deal, Fielding. But for now, I'll hang up because I can hear you yawning and know you need to go to sleep. Goodnight Jim, pleasant dreams."

"Goodnight, Katie," he replied reluctantly. "I..." he started to say, but she had already hung up the phone.

* * *

"Good morning, Miss Katie," said Andrews, entering the dining room just as Katie was sliding into her chair at the breakfast table across from Gran. Ruth had not come down yet.

"My apologies, but you have a telephone call. A young man, calling himself your fiancé, told me it's rather urgent."

"Oh, for heaven's sake!" exclaimed Katie, getting to her feet.

She went into the hall and snapped up the telephone receiver. "What do you want, Tom White? And, for the millionth time, you are NOT my fiancé. Besides, isn't it your sister you should be calling?"

"And good morning to you too, dear Katie," said Tom. "Of course I'll talk to my sister but it's you that I need to speak to first."

"OK, you've got me, so what is it you want?"

"Got you? If only that were true, my love," replied Tom, giving her a dramatic sigh. "But look here," he continued, finally getting to the reason for his call, "I wonder if I might use one of your garden sheds? The small one up from the tennis courts will do nicely."

"Yes, that's fine but let me double check with Mr. McKinney first," she replied. "May I ask why you need to use one of my sheds and not one of your own?"

"Poppy tells me that ours are crammed full until we can rebuild the greenhouse," he answered. "Remember you burned it down a while back."

Katie sighed. "I did not, Tom White, and you know it. That German spy, Kenneth West, set it on fire trying to kill me."

"Yes, well, whatever," replied Tom dismissively. Katie could hear the rustling of papers in the background. "Listen, future wife, I'm working on something that could pay off big. Call it a type of science project. And I'd be willing to cut you in if you play your cards right."

"Play my…" sputtered Katie, looking up just in time to see Ruth descending the staircase. "Oh, thank goodness! Here, Ruthie, take the phone before I start using language that my grandmother doesn't permit in this house. It's your brother and he's working on another one of his schemes."

Ruth walked over and took the phone from her. Covering the mouthpiece with her hand, she whispered to Katie, "I don't know why you let him get to you like this. You know he enjoys getting your goat."

"Well a goat is the only thing he'll ever get from me," huffed Katie, turning back toward the dining room. "Well, that, and the use of a garden shed."

After breakfast, she convinced Ruth to take a ride over to the hardware store with her.

"I'm in search of a ladder," she told her friend, pulling into a parking space along the road near the front of the building.

"Doesn't Rosegate have plenty of ladders already?" Ruth asked, stepping out of Katie's roadster and hurrying alongside her.

"Yes, of course," Katie replied, opening the door of the shop for her friend and then following her inside. "But I'm looking for a special ladder that has round disk's for feet."

Ruth shook her head. "There are times I simply don't understand a word you're saying, Katie dear."

Ruth was not alone. Mr. Fred Miller, owner of Miller's Plumbing and Hardware, didn't have any idea what Katie was talking about either.

"No, Miss Porter," he replied, taking his pipe from his mouth. "We have short ladders, tall ladders, step ladders, rope ladders, hook ladders, swim ladders, attic ladders, wooden ladders, and even aluminum ladders now that the war is over. But I never heard of one that has disks on the bottom of its side rails. Could you be thinking of a shoe?"

To make sure the young women knew exactly to what he was referring, he ushered them into another room where a multitude of ladders were on display.

"If you look here," he said, using the end of his pipe to point to the bottom of a ladder that was leaning against a nearby wall. "This ladder has a flat rectangular piece that acts like a shoe. It gives it a broader base in which to stand and helps make sure the darn thing doesn't slip out from under the climber."

Katie nodded and then glanced around the room. "But no shoes that are circular in design?"

"No, miss," replied Mr. Miller, shrugging his shoulders. "But if I find one that has those on it, I'll certainly give you a call."

Katie's next stop was to the telephone booth directly across the street from the hardware store. While Ruth shopped at a dress shop a few doors down, Katie placed a call to Charlie Grant at the Fairfield police station.

"Hi Charlie," she said, when the detective came on the line. "I would have come to see you in person, but I am rather reluctant to bump into my friend Sergeant Smith."

Detective Grant chuckled. "Yes, I don't blame you. So, what can I do for you Katie?"

"Answer a few quick questions?" she asked.

"Sure. Am I to assume you're still working on the bank burglaries?"

"You bet!" exclaimed Katie. "Unless you've already found and arrested the thieves."

"No such luck," replied Charlie sadly.

"I take that to mean that the culprits were not found hiding out in Rosegate's woods?"

"No," said Charlie. "And honestly, Katie, I didn't expect that they would be. We're still investigating how the money bag and policemen's shirt got there, though. Any ideas?"

"No, but I'll let you know as soon as I find out," Katie promised. "If the thieves dropped the bag on our property, that would indicate that they were there at one time and that makes me very nervous."

"As it should," said the detective.

"Which brings me to my first question. Were the upstairs windows locked in both banks when the break-ins occurred?"

"Yes. Sergeant Smith interviewed the staff at both and they swear to it," replied Charlie. "They told her that those windows are never opened so there would be no reason to unlock them."

"Interesting," Katie said thoughtfully. "I didn't see any broken glass. Did you?"

"I didn't work the bank break-ins, if you remember. But hold on a minute and I'll get the file from Sergeant Smith's desk."

He was back on the phone in less than a minute. "Nope, no broken glass. Sounds like an inside job to me."

"Jim and I thought that as well, at first," Katie remarked. "But it doesn't make sense that the thief would use a window and ladder to get in and out. A person working the heist from the inside would just open the front door. Also, the two bank thefts appear to be connected. It would almost be too much of a coincidence that each bank had an inside person working the job."

"I see your point, Katie," Detective Grant replied, chuckling. "Not impossible but not probable. Your brain always did work faster than mine!"

"I'll take that as a compliment," she replied. "Last question, Detective, does the sergeant's file say if the electricity at the Banking and Trust was off?"

"Hm, let me see," said the detective, turning the pages of the file.

"Yup, here it is. The electricity was off. The lines had been cut."

"Thanks, Charlie!" exclaimed Katie. "You've been a big help!"

"Listen, Katie," he began earnestly. "If things don't work out with you and Fielding, then maybe…"

But Katie had already hung up the phone and was dialing the number to the *Gazette*.

"Hello, Mrs. Mathers," she said into the receiver when the newspaper editor's secretary answered. "This is Katie. May I speak to Mr. Connor, please?"

"He's in a meeting at the moment, Katie," Mrs. Mathers replied. "Does your call have anything to do with the bank heists, by any chance?"

"Yes," replied Katie. "I wanted to let him know that I'm still following some leads since the thieves have not yet been caught. I hope to write a follow-up to my original article."

"That's very interesting," said Mrs. Mathers, lowering her voice to nearly a whisper. "And might be harder than you think."

"It might? Why do you say that, Mrs. Mathers? Didn't Mr. Connor like my article?"

"Oh yes, he thought it excellent, which is why it made the front page."

"Then I don't understand," replied Katie, puzzled.

"The meeting that Mr. Connor is in at the moment is with the Fairfield police," Mrs. Mathers informed her. "They're insisting that you be taken off the bank story immediately."

Katie was stunned. "Why the very nerve! They can't demand that I be removed, can they?"

"Oh, they can demand anything they want," replied the secretary calmly. "But it won't do them any good. I've worked for Mr. Connor long enough to know he won't be bullied. In fact, he'll most likely insist that you continue."

Katie said nothing for a moment and then asked, "Mrs. Mathers, is one of the officers a female police sergeant?"

"Yes, how did you know?"

"Let's just say she's had it in for me ever since I showed up at the first break-in," replied Katie. "I believe she thinks I'm one of the thieves or at least in league with them."

"Why would she think a thing like that?"

"Well, some evidence showed up in my back yard, which I can't explain. And then my dog tried to bite her. But it may be her dislike of my dinner attire that sealed my fate."

"That will do it," replied Mrs. Mathers, chuckling. "I'll tell Mr. Connor you called. Please be careful, Katie."

After assuring the secretary that she would, Katie hung up the phone and went in search of Ruth, finding her just in time to be rescued from the clutches of a hat shop salesman.

"We've got to drop by and check on E.M.," said Katie, once they were back in the car. "I hope Robert's been checking on him as well."

"I spoke with Robert early this morning and he mentioned seeing E.M.," replied Ruth. "He says he's doing much better but should remain in bed for at least another day."

"I imagine that Robert didn't have time to give the patient breakfast," Katie remarked.

"No, probably not," agreed Ruth. "Let's stop by the pastry shop and pick something up."

"Excellent plan!" exclaimed Katie, turning the car in the direction of the shop.

Soon the women were climbing the stairs to E.M.'s third floor apartment, a large bag of pastries in hand.

"Jim!" exclaimed Katie, as she and Ruth opened their friend's door and stepped inside. Jim was sitting in an overstuffed chair across from E.M. who was propped up in bed. "How long have you been here?"

"Oh, about half an hour," he replied, getting to his feet as the women entered, and then glancing at his watch. "Unfortunately, I should be going. I'm already late for work."

"What a shame," said Ruth, walking past him on her way to E.M.'s tiny kitchen. "We've brought pastries for breakfast. I'll just put on some coffee."

"I think we can spare an éclair," remarked Katie, stopping in front of Jim and reaching into the bag. He stood with his mouth open ready to accept the offering, causing Katie to giggle as she gently placed it into his mouth. Suddenly, he slipped his hands around her waist and pulled her to him in a tight hug.

"Careful, Jim," warned Ruth, glancing back over her shoulder. "You're getting éclair in Katie's hair."

"Not to mention squashing the bag of pastries," croaked E.M.

from his bed.

Jim released one hand from around Katie and, bringing it up to take the pastry from his mouth, leaned close to her ear and whispered, "Good morning, beautiful," which sent a shiver all the way down to her toes.

Katie stood blushing as Jim then backed away from her and turned to pick up his hat from a side table. Plopping it at a tilt on his head and waving goodbye with the éclair still in his hand, he left the apartment, gently closing the door behind him.

"I would say that Jim was very grateful to get that pastry," teased E.M., reaching for the water glass beside him.

Still blushing, Katie stuck her tongue out at him but said nothing as she joined Ruthie in the kitchen.

Twenty minutes later they were just finishing their coffee when the phone rang.

"Katie, it's Jim," said Ruth, holding the phone out to her.

Puzzled, Katie stood quickly and took the receiver from Ruth. "Katie?" she heard Jim's voice say. "Did you and Ruth drive over together to E.M.'s this morning or separately?"

"We came together in my car. Why?"

"Well give her your car keys and wait for me outside E.M.'s apartment building," he replied. "I'll be there in five minutes to pick you up."

"OK, Jim," Katie answered. "But can you tell me what's up?"

"The Fairfield Savings and Loan has just been hit," he replied. "In broad daylight!"

CHAPTER 5
A SECOND HIT

"This is getting ridiculous, Jim," sighed Katie, as he drove them to the Fairfield Saving and Loan building. "I'm beginning to think these thieves are going out of their way to mock us."

"It is extremely frustrating," replied Jim, nodding. "Probably more so for the police than for us. I do find it very interesting that they attempted a heist in the middle of the day."

"Yes, that is very interesting," agreed Katie. "I'm rather surprised that they would risk it."

"Well, my guess is that they've either become very confident due to their string of successes," he replied. "Or so desperate that they're willing to take a chance."

They pulled into the parking lot of the Savings and Loan and quickly jumped out of Jim's sedan. As they entered the building, they could hear Sergeant Smith loudly questioning a worried bank clerk.

"You say you saw them?"

"Yes," replied the clerk, mopping his forehead with a handkerchief. "I came up to the second floor to retrieve some files for Mr. Mosely, our vice president, and there he was, standing in the middle of the floor looking at me. The other guy was at the window."

"What did they look like?"

"Well, the one standing in the room was short...for a man, I mean. Maybe about your height, sergeant."

"And the other guy?" Sergeant Smith asked. She leaned over the nervous man and placed her hands on the arms of his chair.

"I couldn't tell how tall the other guy was," replied the clerk.

"Why not? You were there in the room, weren't you?"

"Yes, but that guy never made it in through the window," said the clerk. "He kind of hovered outside. I only saw him from the chest up."

"Hovered? What do you mean when you say he hovered outside?" snarled the sergeant. "That window is on the second floor. Are you saying that he was floating up there in midair, Mr. Cohen?" she added mockingly.

"No, ma'am. I mean, yes, ma'am," replied the bank clerk, now looking as if he was about to faint.

"Not floating," whispered Katie to Jim. "But resting on the upper rungs of a ladder. Perhaps there are three guys. One goes through the window and cracks the safe. A second waits just outside the window and takes the money bags as the first guy runs back and forth from the safe. A third guy waits at the bottom and catches each bag dropped to him from the top of the ladder."

"So, we have a window-man, a ladder-man, and a ground-man," replied Jim thoughtfully. "It would make sense especially since they seem to be in and out so quickly."

"Quicker than all three using the front door and running up and down the stairs," Katie added.

Detective Charlie Grant looked over and saw Jim and Katie standing just inside the front door of the lobby. As he nodded his head at the them, Katie brought her finger to her lips signaling that they did not wish to be noticed. The police detective gave her a wink and tilted his head in the direction of Sergeant Smith, indicating that he understood.

"How were these mysterious bandits dressed?" Sergeant Smith continued.

"The short guy wore dark clothes and a mask over his face."

"What color was his hair?" asked Smith.

"I don't know. He was also wearing a hat." replied the clerk.

"A fedora? A baseball cap? A top hat?" mocked the sergeant. "What kind of hat was he wearing, Mr. Cohen?"

"Easy Sergeant," warned Detective Grant softly.

The clerk paused for a moment, thinking. "A knitted hat, Sergeant. Pulled low over his forehead."

"OK, what about the floating guy?" continued Sergeant Smith.

"What was he wearing?"

"I hardly got a look at him at all," replied Mr. Cohen. "I think he was dressed just like the other guy but, honestly Sergeant, he swung away before I could get a good look at him."

"Swung away?" repeated the police sergeant, puzzled. "What do you mean?"

"I mean, he was there and then he wasn't," replied the clerk. "He kind of swung out of the view of the window."

"That's very odd," whispered Katie as Jim nodded his head.

"What happened to the first guy once you saw him, Mr. Cohen?" asked Detective Grant, gently tapping Sergeant Smith on the shoulder and signaling her to step aside. "He didn't push past you and run downstairs because no one on the ground floor saw him."

"No, he laughed at me and just walked straight out the window!" exclaimed Mr. Cohen. "It scared me half to death and I don't mind telling you it took me a minute to collect my wits! I yelled down the staircase for help and then looked out the window expecting to see his body laying crumpled on the ground below. But he was gone. No sign of him. I can't explain it!"

"I'm beginning to think you imagined the whole thing, Mr. Cohen," said Sergeant Smith sarcastically. "Or perhaps you've been drinking?"

"We could check for tracks under the window," shouted Katie from across the room. Sergeant's Smith treatment of the witness greatly disturbed her. Katie approached with Jim following close behind.

"Well, if it isn't the unmarried reporting team of Porter and Fielding," announced Sergeant Smith, looking up and glaring at Katie. "I thought I told you to stay away from this story."

"No, Sergeant," countered Katie evenly. "You warned me to stay out of your way or else. And I intend on staying out of your way. But I'm a reporter for the *Fairfield Gazette* and have a right to cover a newsworthy story such as this one."

"She's right, Smith," remarked Detective Grant. "Freedom of the press and all that."

Sergeant Smith said nothing but shook her head and walked away.

"So, they never got to the safe?" Jim asked the detective.

"No," replied Charlie. "The clerk accidently surprised them before they had a chance."

"And they didn't have to concern themselves with an alarm system since the Savings and Loan is open for business during these hours," Jim pointed out.

"Yes, that's true," agreed Detective Grant.

"It's fortunate for Mr. Cohen that the culprits didn't try to harm him. They certainly had the opportunity since he was the only one on this floor," observed Katie.

"Yes. Which tells us that their interest is in stealing the money and not to harm anyone if possible," replied the detective.

"An encouraging thought," murmured Jim, glancing at Katie.

Suddenly there was the clamoring of noise coming from the front door as a dozen reporters and photographers pushed their way into the lobby.

"How is it that you two always manage to beat everyone else here?" teased Howard McBride of Wakefield's *Time Sentinel.* He had rushed over from the neighboring town to cover the story.

"We work for better newspapers?" joked Katie loudly, as she and Jim gradually made their way in the direction of the front door.

Then, while everyone else scattered throughout the lobby, they quietly ducked out and moved around the corner of the building to look for tracks under the open window.

"Just as we suspected, Katie," said Jim, couching down to exam the ground. "Here are those strange circular prints again!"

"But look here, Jim," Katie said turning away from the building and pointing to the ground. "There are more! It looks like they're coming from that direction."

The couple slowly followed the tracks that led about six feet from the building before completely disappearing.

"How strange," murmured Katie. "I don't understand."

"Looks like someone might have been "walking" a ladder," Jim remarked, taking his hat from his head and fanning himself with it.

"Walking a ladder?" asked Katie.

"Yes, I saw it done in the circus once," nodded Jim. "An acrobat climbs near the top of a ladder and then leans from side to side causing the ladder to teeter on each leg and move forward. It takes quite a lot of agility and balance."

"Seems like a very awkward way to approach a window," said Katie thoughtfully.

"To hide footprints, perhaps?" replied Jim.

"There is also the matter of carrying several bags of money," Katie countered.

"But we said that the bags could have been tossed to the man on the ground who would have carried them away," Jim pointed out.

"Leaving footprints that are not here," replied Katie, looking around.

"Yes, it appears you are correct as usual, Ace," sighed Jim, returning his hat to his head. "Now what?"

"I'd like to go back inside and take a look at that window," said Katie. "I've been wondering how the burglars have been opening locked windows without breaking the glass."

They walked back inside the Savings and Loan and made their way up to the second floor. Several other reporters and a group of police officers were already there taking pictures and asking questions. Katie approached the window and carefully examined the casing, sash, and lock. She reached over and tried to wiggle the glass panes, but they didn't budge.

"You think they may have lifted out a pane and then reached in and turned the latch?" asked Jim.

"That's what I was hoping but all the panes seem secure," she sighed, looking around the floor near the window.

"They certainly don't keep this area of the bank very clean, do they?" remarked Jim, looking down at a pencil, some odd screws, a magnet in the shape of a horseshoe, scattered paperclips, a wooden ruler, and some dust balls.

"I suppose there's no need as few people come up here," replied Katie, turning and moving away from the window. "It's mostly storage."

"Ed!" shouted Sergeant Smith, moving to the window that Katie and Jim had just left. "Bring me some small evidence bags."

Katie turned and watched as the police sergeant pulled on a rubber glove and carefully dropped the pencil into a small evidence bag. She handed it to officer Ed. Then she stooped down and picked up the screws, one by one, and dropped them into a second evidence back. This, too, went to Ed.

"Here, bag that ruler and take everything to the lab," the sergeant instructed the officer.

While Ed was turning to leave, Sergeant Smith leaned over and picked up the magnet, dropping it into her coat pocket.

"Perhaps our friend the sergeant is working on the theory that the thieves unscrewed the window from the outside using a pencil," whispered Jim in Katie's ear.

"Well I suppose anything's possible," replied Katie, smiling up at him.

Deciding that there was nothing more to see, they left the bank and stood for a moment on the sidewalk out front.

"Now what, Miss Porter?" Jim asked, his eyebrows raised.

"Lunch!" she announced. "Polly's?"

"Sounds good," Jim chuckled, taking her arm and steering her toward his car. Ten minutes later they were seated in their usual booth by the window in the coffee shop. After they gave their order to the waitress, Jim looked over at Katie to see that she was looking intently at him, a worried expression reflecting in her blue eyes.

"What?" he asked her.

"Jim, I...," she began and then paused and looked down at her hands resting on the table.

"Katie?" he asked again, a sense of dread settling in his stomach. *She doesn't want to see me anymore,* he thought to himself.

"Jim," she began again. "Would it be all right with you if I picked up the check this time?"

He sat looking at her for a moment, his eyebrows knitted together and his jaw tight.

Oh, dear, she thought. *I've hurt him.*

"The check?" he stammered. Then, suddenly, a wave of relief washed over him. He reached over and took hold her hand. "Katie, darling, you just scared the life out of me."

She searched his eyes. "I did?"

"Yes," he replied, finding his breath. "If you really want to pay for lunch, that's fine, but why the worried look?"

"Well, it's been on my mind and something I wanted to talk to you about," she replied, catching her own breath. "You see, you pay for everything when we go out, and bring me nice gifts as well. And it's awfully nice of you and I do appreciate it. But, is this something you can afford to do?"

"Katie..." he began, shaking his head and gently squeezing her hand.

"I know that you're not a rich man and that you even send money home to your mother and I don't want you to ever feel as though you need to buy me things."

"Katie," he said again. He reached over and took her other hand in his. "You are correct. I am not a rich man. Well, not as far as having money, that is. However, I live simply and make enough as a reporter to be comfortable. I also make enough to spoil you occasionally. Besides, you have me over for meals at Rosegate regularly. You've paid for tickets to charity events which I attend as your escort. And, you've paid for my guest membership at the country club so that I can participate in the tennis tournament. I would say, Katie Porter, that we're quite even."

"But, we're not," replied Katie earnestly. "That's the point. Paying for things like tickets and club memberships is nothing for me but if you keep paying for things you can't afford…"

"Katie," he interrupted, smiling warmly at her. "I have very little to offer you except occasional meals, nights out dancing, and my charming personality. If you are OK with that then everything will be all right with me."

She didn't answer for a moment as she contemplated his words.

"Well, Jim Fielding," she finally replied with a smile. "I can definitely say that I'm OK with that."

At that moment their lunch arrived, and they let go of their hands so that the waitress could place their plates on the table. She smiled at them. "Anything else I can get for you?"

"No, I think we're fine for now," Jim answered, glancing over at Katie.

"Yes, just fine," she replied, smiling warmly back at him.

* * *

"Don't hurt yourself, Jim," said Gran loudly from the back patio of the Rosegate mansion. It was late afternoon and she, Katie, and Ruth were watching as Jim tried unsuccessfully to walk a ladder.

He was out on the grass a few feet away with Robert, the stable hand, and the young redheaded Thomas holding each side of the wooden ladder. Jim would climb nearly to the top and then, when he was ready, the young man and the boy would let go. Jim would sway from side to side, attempting to propel the ladder forward, but only succeeding in crashing to the ground.

"You're going to break your leg," shouted Katie. "And leave me without a partner for the tennis tournament."

"Maybe that is exactly what he's trying to do," said a voice coming up behind them. They turned to see Dr. Robert Reed walking out through the patio doors.

"Robert! What are you doing here?" said his fiancée, reaching her hand out to him.

"Robert! How did you escape without the guards seeing you climb over the wall?" teased Katie.

"You tease but I almost feel that way," Robert replied, leaning over to give Ruth a kiss. "The flu cases have finally diminished enough for the hospital to give me a night off. I was going to see if anyone wanted to get in a few practice games of tennis. We don't have many more days before the tournament, but I see that Jim is busy trying to kill himself."

"We're running an experiment," said Katie. "Jim is trying to see if the bank burglars might have walked a ladder up to the side of a building so as not to leave any footprints, but he hasn't been able to make the ladder cooperate."

"Let me try," said the doctor, walking over as Jim hit the ground once again. "My brothers and I taught ourselves how to do this when we were kids. I think I can remember."

"It's all yours, pal," replied Jim, breathing heavily as he brushed dirt from his clothing. "I'm done being thrown to the ground."

Robert Reed studied the ladder for a minute, rubbing his hands over several of the rungs before signaling to the young stable hands to hold the side rails.

"First I've got to see if I can balance it," he explained, slowly climbing the ladder and then stopping two rungs down from the top. Holding tightly to the end of the rails, he told young Robert and Thomas to let go. As they carefully backed away from him, Robert concentrated and, although he swayed involuntarily twice, was able to steady the ladder and balance perfectly on it for several minutes.

"Bravo, Robert!" shouted the group on the patio, clapping their hands. Robert released his grasp and hopped backwards to the ground, letting the ladder fall of its own accord in front of him.

"Now to see if I can walk it," said the doctor, helping Robert and Thomas lift the ladder into place. He took a breath and climbed up the rungs, grasping the end of the side rails once again. He nodded to the two young men below and they let go of the ladder and backed away. Robert balanced for a moment and then started to sway the ladder from side to side, each time leaning his body in the opposite direction, acting as a counterweight. Katie held her breath as it looked as though the ladder would topple at any moment but then, as if by magic, it started to rock forward on one leg and then on the other. Soon, Robert had managed to travel several feet before letting go and hopping to the ground.

"Phew!" he exclaimed, rubbing his hands together. "That took more strength then I remember. Of course, I'm much older now."

"Robert, darling, you were amazing!" remarked Ruth, jumping up from her chair and sliding her arms around him.

"Yes, that was wonderful, Robert," nodded Katie. "But also disappointing."

"Why?" exclaimed Robert. "I just proved that it's possible to make a ladder walk."

"Yes, but the thieves would not be able to carry money bags and still walk the ladder," explained Jim, looking at Katie. "Isn't that right?"

"Yes," she replied, sighing. "You see, you had to keep a tight grip on the top part of the side rails in order to progress forward. Your hands were not free to carry the money. But tell me, Robert, would it have been easier to walk the ladder if it had disk-like shoes on the bottom of it."

"Easier to balance, perhaps," replied Robert. "But harder to walk as it would require lifting each leg that much higher in order to clear the ground and move forward."

"Sorry Katie," said Jim softly. "Looks like we're back to square one."

Katie was nodding in agreement when Gran suddenly pointed across the way. "What on earth is Thomas White doing?" she cried.

Everyone looked in the distance to see Tom strolling across the lawn carrying an armful of tubes, buckets, wires, and a long sheet of aluminum foil that was dragging behind him.

"Oh, I forgot to tell you Gran," admitted Katie, placing a hand over her eyes to shield them against the sun. "I've given him permission to use one of our garden sheds. He's doing a science project."

"Oh dear," muttered Gran. "Well I suppose it's only fair since you burned down the White's greenhouse."

"Gran!" exclaimed Katie, getting ready to defend herself before realizing that her grandmother was teasing her.

"The sun is setting. Time for cocktails, everyone," said Mrs. Porter, getting up from her chair and motioning everyone inside the house.

Half an hour later, with everyone seated comfortably in the game room and enjoying their drinks, Katie asked Jim to sing for them.

"I remember you singing for us before, and in this very room, in fact. You were wonderful!" she said, glancing into his soft blue eyes. She could remember quite vividly how the beauty of his voice had moved her those many months ago. "Besides, we'll feed you if you do," she added, jokingly. "And Ruthie is here to accompany you on the piano, just like she did then."

"Singing for my supper, huh?" replied Jim, smiling. "OK, Miss Porter, what would you like to hear?"

Ruth walked over to the piano and lifted the bench to look through several pieces of sheet music.

"There's quite a lot to choose from, Jim," she remarked, handing several songs to him for his review.

But Jim wasn't looking and instead whispered, "Good God!" as he stared out the window.

"What is it?" asked Katie, quickly standing.

"Quick, Katie," he exclaimed. "Do you have a pair of binoculars close by?"

"Yes, right here in the credenza. What's wrong?" She brought out the binoculars and walked over to him and Ruth at the piano.

Jim lifted the binoculars to his eyes and focused them for a moment. "Yes, there it is," he said, handing them back to Katie and pointing out the window in the direction of the tree line far off in the distance. "Look at the north side of the trees."

"I can't see any...," began Katie. "Oh wait! I see it!"

Barely visible, a tiny light was dancing among the trees. "Golden Joe," she whispered.

CHAPTER 6
THE GHOST APPEARS

"You don't really think it's the ghost of Golden Joe, do you?" asked Ruth, as she, Katie, Jim, and Robert Reed ran the quarter mile from the Rosegate mansion to the estate's wooded area.

"No, of course not," replied Katie breathlessly. "But it does make me wonder if it's the bank thieves or Jim's youngsters from the Boys Club. It's very suspicious for someone to be out in the woods after dark."

They had nearly caught up with Jim and Robert who had run ahead and were waiting for the two women at the tree line.

"I agree," said Ruth, increasing her pace slightly to keep up with her friend. "We are going to be careful, right?"

"Yes, of course," nodded Katie as they reached the others. She had thought to grab a flashlight when the four of them had dashed out the back door of the Rosegate mansion and now she pointed it down at the ground and clicked it on.

"You lead the way, Katie," whispered Jim, stepping behind her. "These are your woods. You know them better than we do."

"Right," she responded. "Stay close, everyone. We don't want to get separated or be spotted."

They proceeded quietly along a wooded path in the general direction of the light, which could still be seen a short distance ahead. It was headed north, away from them, but the group had no trouble keeping up all the while maintaining a safe distance.

"This is the way to the creek," said Jim quietly, after they had walked for several minutes.

"Yes," Katie whispered. "Looks like our trespassers are making their way to the stump. I hope it's not your boys."

"No, they gave me their Badger Tribe promise," he whispered back to her and shook his head. "I'd be very surprised if they broke it."

"Badger Tribe promise?" Robert whispered to Ruth, but she only shrugged her shoulders.

As they came closer to the creek they saw that the light, which they could now see was a flaming torch on a long wooden stake, had stopped. Katie switched off her flashlight and the group was thrown into total darkness.

"Whoever it is definitely stopped at the stump," she whispered. "Let's climb up the hill that overlooks it, just like the boys have done. That way we can watch from above and stay out of sight. Follow me and be careful."

They followed Katie up the wooded hillside, careful not to step on twigs or trip over tree roots, which was quite difficult given that they were proceeding in near pitch darkness. Finally, they reached halfway up and found a spot behind a large rock and several large tree trunks. Gazing down below, they could just detect two men dressed in black clothing that made them blend into their dark surroundings. They wore hats pulled low over their foreheads, hiding their faces. Had they not been seated on either side of the torch, the end of which had been jammed into the ground, they would have been invisible to the group above. The flickering of the torch's flame cast dancing shadows across their bodies, adding to the eeriness of the encounter. They sat about four feet from the stump.

"I hope it comes soon this time," said the taller of the two. "This place always gives me the creeps."

"Yeah, I know what you mean," said the other, glancing around. "But it's paying off, remember."

Katie was surprised to hear the voices. Instead of the deep tone of mature men, these two sounded like they were in their early to middle teens. She glanced over at Jim from her hiding place behind one of the tree trunks. He had heard the same thing and looked back at her, his eyebrows raised.

"Did you destroy the last message like you were supposed to?" asked the shorter man.

"Nope. I forgot," said the taller one. "It's here in my pocket. I'll do it now." And he reached into his trouser pocket and pulled out a single piece of paper. Katie and her friends were too far away to see what was on it and Katie sighed in frustration as the man reached up and started to place the edge of the paper into the flame of the torch. At that moment, however, a strange eerie animal-like screech echoed through the trees. It sent shivers up Katie's spine and she looked over at Ruth and Robert hiding behind the large rock, and saw Robert grab Ruth's hand.

"Ah, gee whiz," the startled taller man exclaimed, dropping the message before it could light. It was caught by a slight gust of breeze and blew away, disappearing into the bushes. "Now look what happened."

"Don't worry," said the short man anxiously. "No one will find it way out here. Now get ready because here it comes."

Katie followed their gaze and suddenly gasped. Floating a foot or two off the ground and coming towards the two men was a formless figure, gold in color, with billowing strands of what could be a robe or other type of flowing garment. Katie thought she could make out the semblance of a cape, but she wasn't sure. She heard Ruth take a sharp intake of breath and, glancing over at her, saw her lean closer to Robert. Both he and Jim stared, transfixed, at the figure, Jim's eyes narrowing.

The ghostly form came closer and then stopped about four feet on the opposite side of the stump from the two men. Katie trained her eyes and could now make out, in the middle of it, the very faint outline of what appeared to be an old miner, his clothes ragged and a mining helmet on his head. The ghost slowly held up its hand and pointed to the stump.

"Please, Golden Joe," pleaded the taller man. "Don't hurt us! We tried to get the money, but someone saw us! We had to make a run for it before we got caught. We didn't have a chance to crack the safe."

The ghost said nothing but slowly shook its head and pointed again at the stump.

"We don't have the money," argued the shorter man, his voice cracking. "They almost caught us. I told Frankie here that it was a bad idea to go there in the middle of the day but..."

Suddenly the ghost of Golden Joe tipped back its head and let out a loud screech that made the hair on the back of Katie's neck stand up. It must have had the same effect on the shorter man because he stopped talking and cowered on the ground, his arms covering his head.

"Please, Golden Joe, please…" murmured the taller man, over and over. He, too, was cowering but held his hands straight up in the air.

The apparition hovered for a moment and then slowly held up one finger.

"You're going to give us one more chance?" said the taller man hopefully.

Golden Joe slowly nodded yes.

"Oh, thank you, thank you, Golden Joe," said the shorter man, nearly crying with relief.

The ghost slid its finger across its neck as if to cut its own throat. The two men understood the meaning of the gesture.

"We won't fail you this time, Golden Joe. We promise," said the taller man. "You'll get your money."

Golden Joe held up its hand to silence them and then, with a twist of its wrist, and as if by magic, a single sheet of paper appeared in its hand.

"Their coded message," thought Katie to herself. "The instructions for their next bank heist."

The ghost floated over to the stump and, bending down, placed the message in the hollow space before straightening and slowly floating backwards in the direction in which it had first appeared. Then, with one dramatic swoop of an arm, it completely vanished.

Robert signaled to Jim, catching his eye. He gestured that they should rush down the hill and capture the two men below. Jim looked over at Katie, but she shook her head. The recipients of the messages were only stooges. It was the ghost of Golden Joe who appeared to be giving the orders and she wanted to find out more. They needed a plan, one that would uncover the entire scheme and enable the police to round up the whole gang.

Katie and her friends remained in their hiding places, watching, as the two men looked around and then scampered over to the stump.

"I'm sure glad it's gone," said the short one, pulling out the message. "Seeing Golden Joe always creeps me out a little."

"A little!" mocked the taller man. "I've never seen you so scared! You were crying!"

"Was not!" shouted the shorter fellow. "Besides, you weren't acting so brave yourself. Please, Golden Joe, please!" he mocked, his voice cracking once again.

"Shut up!" scowled the taller one, punching the shorter man in the shoulder. "Come on, we've got to get out of here. And be quiet! Do you want to wake the whole neighborhood?"

The men pulled up the torch from the ground and headed down the path in the direction of the clearing and the Rosegate mansion. Katie could see the light from the torch dancing through the trees before finally disappearing. Jim started to come from behind the tree where he had been hiding but Katie motioned for him to stay still. She pointed to her wristwatch and then held up five fingers, signaling that they should let some minutes pass in order to make sure that Golden Joe was not still around to discover them.

They waited five minutes and then came out of their hiding places.

"Can you believe it?" whispered Robert. "That was certainly one of the strangest things I've ever seen in my life!"

"Strange, yes," nodded Katie. "But, no, I don't believe it. None of it. There is no such thing as a ghost. And even if there were, there is no ghost of Golden Joe. That's just a fairy tale. And, besides, ghosts do not give instructions concerning bank heists, which I believe was what was going on here."

"You seem sure about all of this, Katie," smiled Ruth, brushing the dirt from her skirt.

"Only because the attempt at the Savings and Loan didn't get them any money," replied Katie. "Remember, those two guys said that someone saw them before they could crack open the safe and they were forced to make a run for it. That sounds a lot like what happened today."

"True," said Jim, taking Katie's hand. "We also heard them say that coming into these woods, although creepy, was paying off. This might indicate that they have had success with other jobs. We know of at least two banks where money was taken."

"It's too bad that we didn't have a chance to see the message the ghost put in the stump," said Ruth as the group carefully made its way back down the hill.

"We may still be in luck, Ruthie," replied Katie. "As long as we can find the note that blew away and into the bushes."

She flicked on her flashlight and the group searched the area for nearly half an hour before Jim found the piece of paper caught in a tree branch.

"Bingo!" he shouted, handing it to Katie. "Here you go. I'll hold the flashlight while you read it aloud."

"I can't," replied Katie, glancing down at the message.

"Why not?" asked Jim, giving her a puzzled look as he held the flashlight over the paper. Ruth and Robert moved closer to peek over her shoulder.

"Because it's in code. We'll have to figure this out when we get back home," she replied, folding the paper into her pocket and following behind Jim as he led the way back through the woods.

* * *

"Thank goodness you're back and unharmed," said Gran, coming up to the group as they entered the mansion through the patio doors. "I was getting worried!"

"I'm sorry we worried you, Gran, but we've discovered quite a lot," Katie reported. "Can I tell you over dinner? Have you already eaten? I'm sure we're all very hungry," she added, looking over at her friends.

"Of course. I told Gertie to hold dinner until your return," Gran replied, guiding everyone into the dining room.

Soon Gran, Katie, and their guests were seated around the table enjoying a nice, albeit late, dinner. As they ate, Katie told her grandmother all that had occurred in the woods on their estate.

"Katie, dear," said Gran, calmly when Katie had finished. "There is no Golden Joe or his ghost, for that matter. I just told you that to make you eat your Brussel sprouts."

"Which I still don't like!" groaned Katie, but she was smiling. "I know there is no ghost of Golden Joe, but someone is doing an excellent job in pretending there is."

"Yes, he was very believable," remarked Ruth. "Quite scary, in fact. I can't imagine what kind of effect seeing what we saw tonight might have on a person more gullible."

"Like the two fellows who apparently carry out Golden Joe's instructions," added Jim.

"Which reminds me," said Katie suddenly. "Jim, how old were you when your voice started to change."

Startled at first, Jim stared at her, his fork paused in mid-air. Then he chuckled. "Oh, I see," he replied. "Well, I believe I was around thirteen. Yes, that's it. I remember because my mother was worried that I wouldn't be able to sing in the church choir any longer. But she needn't have, because when it finally changed for good, I sang even better than before although a few octaves lower, of course."

His friends chuckled and Katie imagined a young Jim Fielding singing in his church choir, his beautiful youthful voice, adored by his mother, rising above the organ. She bet he was a knockout even then.

"And at what age was this wonderful transformation completed?" asked Katie, her eyes bright and twinkling.

Jim smiled warmly at her. "Fifteen. The full Fielding voice transformation that you enjoy now was completed by the time I reached age fifteen."

"Interesting," replied Katie. "And you, Robert?" she asked, looking over at the doctor.

"I was a bit slower than Jim," Robert replied. "It took me from age ten until I was nearly sixteen before I could finally depend on my voice not slipping into a croak; a dilemma that you women are fortunately spared."

"We have other dilemmas that we must deal with," responded Ruth, smiling over at him. Then turning to her friend, she asked, "Katie, why all this interest in Jim and Robert's voices?"

"I believe I know the answer to that," replied Jim, winking at Katie. "When we were listening to those two fellows in the woods, I recall thinking that they sounded awfully young. Katie heard it too. Then the shorter man's voice cracked, not once but twice, in a way that indicated that his voice was still changing. That means that he most likely wasn't older than fifteen, if even that."

"Exactly," nodded Katie. "The taller man's voice sounded more mature, as if it's already changed, but still on the young side. I would guess that he's a few years older. Probably in his mid-teens."

"Do you think they are from the same group of boys that drank lemonade out on our patio yesterday?" asked Gran.

"No, Gran," replied Katie, shaking her head. "All of those boys looked to be under the age of ten, isn't that right Jim?"

"Yes," he answered. "All but Bobby and Thomas, who are the oldest in that group. And they've just now turned ten. Neither one of their voices has begun to change yet."

"I'm not sure I like the idea of youngsters camping out in our woods and picking up messages from ghosts," sighed Gran, reaching for her wine glass.

"That's another thing I find interesting," Katie remarked. "I don't believe anyone, including our ghost, *is* camping in our woods. Those two young men came on and off our property carrying a torch, which we saw from our game room window. Jim could see the flame even before we looked through the binoculars. Our ghost is bright gold in color. We most likely would have seen its glow by now if it was living in our woods. No, I think the bank thieves are only using Rosegate as their pickup place for the messages. That's why the police haven't been able to find any trace of them."

"Except the policeman's uniform shirt," Jim reminded them. "I wonder where that fits in?"

"Perhaps it doesn't," replied Ruth. "It could be left over from a costume party or parade and was dropped by a passerby."

"True," said Katie. "But it does make one wonder."

It was long after Jim and Robert left for their homes that Katie and Ruth sat down with the coded message and tried to decipher it.

"This resembles the description of the one that Jim's boys looked at when they were caught by Golden Joe," said Katie, unfolding the paper and spreading it out on the table.

"There seems so little to go on," observed Ruth, gazing down at it. "And what we do have doesn't make any sense at all."

Along one side of the paper was a column containing pictures of ten creatures, with a number assigned to each. The list started with a Scorpion which had the number 1 next to it. There was also a Tiger with the number 2, a Seagull with number 4, an Owl with number 3, a Kangaroo with number 8, a Panther with number 2, and a Raccoon with number 7. Three of the creatures were difficult to identify and had the numbers 5, 1, and 4 next to them.

"What are these birds here, I wonder?" Katie pondered, pointing to the third and fifth pictures in the column.

"That one looks like a Buzzard," replied Ruth, placing a finger on the third one. "Ugly looking, isn't he?"

"Yes," Katie nodded.

"That bird is a Vulture," remarked Andrews, coming around the couch where the two women were seated. He had entered the room carrying a tray of sherry and was placing it on the coffee table in front of them. "A Turkey Vulture to be exact."

"Wonderful, Andrews!" exclaimed Katie, looking up at the butler and smiling. "Would you happen to know what type of bird this is?" she asked, pointing to the fifth image.

Andrews bent slightly over to take a better look. "That, Miss Katie, is a Loon. It is a type of aquatic bird."

"Andrews, you're brilliant! Thank you!" cried Katie, grabbing a pencil and writing the identifications next to the pictures as the butler bowed slightly and retreated from the room. "So, the number 1 is with the Vulture and the number 4 is with the Loon," Katie added.

"These all appear to have been cut out of magazines, or books, and pasted to the paper," noted Ruth. "Do we have any idea if the order of the pictures means anything?"

"Not that I can determine as yet," sighed Katie, running her thumb over several of them. "And I wonder why these particular creatures were selected. Some are jungle animals and others are birds and one an arachnid. Very odd."

"Perhaps the numbers beside each is the key," suggested Ruth. "Even though they are not in numerical order. Perhaps it's the amount of each that matters. You know, like 1 scorpion and 4 seagulls and 7 raccoons."

"And, if a partridge was on the list then we might have some new lyrics to *The Twelve Days of Christmas*. Unfortunately, we don't and, besides, Ruthie, several of the numbers repeat themselves."

"Yes, that's true," sighed Ruth, leaning back on the sofa cushions.

"We also still haven't identified the strange creature in the second picture," Katie pointed out. "Oh dear."

They studied the message for another half hour before giving up for the night. As they made their way upstairs to their respective bedrooms, Ruth stopped and turned to Katie.

"Do you have a minute?" she asked her friend. "I'd like to talk to you about something."

"Sure, Ruth," replied Katie, somewhat puzzled. She turned and followed her friend into the guest room.

"I just wanted to tell you," began Ruth as the two women settled on the edge of Ruth's bed. "How happy I am to see you and Jim together."

"Together?" replied Katie, blushing.

"Well, you know what I mean. Dating," smiled Ruth, leaning over and taking Katie's hand. "It's been three years since Ruddy was killed and you've never seemed very interested in seeing anyone else since then. I know you loved my brother but, well, I just wanted you to know that I'm glad that you've finally decided to move on with your life."

"Ruthie," Katie stammered. "I do like Jim an awful lot and I go out with him when he asks me…but…"

"But what?" Ruth asked, interrupting. "Please tell me that you're not trying to talk yourself out of seeing him because, I must tell you Katie Porter, Jim's not just anyone. He's very special. And it's obvious that he's head-over-heels in love with you and anyone with eyes can see that you feel the same way about him. Why Katie, you just light up when he's around!"

Katie didn't reply and looked down at the floor. They sat in silence for a minute before Ruth bent down and, tilting her head to one side, looked into Katie eyes.

"What is it?" Ruth asked softly. "Can you tell me?"

Katie hesitated for a moment and then took a breath and nodded. "I don't want to fall in love with Jim Fielding."

"Why not?" replied Ruth, puzzled.

"Because the thought of it scares the hell out of me."

Ruth did not reply and sat gazing at her friend, waiting.

"I know it doesn't make much sense, Ruthie," Katie finally said. "But I grew up with Ruddy. He was my friend before he ever became my fiancé. Falling in love with him was easy and felt comfortable."

"Yes, I can understand that," Ruth agreed, nodding. Katie had always seemed a part of the White family and no one was surprised when she and Ruddy became engaged. In fact, it would have seemed strange if they hadn't.

"And then he was gone," Katie whispered.

"Yes," replied Ruth, holding tightly to her friend's hand.

"I didn't know if I could go on," continued Katie. "Much less…"

"Fall in love again?" added Ruth.

"Yes," replied Katie. "I can't go through that pain again, Ruth. If something should happen…"

"Yes, of course," said Ruth when Katie didn't finish. They sat in silence once again, both remembering how they felt when they received the news that Ruddy had been killed on Omaha Beach. Jim had been beside him and was, himself, severely wounded.

"Katie, dear," Ruth began softly and thoughtfully. "I don't believe we can live our lives based on what might happen to us, or to those we love, because we'll never know what that'll be. We only have what we know now. Jim Fielding was a close friend to Ruddy. From Ruddy's letters, one could say they were best friends. Jim lost Ruddy too. Watched him die, in fact. All the while, he lay wounded in the sand and waited for his own death. He once told E.M. that he wanted his last thoughts to be of you, a woman he thought he would never meet."

Katie looked at Ruth, her eyes wide and misty. She hadn't known this last bit of information.

"Besides me, Jim is the only other person who truly knows what it was like for you to lose Ruddy. But just think of his dilemma! He knows that he is in love with his best friend's fiancée and has been for a very long time. I can't begin to imagine the guilt he must feel."

"He's never said anything about this to me," replied Katie, somewhat defensively.

"No. He's been sensitive to your feelings with little regard for his own," said Ruth. "The irony here is that you are afraid to admit your love for Jim out of fear of losing him. And he believes that he will never be yours because your heart will always belong to Ruddy."

Katie smiled weakly at Ruth. "Quite a mess, isn't it?"

"Yes, but it doesn't have to be that way, Katie," replied her friend warmly. "I hope that someday soon the two of you will be able to be honest about your feelings for each other because you truly belong together."

CHAPTER 7
THE CLUE OF THE DISKS

"Good news, Katie!" exclaimed Ruth the next morning when Katie joined her and Gran for breakfast.

"Oh, yes?" replied Katie with a yawn. She had slept rather badly, plagued by strange dreams in which Ruddy, after fighting in the war, had been the one to return home and with the news that Jim Fielding had been killed.

"I just received a call from Poppy. Mother and Boots are well enough for me to come home," said Ruth, placing her napkin in her lap. "I have enjoyed my stay here at Rosegate, of course, but I've missed my family."

"That *is* good news, indeed, Ruthie!" replied Katie, smiling fondly at her friend. "Although I have loved having you here with me. It's been like having a sister that I could see every day. Being an only child can be lonely sometimes."

"I'm afraid, granddaughter, that your only child status will remain," said Gran dryly. "Having a sibling now is fairly impossible. That ship has sailed unless your parents can stop long enough in their travels to produce one. And, even then, you'd be at least 21 years its senior, making you more of a mother to it than a sister."

Katie chuckled. "I was only joking, Gran. You know that I'm very happy being the center of attention in this household. Besides, Ruthie is only three miles down the road should I need the guidance of an older sister," she added, giving her friend a wink.

They were chatting on the front steps while watching Andrews load Ruth's luggage into her car when Jim drove up.

"I have some information, Katie," he began, stepping out of his car. He stopped and looked over at Ruth. "You're not leaving, are you?"

"Yes, I'm afraid I must," she replied. "My family is free of the flu but my father reports that the household is in shambles. He needs my help getting everything back to normal. Well, as normal as anything can be at Sunset Hill," she added with a chuckle.

"But Poppy will spare you for tennis practice on Saturday morning?" Katie asked hopefully, as she kissed her friend goodbye. "The tournament is the following weekend, you know."

"Yes, I'll be over," Ruth confirmed, sliding behind the wheel of her silver Ford Anglia. Then, with a quick wave of the hand and a toot of the horn, she was on her way down the drive, quickly disappearing out of sight.

"Good morning, competitor," Katie said, now turning to Jim. "So, what's the scoop?"

"Can we walk and talk, Katie?" Jim asked, sliding her arm through his. "The weather is beautiful today and I could use a good stretch of the legs."

"Sure," she replied, turning first toward the front door of the mansion. "Let me get Nugget. He'd like a nice walk."

Soon they were making their way along one of the walking paths that ran to the west side of the estate. Nugget, his ears twitching, ever alert for the sound of a scampering squirrel, trotted happily along in front of them.

"You look worried, Jim," remarked Katie, glancing up at him. "Bad news?"

"Well, yes and no," he replied, looking down at the path. "I believe I may have found our two thieves, which is good news, of course."

"But?"

"They may be two of the boys from the Boys Club. Not the Badger Tribe kids, thankfully, but from the older boy's group."

"Oh dear," Katie replied with a sigh.

"Yes," he nodded. "I don't have any proof, as yet, but you remember that the shorter boy called the taller one Frankie?"

"Yes, but there are a lot of boys with that name," Katie replied, slipping her arm back through his as they walked. "Could be just a coincidence."

"Could be," Jim nodded. "Except this one showed me a small picture of an animal and asked me what I thought it might be."

"And did it have numbers beside it and look like it might have been torn from a magazine?" she asked.

"Yes, I'm afraid so," replied Jim.

They walked along in silence for several minutes contemplating the impact of this new bit of information. If Jim's suspicions were right, it would be easy enough to arrest the boys at the Boys Club building. But it also meant that at least one of the them was fairly young and that could lead to complications.

"Do you think you might know the identity of the other boy?" asked Katie. "The shorter one?"

"Frankie has a friend that hangs out with him quite a lot," replied Jim. "His name is Walter Issacs. His father was killed during the war while serving in Italy. His mother hasn't handled it well and drinks more than she should. He has two younger sisters. The family is dirt poor and I hear Walter does odd jobs to help put food on the table. Getting arrested would not be good."

Katie sighed. "The effects of the war seem never ending, don't they?"

"Yes," Jim replied. He glanced over at her but said nothing more.

They continued in silence for several more yards when, nearing the garden shed which housed Tom's science project, Jim stopped and turned to Katie.

"Katie," he began, taking her hand in his. "I've been meaning to tell you…"

KABOOM! Suddenly there was a tremendous explosion, knocking them to the ground and filling the air with smoke. Nugget crouched and pinned his ears back as a blast of hot air flew over him. Katie and Jim managed to look up and see Tom emerge from the shed surrounded by thick smoke. He was waving his arms and coughing, and Jim noticed wisps of fire creeping up the hem of a lab coat that Tom was wearing.

"Tom!" Jim yelled. "Your coat!" He jumped to his feet and ran over, grabbing the lab coat by the collar and tugging it off the startled Tom. He threw it to the ground and stomped out the flames.

Meanwhile, Katie too, had picked herself off the ground and, after checking on Nugget, ran over to the two men.

"Are you all right?" she started to say to Tom when, quite suddenly, they were pelted by a spray of warm liquid raining down on them. But it didn't smell like rainwater. It smelled like...

"Beer!" cried Jim, bringing his wet hand to his lips and licking his palm. "Tom White! Have you been brewing beer?"

"Save my manual!" shouted Tom, ignoring Jim's question. "I've got to save my manual!"

Katie glanced around and saw dozens of papers scattered across the lawn. The explosion had blown the manual clear of the shed which was now engulfed in flames. She joined the men in picking up the pages and was just about to tell Tom that they were now even as far as burning buildings go when she happened to look down at one of the papers in her hand.

"Oh my!" she exclaimed, holding it up. "Of course! Why of all the..."

Jim straightened and turned to look at her. "What is it, Katie? What's wrong?"

"Thomas White!" she shouted excitedly, rushing over to him and throwing her arms around his shoulders. "I could just kiss you!" And with that, she did, giving him a quick peck on his lips, causing the shocked young man to collapse out of her arms and onto the ground. The papers he had been holding fell from his hands, scattering once again over the grass.

"Hey, don't I get one?" teased Jim, his eyes twinkling.

"Look at this, Jim," replied Katie, ignoring his comment and walking over to show him the paper.

On it was a picture of two men working on some sort of a farm. They appeared to be in the process of picking something from very tall vines, which were attached to cross wires. In order to reach the top, the two were strapped to very tall stilts.

"Look at the bottom of the stilts!" smiled Katie.

Jim took the paper from her and glanced down at it. He then looked into her deep blue eyes and chuckled. Each pair of stilts had disk-like feet.

* * *

"They're picking Hops," explained Tom, pointing down at the picture. He was freshly showered and wearing a flannel work shirt and overalls belonging to young Robert, the stable hand, who kept spare clothing in the tack room just in case his got soiled from cleaning out the horse stalls.

Gran had announced that the three of them smelled like burnt beer and would not permit them to enter the house without agreeing to bathe. Tom had offered to drive home to Sunset Hill and come back once he had cleaned-up, but Katie and Jim were anxious to interrogate him before he got away, not trusting that the young man might not get distracted by another project and fail to return to Rosegate.

Jim, who lived in town, did not have the luxury of running home and readily handed over his clothing to Andrews before stepping into the guest room bathtub. Twenty minutes later, he joined Katie, Tom, and Gran in the library, dressed in a pair of light gray trousers, creased down the middle of each leg and cuffed at the bottom. He wore no tie over his crisp white shirt but did have on a dark gray single-breasted blazer. Although he looked as handsome as ever, the outfit was one from the 1930's era as opposed to 1947 and was one size larger than Jim usually wore. Katie wondered to whom in the Rosegate household the clothing belonged.

"Mr. Porter's," said Andrews, reading Katie's expression as her gaze went from Jim to him. He placed a tray of cookies and hot tea on the table in front of them.

"Your father," clarified Gran. "He sent a trunk full of clothes home over a decade ago in anticipation of returning to Fairfield with your mother but, of course, they ended up going to South Africa instead."

Katie had no real clear picture of her world travelling parents, having not seen them since she was around the age of five. She had a vague memory of her father towering above her, like a giant, but no memory of her mother at all. Through the years they had kept in touch, sending her letters and, on occasion, gifts but, strangely, never actual pictures of themselves. It was mind boggling to now realize that her father would be only slightly larger than the lean athletically built young man who sat next to her.

"I'm grateful for the clothing," said Jim, smiling at Gran. "I had images of me coming down in one of Katie's bathrobes."

"I have one that would have looked stunning on you," teased Katie, reaching for a cookie before turning back to Tom. "Now, educate me. What, exactly, are Hops?"

"Hops are part of the hop plant. The flowers, actually," replied Tom, spreading out the pages of his torn manual over the table. "You need them to bitter and flavor the beer. They also help to stabilize the brew, but I think I got that part wrong."

"Indeed," remarked Jim. "Or the fermentation process. It's pretty hot in that shed. How much yeast did you add?"

"Well, I'm not exactly sure," Tom answered, smiling weakly. "That's the part of the process I've been experimenting with."

"Well, it looks like you not only blew the lid off the container, but you managed to set the entire shed on fire," replied Jim, shaking his head.

"Yes, but I believe I'm really on to something! Something big!" Tom exclaimed with enthusiasm. "The last batch was nearly done and..."

He looked over to see Jim, Katie, and Gran staring at him and shaking their heads.

"...lots of money to be made..." he continued softly and then stopped.

"Your beer business days are over, young Tom," said Mrs. Porter firmly. "At least at Rosegate."

"Yes, ma'am," replied Tom sadly. "And I am very sorry for the shed. I had no idea it might explode."

"You are very lucky you weren't seriously hurt," Katie reminded him, looking back at the picture. "Now why are these men on stilts? I suppose the hop plants grow very tall?"

"Yes," Jim answered this time. "When I was on leave in England during the war, I saw fields of them. They are climbing plants that grow up trellises made from wires and string. The higher the better because that enables each plant to get the same amount of sunlight, which contributes to their growth. Looks like these fellows are examining the hops or making repairs to the trellis."

"I imagine that the disked shoes stabilize the stilts so that it is easier to walk in the loose soil," Katie remarked, placing her chin in her hand.

"Yes, I would think so," replied Jim, nodding. "Just before planting, they would need to add the string lines on which the hop plants will grow and that means stepping from side to side, with heavy bundles of string in their arms."

"Or heavy bags of money," said Katie, giving him a meaningful look.

"Gosh, that's right!" exclaimed Jim, smiling at her.

"What on earth are you two talking about?" asked Gran, calmly sipping her tea.

"The bank heists" Jim and Katie replied in unison and then both laughed.

"You see, Gran," explained Katie. "There were disk-like prints at the bottom of each open window at both banks."

"And the break-ins through the upstair windows could have been done from someone on stilts as opposed to a ladder," chimed in Jim.

"Allowing the thieves to leave holding several money bags without having to drop them to someone on the ground," added Katie, getting excited as the scenario was becoming clearer.

"And no need to carry and dispose of a ladder," said Jim. "Although it doesn't explain what the safe cracking man did with his stilts once he entered the building. Surely, he didn't walk around with them on. His head would have hit the ceiling and he would have had to remove them in order to work the combination lock on the safe. That would have taken quite a lot of time."

"What if he didn't have stilts on at all?" replied Katie, getting to her feet and pacing back and forth. "What if he rode on his partner's shoulders?"

"I don't get it," said Tom. "Why would they do that when they could use a perfectly good ladder."

"Because, if they were very good at stilt walking, they could approach the window at the needed height without having to lean a ladder against the building, climb up, and then fiddle with the lock. It would also be quicker to hand over the bags of money, and then climb aboard and off they go leaving only one set of very odd-looking imprints in the ground."

"Here," Jim said to Tom. "Stand up and we'll demonstrate."

Tom stood and then, as Jim stooped down, Katie instructed Tom to climbed upon Jim's shoulders. It took Jim a few seconds to balance Tom, but soon he was able to straighten up and walk a few paces.

"Now let's go out into the hallway," Katie directed. "And alongside the staircase."

Jim followed Katie, bending slightly so as not to bang Tom's body on the top of the library's door frame.

"Over here," Katie pointed, walking over to the staircase's outer railing. "Let's pretend this is a second story window. Jim walk over and let Tom climb off. Careful Tom. You're on the edge of a step so make sure to hang onto the railing. If this was the bank, you would be opening the window latch and stepping inside."

Jim followed Katie's instruction and walked over to the outer side of the staircase. Once there, Tom carefully slid off Jim's shoulders and onto the outer edge of the step.

Katie narrated the imaginary break-in as Gran stood nearby watching in amazement. "Tom somehow unlocks the window. We haven't figured that part out yet. The window opens, Tom steps in and rushes to the safe. He cracks it in less than 5 minutes. He swings open the safe door, dashes in, stuffs money into bank bags found within, and carries them out to Jim who is waiting just outside the window. Jim holds at least one bag in each hand...perhaps two, depending on the size of the bags,...as Tom, carrying bags of his own, climbs back out the window and onto Jim's shoulders," and here Tom carefully slid back onto Jim's shoulders, "and they calmly walk away leaving two local newspaper reporters and the Fairfield Police Department completely puzzled."

At this, Jim carried Tom back through the library door and, bending over, playfully tossed him onto the couch cushions.

"Would be awkward but it would certainly work," said Jim, nodding.

"Yes," replied Katie. "It also explains what the clerk at the Savings and Loan described. If you remember, Jim," she continued, looking up at him as she sat back down on the couch next to Tom, "the man said that the guy at the window swung away. That's not likely if one is standing on a ladder but it is possible to create that effect if one is on stilts. Simply lift one leg and pivot on the other."

"True," agreed Jim, now pacing the floor in front of them.

"The clerk also said that the man standing in the middle of the floor, the safe man, stepped out of the window and was gone. The poor clerk expected to see the fellow dead on the ground but what if the culprit just stepped onto the other man's shoulders and they simply walked away?"

"Yes, that would explain it! Katie, you're a genius!" Jim declared, rubbing his hands together.

"No. Not really. I would never have figured it out had Tom not tried his hand at brewing beer," she replied. She leaned over and gave Tom a poke in his ribs. "You were right, Tom. Your science project might just pay off after all!"

"Ouch!" was all Tom said, looking forlornly at Katie.

"But this is only a theory, after all," Katie remarked. "We don't have any proof unless we can find the stilts and the culprits."

"And there is one more troubling thing about this," said Jim, flopping down in a chair by Gran. "In your article, Katie, you mention that it was a third story window that was broken into at the First National Bank. That would mean that the stilts would have to be at least 30 feet tall, making them very hard to balance. Especially carrying a second person and bags of money. I'm not even sure they make them that tall."

"Yes, there is that," Katie replied, nodding thoughtfully. "Well, we'll just have to drive over to the First National and have a look. Perhaps the bank president was wrong about the location of the window."

"After I stop off at my house and change clothes," remarked Jim, smiling.

They decided it would be less cumbersome it they took one car, so Katie and Jim piled into Jim's Renault Sedan and headed to town, leaving Tom to clean up the burned mess left behind by the fire. After stopping first at Jim's so that he could change into his own suit of clothes, they decided to check in on E.M. before proceeding to the bank. They found him out of bed and working away at his typewriter.

"I called Midge and had her bring me my notes on the Hopkins anniversary party. I should have my article completed by this evening," he announced happily. His voice was still raspy, but the color had returned to his face and his cough appeared to be gone.

"Didn't Robert say that you should be resting in bed for one more day?" asked Katie, scolding him mildly.

"Yes, but what do doctors know, anyway," E.M. replied, feeding another sheet of paper into his typewriter.

"Certainly not how to keep a patient in his bed," chuckled Katie, although she was happy to see her friend feeling so much better. "We'll leave you to work on your article but please do not come into the office today. We don't want you to relapse."

"Yes, dear," he teased, and then muttered under his breath. "Now

I know why I'm not married."

They finally made their way to the First National Bank where Jim pulled in and parked halfway down from the front door. Katie stepped out before he could come around and open her door and he saw that she was pointing to the rear of the building.

"Look Jim," she said, starting to walk in that direction. "I think we've already found the answer to our question. I should have seen this when I was here before instead of taking Mr. Martin's word for it."

Puzzled, Jim followed her along a small walkway, up several steps, and around the corner.

"Ah," he nodded, as he saw that the bank building was built into a small hillside, the ground at the back being much higher than in the front. As they studied the building, they could see what appeared to be two floors with windows.

"See Jim," said Katie. "The thieves thought they were breaking into a second story window but, in reality, it was the third story window they were using."

"Making the distance from the ground to this window the same as in the other banks. No need for extra tall stilts. The actual story doesn't matter as long as the distance from the ground is right."

"Yes, I believe so," replied Katie. "Probably no higher than fifteen feet, I would guess."

"If so, the lobby would have no windows at all."

"Yes," Katie nodded. "But let's go in and make sure."

They walked back around the building and entered the lobby. Sure enough, the first floor, which consisted of the teller's windows and account manager's offices, had no outside windows.

"Jim," said Katie, as they left the bank building and turned toward his parked car. "I've been wondering about something."

"Yes?"

"Why do the Fairfield banks have their safes on the second floor? One would think that they would have them in basements?"

"I see what you mean," Jim nodded, closing the car door behind her before sliding into the driver's seat. "I suppose the climate here in Fairfield makes having a basement impractical and expensive. You see, the building's foundation would have to sit below the frost line which is nearly two feet down."

"Hm, yes, that makes sense," she nodded. "Although we have a wine cellar at Rosegate which is a basement of sorts."

"Well, either nobody cared about frost lines and foundations many years ago when the Rosegate mansion was built, or your ancestors could afford the cost of putting in a wine cellar."

"So, if not in a basement, the next best place might well be up on the second floor," mused Katie. "Much harder to steal a safe or even break into it unless one was willing to go through an upstairs window. Speaking of windows, do you have time to take me over to the police station? I don't want to keep you if you need to get to the *Times*, but I would like to examine the evidence that Sergeant Smith picked up at the scene of the Savings and Loan. We need to figure out how our thieves are unlocking the window latches without breaking the glass."

"Certainly," replied Jim. "When we stopped at my place earlier, I called my editor and told him that I was working on a follow-up article on the bank heist story. I'm yours for the entire day if you like."

"Wonderful," she replied, smiling warmly at him.

Five minutes later they were in the Fairfield Police Department seated across the desk from Detective Grant.

"Charlie," Katie began. "I'm not sure if you've officially met, but this is Jim Fielding, investigative reporter for the *Middleton Times*."

"Ah, yes, the boyfriend," replied the detective, reaching over and shaking Jim's hand. "Saw you at Rosegate during the Yorkie incident and then again at the Savings and Loan heist. How do you do?"

Katie blushed and could not look at Jim, but she heard him reply calmly, "Nice to meet you. And thanks for your help at Rosegate. I think Sergeant Smith might have shot us if you hadn't been there. She most certainly would have killed Nugget."

"Yes, the Sergeant has a rather bad temper," chuckled Charlie Grant. "She hasn't been with us for very long and it's taking the rest of the force quite a bit of time getting used to her."

"Really?" replied Katie, looking up at him. "When did she arrive?"

"Oh, only about two weeks ago," Charlie answered. "She was working on the bank heist cases in Wakefield and Cumberland and someone high up thought it best to loan her to us in Fairfield to work on the heists here since they appear to be connected."

"Interesting," replied Katie, making a note in her reporter's notepad.

"Yes," nodded Charlie. "I don't expect that she'll be with us for very long, especially when we catch the thieves or they move on."

"Do you know where she's from originally?" asked Jim.

"Nope," replied the detective, seemingly uninterested. "Not a clue. So, what can I do for you folks?"

"We'd like to see all of the evidence that Sergeant Smith picked up at the Savings and Loan, if that's all right Charlie."

"Well, it not something we usually do," he replied, shrugging. "But it's already bagged and been recorded so I guess it'll be OK." He picked up the phone and called over to the evidence room. "Bob, would you bring over all the evidence collected from the Savings and Loan job. Oh, on second thought, bring all evidence collected by Sergeant Smith during her investigations of the bank heists here in Fairfield. Yes? That's fine. See you in ten." And he hung up the phone.

"Bob will have everything here in ten minutes," Detective Grant explained. "Can I get either of you a cup of coffee while we wait?"

Jim and Katie declined and spent the time chatting with the friendly detective while they waited. Charlie and Jim found that, although in different army units, they had been aboard the same ship on their way to Normandy and had been in the waves of troops that stormed Omaha Beach. When Charlie began to describe the invasion in painful detail, Jim quietly slid his hand over Katie's.

"Katie lost her fiancé on that beach," he said softly, signaling that the detective might want to limit the details of his recollection.

"Oh! I'm terribly sorry Katie," responded Charlie, turning to her, a look of sadness in his eyes. "I didn't know. You never told me while we were going out."

She felt Jim stiffen ever so slightly but before she had a chance to reply, they were interrupted by an officer entering the room carrying a large black satchel.

"Put the bag over here, Bob," said Charlie, getting up from his chair and walking over to an empty table by the window. "Is that everything?"

"Yeah, Charlie," Bob replied. "That's everything. I did a double check. Sign here," he added, handing a clipboard to the detective.

"Wait a minute," remarked Charlie, taking small bags of items from the satchel and placing them out on the table. "Where's the policeman's shirt? The one we found in the woods at Rosegate?"

"Don't know what you're talking about. This is all we've got," replied Bob. He took back the clipboard and ruffled through several sheets of paper. "Nope. I've got no record of a policeman's shirt. Looks like the sergeant might have forgotten to turn it in."

"Yes, that must be it," muttered Detective Grant, giving Officer Bob a suspicious glance.

The other officer just shrugged his shoulders. "Well, call me when you need me to pick everything up."

Katie and Jim looked over the small clear bags containing evidence as Detective Grant dropped the empty satchel on the floor beside them. On the table lay the pencil, screws, paperclips, and the wooden ruler all collected from the Savings and Loan. A pair of scissors, labeled "First National" was also there along with a hair comb and nail file, both from the Banking and Trust heist.

"There's one other thing missing besides the shirt," Katie said, scanning the items once again.

"And what's that?" asked Jim.

"The magnet," she replied. "I saw Sergeant Smith drop it into her coat pocket after collecting the other pieces of evidence at the Savings and Loan. Looks like she forgot to turn this piece of evidence in, as well. The question is why?"

CHAPTER 8
THE CODE IS BROKEN

"I have one more stop to make before lunch, Jim, if that's OK," said Katie, as they left the police station and stepped into his car.

"Sure thing, Ace," he replied, starting up the car and pulling away from the curb. "Where to?"

"Miller's Plumbing and Hardware."

"I have the distinct feeling that you don't believe Sergeant Smith just forgot to turn in the shirt and the magnet," Jim mentioned.

"Right you are, competitor," replied Katie, giving him a warm smile. "There's something very strange going on here. Why hold these two particular items back?"

"You don't like her very much, do you?" he asked, coming to a stop at a red light a few blocks from the hardware store.

"I have no real opinion of her at all," answered Katie, shrugging her shoulders. "Other than being rather put-out that she insisted I come down to the police station for questioning and the fact she wanted to shoot Nugget."

Jim chuckled. "Yes, I could see why that might bother you." He turned into the parking lot of Miller's Plumbing and Hardware and parked the car.

"You don't need to come in," said Katie, stepping quickly from the car. "I'll just be a moment."

As he sat and waited, Jim chided himself for his impulsive jealous reaction to Detective Grant's statement about having dated Katie. Of course Katie had dated before she met him. She was the most wonderful, intriguing, and beautiful woman he had ever met. He, himself, had dated before he met Katie. Quite a lot, in fact. But they were together now and although she had never actually said how she felt, he believed that Katie was fond of him. Maybe not in love but she certainly cared for him. Yes, that was it. So, there was nothing to worry about. He would force himself to ignore these feelings of uneasiness. He would stop thinking about it. Katie was his and he was hers and that was all there was to it.

True to her word, Katie returned in a matter of minutes carrying a brown paper bag with a horseshoe shaped magnet in it.

"Got the best one they had," she told Jim taking it out and holding it up for him to see.

"That you did," he replied. "Now what are you going to do with it?"

"I'm not sure," Katie sighed. "But I certainly can't think on an empty stomach. Let's have lunch at Rosegate instead of Polly's today. I left the coded message we found in the woods there and I need your help identifying one of the animals."

"You sound like Frankie from the Boys Club," Jim replied, giving her a smile. "But I'm game." He turned in the direction of the country road that led to Rosegate and, as they left the city limits, increased the speed of the Renault.

"Speaking of Frankie," Katie continued, glancing over at him. "When you mentioned him this morning, you didn't tell me if you recognized the animal in his picture?"

Jim nodded. "It was a dingo. And before you ask, the number beside it was 1."

"A picture of a dingo with the number 1 beside it," repeated Katie thoughtfully. "I don't get it, do you?"

"No, I don't have a clue," replied Jim, shaking his head. "But it's obvious that our ghost is giving our boys a bit of an education. It would have been easier to cut out a picture of a dog instead of a dingo."

"Yes," agreed Katie, sweeping a strand of hair from her face. "I wonder."

They arrived at the estate just as Katie's grandmother was sitting down to lunch.

"Ah, you're just in time," she announced as the two entered the dining room. "Andrews, tell Gertie to bring more sandwiches unless you require something more substantial, Jim?"

"No, ma'am," replied Jim, sliding into the chair next to Katie. "A sandwich would be great."

"If Gertie could add a slice of pie to that, Jim will be in heaven," chuckled Katie, laying her napkin on her lap. "Apple if she's got it."

"Certainly, Miss," replied Andrews as he left the room.

"So, what mischief have the two of you been up to?" asked Gran, folding her hands across her lap and raising her eyebrows.

"Well, let's see," replied Katie, gazing over at Jim and then back to her grandmother. "We've been in search of a third story window that ended up being on the second story. We discovered E.M. out of bed and working despite doctor's orders. We stopped by the Fairfield police station and found out that the bad-tempered Sergeant Smith is on temporary loan to the department and that she failed to turn in two pieces of vital evidence. This has compelled me to purchase a magnet from Miller's Plumbing and Hardware. Oh, yes, and we also discovered that Detective Grant doesn't mind sharing information with two nosy newspaper reporters."

At that moment Gertie entered the dining room carrying a large tray of sandwiches and an apple pie. Andrews, following close behind, held two carafes of iced tea which he placed in the center of the table.

"I baked it fresh this morning," said Gertie, setting the pie on the sideboard and turning to Jim. "I had a feeling you'd be eating at least one meal with us today."

"Thank you, Gertie!" exclaimed Jim, smiling warmly at her. "You must have a sixth sense."

"Yes, I suppose I do," she replied, glancing at Katie fondly and then exiting the room.

"Sounds like you've had a busy morning," said Gran, pouring herself a glass of tea. "I'm glad that you took time to come home and have some lunch."

"I wanted to show Jim the coded message that we recovered in the woods. Ruthie and I worked on it for quite a while last night, but we didn't get very far in solving it," replied Katie. "In fact, I'd like to show you as well, Gran. You're good at solving puzzles and this one has me quite stumped."

"I'd be happy to take a look at it, granddaughter," smiled Gran. "The sooner we can extricate the ghost and his culprits from our woods, the better."

The lunch topic now turned to the growing of roses, a hobby which both Jim and Gran were passionate about. This left Katie time to quietly ponder the aspects of the bank heist story since her involvement in the conversation would be limited.

To start with, she knew that the ghost of Golden Joe, or someone pretending to be, was directing the bank break-in operation. But why the elaborate set up? Why not just meet in some alleyway or warehouse?

"Unless the ringleader doesn't want to be identified," she thought to herself. Even to the rest of the gang. It was obvious that the two young thieves didn't know the ghost. In fact, they were quite fearful of him. Then there was the matter of the instructions being given in code, a seemingly unnecessary risk given that the young men may not be able to break it. Since the message appeared to be quite short, maybe only a few words, why not just tell them? But she remembered that the ghost motioned his intentions and never spoke.

Then there was the use of stilts instead of a ladder. Ingenious but requiring special training. She couldn't imagine that there was a hop farm nearby, but she did make a mental note to check for any circuses that might be performing in the surrounding area.

"I find Godby's horse manure to be the best," Gran was saying. "Don't you agree, Katie?"

"What?"

"Horse manure," repeated Gran, glancing at Katie, her eyes twinkling.

"We noticed that you were worlds away," chuckled Jim as he placed his fork down beside his empty plate. "I believe your grandmother was trying to bring you back to this one."

"Indeed," smiled Mrs. Porter.

"I'm terribly sorry," replied Katie, smiling. "I'm afraid you are correct. I was thinking about the bank heists and the ghost of Golden Joe."

"Well then," said Gran, standing up from the dining table. "How about we have our coffee in the library and try to solve Katie's coded message?"

Jim and Mrs. Porter walked across the hall to the library as Katie ran upstairs to her bedroom to retrieve it. She soon joined them and placed the message on the table in front of them.

"We've guessed at the identity of all of the pictures except the second one," she explained. "What on earth is this sinister fellow?"

"Good gracious!" exclaimed Gran, studying the picture.

The creature walked on all fours, its legs long and furry. It had a small angular face with an extremely long snot that was nearly the same size as its legs. It looked like a cross between a sloth and a small hairy elephant. Jim started to laugh.

"Do you have an encyclopedia?" he asked, glancing around.

"Yes, of course," replied Katie, waving to a section of shelving across the library where a complete set could be seen.

Jim walked over and selected the first volume. He opened it and turned the pages until he reached the one he wanted and then walked back to Katie and her grandmother.

"Ah, here he is," said Jim, setting the book down beside the coded message. "Our strange looking fellow is an anteater."

"Really?" responded Katie, puzzled. "He doesn't look like any picture of an anteater I've ever seen."

"That's because you've most likely been looking at a small anteater," replied Jim. "There are several different types. The one shown in the message is a giant anteater, the strangest looking of the species. Which makes me wonder why Golden Joe chose this picture instead of the smaller anteater which would have been more recognizable."

"Just like choosing a dingo instead of a dog," added Katie, gazing down at the picture in the encyclopedia.

"Yes, exactly," replied Jim, nodding.

"So, now that we have the identity of the anteater?" asked Gran. "Can you decode the message?"

"No, Gran," replied Katie, dejected. "I still can't make head nor tails out of it," she added as she wrote the name "giant anteater" next to the second picture.

"I find the numbers interesting," remarked Mrs. Porter, leaning closer. "Since we can't figure out why they are there, let's see what they *don't* tell us."

"Like starting backwards," smiled Jim, gazing over Katie's shoulder.

"Yes," replied Gran, picking up Katie's pencil.

"Well, they're not giving us the chronological order," Katie pointed out.

"Or the number of letters in each word," added Jim.

"Or the number of that particular animal that might be needed to do something," said Katie. "Since we know this message has to do with the bank heists, surely the thieves would not need to bring 5 anteaters and 2 tigers with them."

"No indeed," murmured Gran thoughtfully. "Let's try a different approach. What exactly do we need from the message?"

"We need to decipher it," replied Katie, looking at her grandmother.

"Yes, I realize that, dear," smiled Gran fondly. "But think of it this way. If you were the thief, what would you need to know from the start."

"Well," said Katie. "I suppose the first thing would be the location of the bank that I needed to rob."

"That's right," exclaimed Jim, sliding down on the couch next to Katie. "And perhaps the day and time of the hit, although that could come in a later message."

"That's true," agreed Gran, nodding. "Noting the shortness of this message, I would guess our ghost is trying to give the location. That would be a good place for us to start."

They stared at the list of creatures for several minutes.

"What were the three banking institutions that were robbed?" Gran finally asked.

"The First National Bank, the Banking and Trust, and the Savings and Loan, although that heist was only attempted and failed," replied Katie.

"Maybe this message is about a bank that hasn't been robbed yet," suggested Gran.

"No, I don't think so," replied Katie, resting her chin in her hand. "Frankie was attempting to destroy it when it flew out of his hand. Surely he would have wanted to keep it until the job was done."

"Looks like a call for more coffee," announced Jim. "Mrs. Porter, Katie, may I pour you another cup?"

"Yes, please," replied Gran, handing him her empty one but Katie shook her head and continued to study the message.

"Oh!" she suddenly shouted, jumping to her feet and walking quickly over to the desk in the corner. She pulled out a blank piece of paper and returned to the couch. "I think I've figured it out!"

She placed the sheet of paper next to the message and pointed to the third picture. It was of the vulture.

"When Andrews identified the vulture for Ruth and me, I wrote the name out next to the picture. Same with the Loon. That may be our key. Let's disregard the pictures for a moment and look at the actual names of each spelled out. The numbers may indicate the letter in the name of the creature that we are to use," she said, excitedly. "For instance, the number 1 is by the word scorpion so I'll write down the letter "s" as the first letter of my bank location."

"For the second picture do you choose the fifth letter of the word giant or anteater?" asked Jim, pointing to the picture.

"Hm, good point," she replied, tucking a strand of brown hair behind her ear. "Let's skip that one for now." She left a black space after the letter "s" on her paper.

"Then our next letter is "v" as it's the first letter in the word vulture," said Gran.

"Our second letter is the "i" in Tiger," remarked Jim.

"And "n" as the fourth letter in Loon," continued Katie.

Following this process through each of the pictures, Katie was able to spell out the word "s -vingloan."

"If we ignore the word "giant," it looks like the "a" which is the fifth, and first letter for that matter, of the word "anteater" fits right after the "s." Which means that this message refers to the Savings and Loan!" exclaimed Katie proudly.

"You've cracked it, Katie!" shouted Jim, throwing his arm around her shoulders and giving her a hug.

"The three of us solved it," replied Katie, blushing at Jim's reaction and glancing quickly at her grandmother. Mrs. Porter, however, seemed not to notice.

"Is this the only message that you have?" Gran asked.

"Yes, I'm afraid so," replied her granddaughter. "It sure would be nice to have the one indicating the next job."

"Wait a minute," said Jim, snapping his fingers after a moment. "We have at least one letter."

"We do?" asked Katie.

"Yes, remember Frankie asked me to identify a picture of a dingo. If he is indeed one of the thieves, then the next job might begin with a "d"."

"Jim, although I would love to agree with you," replied Katie gently. "It is a bit of a stretch. After all, we have no proof that

Frankie *is* one of our thieves and, besides, the letter "d" could be the middle or end of the code. Do you have any idea where his picture might have been placed in his message?"

"No," replied Jim, reluctantly shaking his head.

"And there is the possibility that it doesn't belong in a message at all," she continued. "Perhaps he was doing his homework or just ran across the picture in a magazine and was curious."

"Hm," replied Jim, giving her a warm smile. "You have a point. And they call me the investigative reporter! I think I've just been dethroned!"

"Well before you put away your crown, let's investigate your theory anyway." Katie chuckled. "You may just be on to something!"

* * *

"I don't have no idea what you're talking about," replied the brash young man named Frankie Cooper.

"You don't have *any* idea," Jim corrected.

"Yeah, like I said," nodded Frankie. He slid his hands into his pockets and shifted his weight from side to side.

Katie and Jim had left Gran and driven over to the Boys Club to see if they could find Frankie and question him. Jim found him shooting pool in the recreation room.

"So, you never asked about a picture of a dingo?" asked Katie.

"Listen doll," replied Frankie, giving Katie a rather suggestive look up and down. "Like I said, I…"

But he didn't get a chance to finish because Jim grabbed him by the back of the jacket collar and yanked him up onto his tiptoes.

"If you will excuse us, Miss Porter," Jim said to Katie politely. "I need to speak with this young man for a minute. We'll be right back." And before she could respond, he dragged Frankie around the corner and out of sight.

Katie took the opportunity to gaze through the open doors that bordered the Boys Club lobby. All but two rooms where empty of activity. In one, she could see a reading circle in progress. A group of young boys were gathered around a young soldier wearing an army corporal's uniform who had joined them on the floor. They sat enraptured as the young man read aloud from Robert Louis Stevenson's Treasure Island.

"Three,' reckoned the captain, 'ourselves make seven, counting Hawkins, here. Now, about the honest hands?" the soldier read, using his best imitation of a sea caption.

Katie smiled to herself as she moved away. She could imagine that the boys would be dreaming tonight of pirates and buried treasures. Peering into the next room, she saw a group of older boys each working behind a row of long tables.

"They're working on their own repair projects," said a middle age man coming towards her. He gave her a warm smile. "May I help you, miss?"

"I don't wish to intrude, sir," began Katie. "I'm here with a friend and he's been detained for a moment. While I was waiting, I couldn't help but notice your activity here and was curious."

"Ah, of course," replied the man in a friendly manner. "My name is Allen. Allen Thompson. Please come in and let me show you around," he added, waving his hand around the room. Katie nodded politely and stepped inside. "Each of these young men have chosen to work on a project for someone in our community," explained Mr. Thompson. "For instance, Pete over here is working on repairing Reverend Martin's push mower. How's it going, Pete?"

"Swell, Mr. Thompson," answered Pete. "I've got the right pinion gear back on and aligned properly. The blades will turn real nice now."

"Let's sharpen them, too, while we've got the mower," replied Mr. Thompson, patting Pete on the shoulder.

"Yes, sir," replied the young man, bending back over his work.

"Sidney is working on Mrs. Webster's oscillating fan," Mr. Thompson pointed out, as he and Katie moved to the next table. "I don't think most folks realize how many things we use daily are mechanical."

"So, all the projects here are mechanical in design?" asked Katie, glancing around the room.

"Yes," replied Mr. Thompson. "This group is learning how to work on small machines while we have other groups learning carpentry, auto repair, and even agriculture. It's all part of our job training program."

"How wonderful!" exclaimed Katie, impressed. "This young man looks like he has quite a task."

They walked over to boy sitting behind a mantel clock. The back of the timepiece was open, and the young man was carefully prodding a small gear with what looked like a jeweler's pick.

"This is Walter," replied Allen Thompson, introducing the boy. "He is a genius when it comes to clocks. This one belongs to the elderly Mrs. Winfield. It stopped working several weeks ago and she misses it terribly. Fortunately, Walter has nearly gotten it working again."

"Really?" inquired Katie, leaning over slightly to get a better look. "That's remarkable. Where on earth did you learn such a thing, Walter?"

"My dad," replied Walter briefly and without looking up. "He taught me."

"Yes," nodded Mr. Thompson. "You see, I'm the shop teacher over at the high school and am able to teach most of these skills to the boys. But clock repair is well beyond my ability. We're fortunate that Walter is learning to carry on his family's trade. Your grandfather was a clock maker, isn't that right, Walter?" he added, turning back to the boy.

"Yeah," was all Walter said as he laid down the jeweler's tool and reached for a stethoscope.

"Let's move away and let Walter listen to the gears," explained Mr. Thompson as the young man placed the earpieces in his ears and raised the end of the stethoscope close to the clock.

"What an excellent trade skill," remarked Katie sincerely. "I'm quite impressed, Mr. Thompson. Walter's father must be very proud of him."

"Unfortunately, Walter lost his father in the war," responded Allen Thompson, his tone growing somber. "As did nearly all of these boys." And then looking up, he exclaimed, "Jim! I didn't know you were coming in today?"

Katie looked over to see Jim standing in the doorway with Frankie directly behind him.

"Hi Allen," he replied, taking a step forward to shake the older man's hand. "I'm actually here on a different matter and seem to have lost my…er…friend," he added, pointing to Katie.

"Oh, how rude of me," interrupted Katie, noting Jim's hesitation. "I failed to introduce myself. My name is Katie Porter. Jim and I just stopped by to speak with Frankie."

"Not *the* Miss Porter, Princess of Rosegate?" joked Mr.

Thompson with a twinkle in his eye. "The Badger Tribe has told us all about you and your wonderful property. Why, you're the talk of the Boys Club!"

Jim looked down at his feet and said nothing, waiting with some apprehension for Katie's response. She replied with a chuckle, however. "Yes, I'm afraid so. I hope you won't hold that against me."

"No, indeed," replied the shop teacher. "In fact, our director and I would love to speak with you sometime in the near future about holding an overnight camping trip in your woods."

"I'd be delighted to hear more about it," replied Katie, reaching into her purse and giving Mr. Thompson her card. "Just give me a call."

Then, giving him a nod goodbye, she and Jim proceeded back out into the lobby to question Frankie. Katie saw immediately that there was a complete change in his demeanor. The young man now stood attentively with his hands resting in front of him.

Jim started the conversation. "I believe that Frankie has something to say to you before we continue."

"Yes, Uncle Jim," nodded Frankie, glancing over at him before returning to Katie. "I want to apologize for my behavior, Miss Porter," said the young man, his tone sounding sincere. "I'm terribly sorry. I meant no harm. Uncle Jim reminded me that this was no way to treat a doll...er, I mean, a lady."

"Or any woman, isn't that right Frankie?" added Jim, raising his eyebrows.

"Yes, sir," nodded Frankie, dropping his gaze to his feet.

"Well then," replied Katie, smiling at the young man and then up at Jim. "I think I can overlook it this time, Frankie. Are you ready to answer a few questions now?"

"Sure, but I don't know if I can help you, miss," answered Frankie in earnest.

"Well, we'll start with an easy one," replied Katie. "Did you ask Jim, I mean Uncle Jim, here, about the identity of a picture?"

"Yes, miss," nodded Frankie.

"Was it a picture of a dingo?" asked Katie.

"Yes," replied Frankie. "I thought it was some kind of a dog, but I wasn't sure. Uncle Jim told me it was a cousin to a dog and that it was found in Australia."

"Uncle Jim is very knowledgeable about such things," she said, shooting a teasing glance at Jim. "Was the picture of the dingo part of a coded message with other pictures on it?"

Frankie didn't answer and stood silently for several minutes. He seemed to be struggling with his conscious before finally saying, "I don't understand what you mean, Miss Porter."

"I think you do, Frankie," countered Katie. "I think you and another boy got the message from the stump by the creek in the woods at Rosegate."

"No, Miss Porter," replied Frankie, now panicked and backing away. "No!"

"You got the message from a ghost," Katie pressed him. "The ghost of Golden Joe, didn't you?"

"No!" the young man shouted. "No! That's not true! I don't know nothin' 'bout any ghost, I tell you!" And suddenly, Frankie turned on his heels and ran out the front door.

"Shall I go after him?" said Jim, starting to move toward the entrance.

"No," sighed Katie, placing a hand on his arm to stop him. "Let him go. We've gotten all we can out of him."

"And what is that, exactly?" replied Jim, holding the door open for her as they left the Boys Club. "He didn't tell us anything."

"Sure he did, Jim," said Katie, slipping her arm through his. "Anyone that frightened could have received instructions from a ghost and would have run away rather than risk telling anyone about it."

CHAPTER 9
THE MAGNET TRICK

"Jim?" said Katie softly, as they drove along the country road back to Rosegate.

"Hm?" he replied, giving her a quick glance before returning his attention to the road ahead.

"I didn't have a chance to explain while we were at the police station, but I never dated Charlie Grant," she remarked. "He took me to the movies twice, and that was well over a year ago. He's a nice guy but we found we had nothing in common and thought it best just to remain friends."

"I admit I'm relieved to hear it, Katie," Jim replied, glancing over at her.

"Jealous?"

"No. Well, yes. A little," he answered, giving her a weak smile. "I'm not normally a jealous guy but hearing Charlie say that he'd gone out with you did give me a jolt." He paused and shook his head.

"Well, I'm dating you now, Jim," she replied casually with a wave of her hand. "If that changes, you'll be the first to know. So there is no need for you to be jealous, okay?"

"Yes, okay," he replied, but an expression of dismay crossed his face. Her offhand manner stung him. He had expected her to take this opportunity to finally admit to some feelings for him, but she had said nothing other than she was fine dating him. Was it possible that he had been kidding himself all this time?

They drove along the country road leading to Rosegate in silence for several miles, their thoughts focused in different directions.

"American Safe Company," Katie suddenly whispered as she absentmindedly gazed at the passing landscape.

"The make of the safes at both banks?" replied Jim, shifting gears in the Renault to make the turn into Rosegate.

"Yes," she answered. "You don't happen to know how to crack a safe by any chance?"

"No," he replied. "I try to avoid anything that has to do with jail, thank you."

"I wonder if it's easier to crack a safe made by the American Safe Company or if we're dealing with a professional who can crack any safe?"

"I read somewhere that safe cracking is actually much more difficult than one imagines," Jim remarked as he drove up to Rosegate's front door and parked. "Come to think of it, it was in an article I read in the *Stars and Stripes* during the war about this guy named Harry C. Miller. He's devised a three-step method of manipulating the combination and is considered the best safecracker ever known. In fact, President Roosevelt had him come to the White House to crack one of his own safes when an aide, the only guy who knew the combination, was killed."

"Not a very good idea to have only one man know the combination," laughed Katie, stepping out of the car as Jim held the door open.

"No, I suppose not," he replied, fumbling with his hat in his hands as he walked her to the front door.

"Would you like to stay for dinner?" Katie asked, glancing at her watch. "It's nearly time for cocktails and…"

Suddenly the door flew open and Andrews stepped out. "Miss Katie," he shouted. "Detective Grant of the Fairfield Police Department just called. The Dempsey house has just been robbed!"

* * *

The Dempsey sisters were considered quite an odd couple in the town of Fairfield. They lived in a large brownstone in an expensive part of town. Margaret, the older of the two, had inherited the house from their father after living there all her life and taking care of both of her parents. Her sister, Eloise, had moved in with her after several years of travelling in anticipation that her stay would be brief. However, that had been twenty years ago and she was now a permanent fixture.

There was plenty of room for the two of them, but it often seemed crowded as Eloise, a larger than life character, seemed to overwhelm any space she inhabited. She was constantly noisy, either by talking loudly to herself or having a radio blaring. She was an avid radio listener and the Dempseys had one in every room of the house. Eloise would leave all of them on as she moved from room to room so as not to miss a minute of a broadcast.

Margaret, herself, had been quite a talker in her youth, but she had grown quiet through the years and folks around town assumed it was because she was unable to get a word in edgewise. But there was also an air of sadness about her which perhaps was the result of a lifetime of disappointment. No one knew exactly what had happened to Margaret and she never talked about her past. However, she did once reveal to Katie that she found solace in her own silence.

"I have great conversations in my head," she confessed. "And I don't have to argue with anyone."

It was dusk when Katie and Jim arrived at the brownstone. The property was surrounded by police cars as well as several neighbors who had come outside to see what all the fuss was about.

The couple had quite a run-in with the officer guarding the front door and it took finding Detective Grant, who fortunately was around the back of the building, before they could gain access to house. The detective, himself, was busy speaking with another officer so just tipped his hat at them and pointed to the back entrance.

As it so happened, coming through to the back also afforded them the opportunity to look at the ground under the second story window and they quickly discovered the same strange disk-like markings.

"Stilts again," Katie whispered to Jim as they bent over to examine the prints.

"Yes," agreed Jim, whispering back. "Looks like our thieves have switched from banks to private residences."

"Perhaps," replied Katie. "Or decided on both in order to keep us guessing." They turned and made their way to the back door, reaching it just as Margaret Dempsey pulled it open.

"Are you all right?" Katie asked the anxious woman who appeared to be very relieved to see them.

"Yes, we're fine" she answered, giving Katie a quick hug. "I'm so glad that Detective Grant was willing to call you when we asked him. My sister and I read your article about the bank robberies in the *Gazette* and, since we know your grandmother so well, hoped that you might be able to help us."

"Well, I'm not sure what I can do," Katie replied, giving Margaret's forearm a gentle squeeze. "But I'll do the best I can."

"There is one thing you might find interesting," Jim interjected over Katie's shoulder. "There are some strange prints found outside your window and they match others found at the banks that have been robbed."

Margaret looked over at Jim, noticing him for the first time.

"Margaret," said Katie. "This is Jim Fielding from the *Middleton Times*. He's been following the same story as I have."

"Oh no!" responded Eloise, entering the room just in time to hear Jim's introduction. "Not the press! We can't have the press! Not yet! Oh dear!"

Jim looked startled and was about to reassure the upset woman when Katie laid her hand on his arm and looked back at both sisters.

"Jim is a friend," she explained softly. "We've been out together following leads and were just returning to Rosegate for dinner when Andrews told us about your call. We came right over."

Margaret nodded in acceptance, but Eloise still looked doubtful.

"Well, they cleaned us out," remarked Margaret pragmatically, as she led them into the library where a police officer was dusting a safe for fingerprints. Another officer was examining the window ledge and, as she turned, Katie suddenly realized that it was Sergeant Smith.

"What are you doing here?" demanded the officer angrily. "I thought I told your editor to take you off this story."

"You did tell my editor," replied Katie calmly. "But after you spoke with him, he insisted I continue to follow all leads. You see, the *Fairfield Gazette* is a legitimate local newspaper and we investigate any story that might reveal a threat to the public."

"As does the *Middleton Times*," added Jim, coming up to stand next to Katie. "Hello, Sergeant. Find anything interesting?"

"Hello Jim," replied Sergeant Smith, ignoring Katie. "The press has a right to report on a story but not until the police clear the crime scene. And that can only be done after we complete our investigation which we haven't done yet. I must ask you both to leave."

"Excuse me, Sergeant," said Margaret stepping forward. "You are in my house and these two young people are my guests. I invited them over. You can instruct them to stay out of the way of the police, but you cannot make them leave."

Sergeant Smith glared at the woman, but Margaret only glared back. "Well, we'll just see about that," the officer replied reaching for her handcuffs.

Fortunately for all, Detective Grant entered the room at that very moment and gave everyone a warm smile.

"Hello Katie. Jim," he said, nodding at them both. "I'm glad you could make it. The Dempseys asked me to call you. We all wondered if you might be able to help."

Sergeant Smith, hearing that a superior officer was involved, turned on her heels and stomped out of the room.

"We'll certainly do what we can, Charlie," Katie replied. "Is it the same MO as the bank heists?"

"Yes, it appears so," nodded the detective. "Open second story window. Same strange marks below. Quite puzzling. Why hit a private residence when there are still several banks left to rob in town?"

"Did they take only what was in the safe?" asked Jim, taking out his reporter's pad.

"Yes," said Charlie. "They…"

"Took everything," interrupted Eloise. "Money, Mother's pearl necklace, Daddy's gold watch, several gold coins…"

"They took jewelry?" asked Katie, looking over at Margaret. "That will be unnecessarily inconvenient for them to handle."

"Why not?" asked Eloise. "The pieces are small and easy to carry. Besides, they're very valuable. I would think the thieves would steal nothing but jewelry!"

"Because selling stolen jewelry usually requires a fence," Jim responded, smiling over at her. "Money can be spent easily and anywhere."

"Yes," added Margaret. "But these thieves will be very disappointed."

"Why?" asked Katie.

"Because the necklace and watch are copies. I had to sell the originals several years ago to help pay for the taxes on the house."

"Margaret!" cried Eloise, bringing her hands to her face. "How could you! Why Mother's necklace…"

"Was needed to keep this roof over our heads, Eloise," replied Margaret, cutting short her sister's protest. "I had the copies made by an expert in New York so that you wouldn't find out and make a fuss. I suppose the cat's out of the bag now," she added, throwing up her hands.

"What time did the theft occur?" asked Jim. "Do you know?"

"Yes. We think just about an hour ago," said Eloise. "The frightening thing is that we were home. I was upstairs taking a nap and my sister was in the kitchen preparing dinner."

"We didn't hear a thing," Margaret added in resignation. "They were here and gone before we knew what was happening."

"Very quiet thieves," muttered Katie, turning and moving to the window.

"Well, they didn't need to be," said Margaret, shooting a glance at her sister. "You see, several radios were on and one really can't hear a bomb go off because Eloise turns them up so high."

"You had the radios on while you were napping?" said Detective Grant, raising his eyebrows.

"Yes, well," replied Eloise sheepishly. "The sound helps me sleep."

"And they came through this window?" Katie asked, peering out and looking down at the ground below where a police officer was taking pictures of the strange prints.

"Yes, that's right," said Eloise. "Although I can't imagine how. We always keep our windows locked."

"I see that there is a chip missing from the latch," observed Katie, running her finger across it.

"Yes, it happened many years ago," replied Margaret. "Very unusual since the latch is made of metal. The tip snapped off in Father's hand one evening. Probably a fault when they made it. I never got it repaired because the latch still works and we're able to lock the window."

"Yes, I see," replied Katie, flipping the latch back and forth. "Very interesting."

"Do you have an alarm system, Miss Dempsey?" Jim asked Margaret.

"No," she replied. "We did at one time, but I had it disconnected. Eloise kept setting it off accidently and, besides, I felt we really didn't need it. After all, we live in a nice neighborhood. Who would steal from us? Ironic, isn't it?"

"How much money was taken?" asked Detective Grant, walking over to the safe as another officer packed up his lab kit and, shaking his head, whispered "no prints" before walking away.

"$500," replied Margaret, plopping down in a chair. "All we had left."

"No, that can't be!" exclaimed Eloise. "What about our annuity? Surely we have that?"

"Not until next year, Eloise," replied her sister quietly. "The next payment is not due until December."

"But, how will we live?" cried Eloise, wringing her hands in distress. "How will we eat?"

"I don't know," replied Margaret softly, and she got up and left the room.

* * *

"Are you all right, Jim? Would you like me to drive?" Katie asked as they left the Dempseys and walked to his car parked at the curb.

"I'm fine," he said, opening the passenger side door for her. "Why do you ask?"

"Because you seem out of sorts," she answered, concerned.

"It's nothing," he replied, coming around the car and sliding behind the wheel. "I've got a bit of a headache. I seem to be prone to them since the war."

"Are you sure? I don't mind driving," she remarked, looking intently into his eyes. She could see that something was bothering him.

"No need, Katie," he answered rather abruptly and then, pausing for a moment, turned to look at her. "Sorry, I didn't mean to be so short." And taking a deep breath, he added, "I'm fine. I'll drop you at Rosegate and then go home, take some aspirin, and relax with a good book."

He started the car and pulled away from the curb. "I'm quite used to taking care of myself, you know," he said so softly that she barely heard him. "Been doing it for years."

Katie looked back at him with raised eyebrows, but he kept his eyes on the road and didn't meet her gaze.

Gran was waiting for them at the end of the walkway when they arrived back at Rosegate. "How are the Dempseys?" she asked anxiously as Katie approached with Jim following a few steps behind. "Was anyone hurt?"

"No, Gran," replied her granddaughter. "No one was hurt but the thieves took all of their cash and a few pieces of jewelry."

"Oh, that's too bad. We must find a way to help them," said Gran, taking Katie by the arm and turning toward the house. "Coming Jim?" she asked, glancing back over her shoulder.

"No, Mrs. Porter," Jim replied, shaking his head. "Thank you, but I must be getting home." And tipping his hat to both women, he quickly turned and walked back to his car, pulling away and disappearing down the driveway in a matter of seconds.

Gran turned and looked at Katie, an expression of concern on her face.

"He's not feeling well," Katie replied, shrugging. "Headache."

Gran studied her granddaughter for a moment before speaking. "How unfortunate," she finally said.

"Yes," replied Katie, feeling a strange sense of guilt. "I'll call him later this evening and see if he's feeling better."

They went directly into the dining room where dinner was waiting for them. Katie noticed the horseshoe shaped magnet that she had left on the sideboard that morning and absentmindedly picked it up and carried it to the table with her, setting it beside her plate as she laid her napkin in her lap.

"Were the Dempseys out when their place was robbed?" asked Gran, still concerned about her friends.

"No, they were home," Katie answered. "Which is rather worrisome because they could have been hurt if they had seen the burglars. Fortunately, several radios were on and the two women never heard a thing."

"Ah, yes," nodded Gran, cutting into her roast beef. "Eloise loves to keep those on throughout the house. I don't know how Margaret stands it. And to think that she's…"

"Hm," replied Katie, her mind a million miles away as Gran continued to speak. She played with the magnet as she pondered her evening with Jim, moving it inch by inch toward her dessert spoon until the utensil was caught in its magnetic field and pulled to it. She released it and repeated the process. "Jim's headache," she was thinking. "Prone to him since the war. Wonder if it has anything to do with his injury. Shows how serious it must have been. He got the purple heart for it. I wonder if it was worth it. After all, it's just a metal. E.M. received a metal also and didn't have to get hurt to earn it. Of course, his is the Bronze Star for valor, a completely different sort of thing. E.M. had to choose to endanger his life in order to save others. It was a choice. Jim didn't choose to get shot, or hit with shrapnel, or whatever it was that nearly killed him. But in the end, they're still just metals. "Oh my goodness!" she exclaimed, startling her grandmother.

"Katie, dear," said Gran. "What is it? What on earth's the matter?"

"Metal," replied Katie, holding up the magnet with the spoon attached. "The window sash latches are metal."

"Yes, I believe that's true."

"And this is a magnet," continued Katie, jumping up from her chair.

"Katie, are you all right? What on earth has gotten into you?"

"Oh Gran! It's been staring me in the face the entire time! What a fool I've been not to see it!"

"I think you've lost your mind, granddaughter," replied Mrs. Porter, putting down her fork and knife and staring at Katie.

But Katie wasn't listening. She walked quickly across the dining room and over to one of its windows. Holding the magnet close to the latch, she slowly moved it from side to side. Nothing happened. She moved the magnet closer. This time, the latch began to quiver slightly.

"Can you tell me what you're doing?" asked Gran, coming over to stand next to her.

"I think the thieves have been using a magnet to unlock the window latches," replied Katie, biting her lower lip as she concentrated on moving the magnet. "If only I can get it to work."

"Maybe the angle is wrong," suggested Gran, now taking an interest and leaning closer.

"Yes, you may be right," replied Katie, raising the magnet up a little higher and moving it closer. It took a few more tries but Katie was finally able to swivel the latch out from under the lip on the opposite sash, thus disengaging the lock.

"You did it!" cheered Gran, patting her granddaughter on the back.

"Yes!" chuckled Katie. "But being able to open it from the inside is not helpful since the thieves would have had to do this from the outside and through a glass pane. I'll need to go out and see if I can unlock it from there." And she turned and started out the doorway.

Gran returned to the table and rang a small dinner bell. Andrews appeared almost immediately.

"Yes, ma'am?" he asked.

"Andrews," replied Gran. "Miss Katie needs a small ladder."

"Yes, ma'am," answered the butler, involuntarily glancing over at Katie's half eaten meal and her empty chair. However, he had been the Porter's butler for well over a decade, so nothing surprised him.

And he asked no questions other than to clarify. "Will she need it inside or out?"

"Outside, Andrews, of course," Gran retorted, although she was smiling. She turned and followed Katie outside and over to the same window.

Within minutes, Katie was braced at the very top of Gertie's small kitchen ladder, slowly and carefully moving the magnet from right to left. She had to repeat the motion twice before the magnet finally caught and the latch swiveled out of its locked position. Then, dropping the magnet into the pocket of her sweater, Katie opened the dining room window and climbed inside.

"Amazing," sighed Gran, shaking her head as she walked back inside the mansion through the front door. "I don't know how she comes up with these things."

Once inside, she found Katie picking up the hallway telephone and dialing a number.

"I've got to call Jim and tell him what I've discovered!" she exclaimed excitedly. "Of course, the thieves would have practiced and most likely been able to unlock the latch in a matter of seconds. And they may have had an even stronger magnet. Oh, pick up Jim! Why isn't he answering the phone?"

"Perhaps he's gone to bed," said Gran, moving toward the dining room. "Remember he isn't feeling well. Come eat your dinner. Your food is getting cold."

"Yes, I'm coming," sighed Katie impatiently. She waited for the answering machine to pick up. "Jim, this is Katie. Please call me. I've discovered how the thieves unlocked the second story windows. OK? Well goodbye. Oh, I hope you're feeling better. Call me. Bye!"

"I wonder if Margaret and Eloise will permit me to send them a check," pondered Gran as Katie returned to the dinner table. "You know, just to tide them over until their annuity arrives."

"I doubt it, Gran, although you know them better than I," replied Katie, taking a sip of her wine.

"There must be some way in which to help them," said Gran softly.

Katie thought for moment. "Well, I could ask Charlie Grant to help. He could deliver the money to the Dempseys and say that it was found dropped in our woods. It wouldn't be too farfetched as the money bag from the Banking and Trust was found there."

"That's true," replied Gran, nodding thoughtfully.

"Of course, we don't know the denominations of their cash," said Katie, shaking her head. "And there'd be no way to ask them without raising their suspicions."

"If they are as desperate as you described," stated Gran. "Then I don't suppose it will really matter. I believe they'll take it. We could start with $50's. I'll phone our bank manager tomorrow."

It was past 11:00 o'clock when Katie finally retired to her bedroom. She was extremely tired but took time to write down her notes on what she had learned that day concerning Frankie Cooper, the Dempsey robbery, and the magnet trick of opening the window latches. Her thoughts drifted to Jim. She sensed that something had happened between them that had bothered him, but she couldn't figure out what it was. Perhaps it was just her imagination? She told herself that he would call her in the morning to see if they were on for lunch and everything would be all right. Still she couldn't shake the feeling of uneasiness as she drifted off into a fitful sleep.

She was in the middle of a nightmare when she was suddenly awakened by a loud crash that sounded like breaking glass coming from somewhere downstairs. She jumped out of bed and looked around for Nugget. The little Yorkie was still in his basket, but had lifted his head, his ears straight up and alert. Katie walked quickly to her bedroom door and opened it.

"What was that?" exclaimed Gran, peering out of her door from across the hall. She was dressed in her robe and sleepers and held her reading glasses in her hand.

"It sounded like someone broke a window," replied Katie, heading down the staircase. "Come on Nugget! Someone may be breaking into the house."

Growling, the little dog dashed past her and down the stairs with Katie following close behind. When he reached the ground floor, he sniffed around and headed down the hallway in the direction of the game room. As he and Katie neared the doorway, they nearly collided with Andrews who was approaching from the opposite direction, an old saber dating back to World War I gripped tightly in his hand.

"Stay back, Miss Katie," said the butler, stepping in front of her and through the door. "Someone may be in there."

Nugget scooted past Andrews and into the game room, barking loudly.

"Nugget, hush!" said Katie, but the Yorkie ignored her and kept barking.

"All's clear," shouted Andrews as Katie entered. She flicked on the light and proceeded to look around the room.

"Nothing seems to be disturbed," she observed. "Are we sure the noise came from here?"

"Yes, miss," replied Andrews, walking around the room. "Ah, here it is," he said, pointing to the rug behind Gran's overstuffed chair.

Katie walked over to where the butler was pointing and, looking down, saw a large rock with what looked to be a note tied around it. She picked it up as Andrews walked over and pulled the curtains open, revealing a broken window.

"Did you find anything?" came a voice from the doorway. Katie looked up to see her grandmother standing there with an antique pistol in her hand.

"I hope that thing isn't loaded," Katie chuckled, nodding at the weapon in Gran's hand.

"No, of course not," replied her grandmother, walking slowly into the room. "It doesn't even fire anymore, but a burglar won't know that."

"Is that great grandfather's civil war revolver?" Katie asked, balancing the rock in her palm.

"Yes, I keep it in my dresser drawer for protection," replied Gran.

"Well, unless you plan on using it to hit the culprit over the head, it's more of a hazard than a help," Katie pointed out. Then she looked over at Andrews' saber. "Your fathers?"

"Yes, Miss Katie," replied Andrews, nodding proudly. "Skewered many a Bulgarian with it," he added, holding it up.

"Well, with all of this ancient weaponry in the house, we don't stand a chance, do we?" smiled Katie.

"Yes, miss. I suppose not. Now, if you will excuse me," said Andrews, looking somewhat deflated. "I'll get some wood to seal up the broken window." And he turned and left the room.

Katie removed the note from the rock and, unfolding it, read "*Stay away! Drop the bank robbery story or else! You've been warned. Signed, a friend.*"

"It looks like someone is getting very nervous about my continued work on the bank heist story," sighed Katie, handing the handwritten note to Gran.

"And I imagine that this note will not deter you," replied Gran, looking at her granddaughter intently as she handed it back.

"No indeed," Katie responded. "Just the opposite, in fact."

"Yes, I thought so," nodded Mrs. Porter. "So what now? Are you going to the police?"

"Not the police as a whole," said Katie thoughtfully. "I think I'll give it to Charlie Grant when I bring him the money for the Dempseys. He can do a discreet investigation of his own. And I believe he should start with his own "on loan" police sergeant."

CHAPTER 10
NO PIE TODAY

"What do you mean, E.M.? I don't understand."

Katie had arrived early to work that morning and was now standing in front of E.M.'s desk trying very hard to follow what her friend was saying to her.

"He told me that he had to go home to East Haddam to settle some business and asked me to drive him to the train station. I was a bit surprised because it was pretty late but there you go," replied E.M. "He took the 8:00 pm to Hartford. I thought you knew?"

"No, he didn't tell me," replied Katie, running her fingers through her hair. "He didn't stay for dinner last night, complaining of a headache. Hopping on a train to Connecticut was the last thing I thought he'd want to do. Perhaps there was an emergency."

"Well, I did manage to get out of him that he was long overdue signing some legal papers for his mother. Something to do with his sister, I believe, and the family lawyer thought it necessary since his close brush with death a few months back when his car crashed," explained E.M.

Katie thought back to the accident that nearly took Jim's life. He had been extremely lucky to have survived and Katie had become so upset while sitting by his bedside, waiting for him to regain consciousness, that she had tried to attack Dr. Timothy Tomasa with a thermometer.

"Apparently he'd been putting it off for quite a while but felt that he had the time now," E.M. continued with a shrug.

"Very strange," replied Katie. "He never said a word. What's more, he didn't ask me to take him to the station although he had just left Rosegate."

"As he was stepping out of the car, he mentioned that he didn't want to bother you since you were busy following up on a newspaper story and then he thanked me for the ride," added E.M. "I'm sure that he'll give you a call sometime today to explain."

"Yes, that's true. I'm sure he will," nodded Katie in agreement and more cheerfully than she felt. The whole thing was very odd. She hoped that some dire emergency hadn't caused Jim to travel home to East Haddam at the spur of the moment, but she had no choice but to await his call.

"So, E.M." she began, deciding to switch gears. "Jim mentioned that he had read an article in the *Stars and Stripes* during the war about a safecracking technique invented by a man named Henry C. Miller. I know you wrote for the paper and wondered if you could tell me how I might get a copy of that article."

"Yes, I happen to know the article you're talking about and where to get it," he replied, pulling open a desk drawer.

"Wonderful!" she exclaimed and then looked down at the drawer. "Don't tell me you keep copies of the *Stars and Stripes* in your desk and happen to have that particular article!"

"Not all copies, dear Katie," he chuckled, pulling out one of the editions and flipping through it. "Only the ones that have articles in them that I wrote." And he stopped at an open page and patted it.

"E.M.!" Katie exclaimed. "You wrote the article? How fortunate!"

"Yes, very," replied her friend. "I happened to be stuck on a train headed for Lisbon when a fellow in the seat next to me introduced himself and struck up a conversation. He said his name was Henry Miller and he was on his way to crack a safe owned by some high official in Portugal. He was excited to try out this new method that he had perfected."

"E.M., this is wonderful!" cried Katie with excitement. She glanced over the article. "It appears that safecracking takes quite a lot of skill, patience, and very good hearing."

E.M. chuckled. "Yes, indeed. And there are several steps involved. Not at all like it's shown in the movies. You see, according to Mr. Miller's system, it's a three-step approach. The first is to determine the contact points inside the lock. The drive cam has a notch in it which is sloped. When the combination dial is turned, the sloped notch allows the correct lever and fence to pass through. When the lever contacts this slope, it makes the sound of a click. That's when the safecracker knows that they've found the right point in which to determine which numbers on the combination dial correspond to the left and right side of the sloped notch. It takes several careful turns of the dial, left and right, to discover all of the numbers in the combination."

"It sounds very confusing," remarked Katie, shaking her head.

"Yes, I imagine it is," replied E.M. nodding. "Because there can be up to eight numbers in a combination and if the safecracker misses one click, he has to start all over again. There are two more steps after that, but you get the basic idea."

"So, our safecracking robbers most likely have quite a lot of experience in this," Katie said thoughtfully. "Especially since they seem to crack the safe in a matter of minutes."

"That is astounding, Katie," said E.M., shaking his head. "Because Harry Miller, himself, has not beaten his own record of 20 minutes."

"I wonder if different combination locks are easier to crack than others," Katie pondered.

"Why not ask Mark Dickson?" suggested E.M. "He might know."

"Good idea!" replied Katie. "I'll hop over to his shop right after I finish up a few things here," she added, turning and walking to her desk. Jim had not called her at Rosegate that morning and now that she knew he was out of town, she figured that he would call her at the *Gazette,* and she didn't want to miss him.

She fabricated things to do all morning while she waited. She went over her notes on the bank heists three times, reread her own article on the story, rearranged her desk twice, filled, dumped out, and refilled her stapler, counted her rubber bands, picked up the phone receiver at least five times to make sure her desk phone was working, reread the morning edition of the *Gazette,* worked the crossword puzzle, sharpened all five of her pencils twice, and made a long chain out of her paperclips. It was nearly lunchtime when Katie finally admitted to herself that Jim was not going to call, and she reluctantly made her way through the lobby of the newspaper building.

"Hello Nancy," she said to the receptionist. "Please take a message should anyone call me."

"Certainly, Katie," replied the young woman. "Are you expecting one in particular?"

"Yes," nodded Katie. "A very important one."

She left the building and headed over to Polly's to grab a bite to eat before seeing the locksmith. As she slid into the booth in which she and Jim usually sat, she was nearly overcome by a sudden feeling of loneliness.

"Your friend not joining you today?" asked the waitress, her pencil poised over her order pad.

"No, he's been called out of town," replied Katie, taking a cursory glance at the menu.

"Oh, that's too bad," said the waitress, scratching something off the pad. "I take it no pie today, then?"

"Yes, no pie," replied Katie, looking up sadly as she gave her usual order to the woman. How unsettling, she thought to herself gazing out of the window, to have one's daily routine altered so much by the absence of another person. One wouldn't think it would matter, really, but it did.

She recalled a school play in which she played a goose. Gosh, she must have been about 6 or 7 years old, she reminded herself. Gertie and Gran had been quite pleased with the costume they had made for her and both had spent several days rehearsing the little goose dance with her that she was to perform. Then they received word that her parents would be in town for the performance and little Katie was nearly beside herself with joy. Three chairs were reserved for the Porter family and Katie snuck several glances out into the audience in hope of catching a glimpse of her elusive parents. But, throughout the entire production, only Gran could be seen sitting next to two empty chairs. Her parents' plans had changed, and they instead were headed to California to watch for whales.

And then there was Ruddy White. She had grown up with him and, through the years, they had developed their own kind of routine. Actually, it was more of Katie blending into the White's daily lives than Ruddy sharing hers. Even after they had become engaged, he seldom came to Rosegate. His sister Ruth was Katie's best friend so it seemed only natural that Katie should be with his family and his life. After they were to wed, it was expected that she would live at his estate although Rosegate was her ancestral home and very much her preference. Still, she had loved him and would have settled at Sunset Hill as best she could. And then, in the blink of an eye, he was gone.

Jim Fielding was very different. Funny, she hadn't thought about it until now. He seemed to fit naturally into her life without much effort. They apparently had the same daily routine perhaps because they had so many things in common; like music, and cooking, and ham sandwiches. She smiled up at the waitress, now, as the woman placed hers down on the table in front of her. They had the same jobs, laughed at the same jokes, enjoyed the same movies. And…well…they respected each other. And Jim and Gran got along famously. Even Nugget adored him. Jim fit…

"Excuse me, miss, but is this seat taken?" came a pleasant male voice, breaking through her thoughts.

"Jim?" she whispered, quickly looking up and into the face of E.M. Butler.

"Sorry, I didn't mean to startle you," said her friend gently. "But I thought you might like some company for lunch."

"Yes," Katie replied, her eyes brimming with tears. "That would be wonderful."

* * *

"Hello Katie," said Mark Dickson. "How are you?"

"I'm fine, Mark," she replied. "And you?"

Mark Dickson and his father owned Dickson's Locksmith and Key Company, providing the only such service in town. The elder Mr. Dickson, now in his 70's, seldom came to the shop these days but Mark could be found there during the week and was on-call on weekends for the poor souls who managed to lock themselves out of their homes or vehicles.

Katie had known the Dickson family for years and saw Mark often at the Fairfield Country Club of which both their families were members.

"Fine, thanks. How's your tennis game coming?" Mark teased. "Hope you're putting in a lot of practice because I saw that you've signed up for mixed doubles. You know my wife and I win that category every year."

"Not this time," smiled Katie. "My partner and I will wipe you off the court."

"Like to make a little wager on that?" challenged the locksmith.

"Fiver?" replied Katie.

"You're on!" Mark agreed, extending his hand and shaking hers. "Now what can I do for you? Have you locked yourself out of the roadster?"

"No," said Katie, smiling. "It's your expertise I'm after. I need some information on the type of locks used on American Sentry safes. Do you know anything about them?"

"Yes, quite a lot actually," he said, moving from behind his counter and over to a cabinet across the room. He opened it and pulled out several combination locksets and then, moving back to the counter, placed them in a row for Katie to see. "These are three types of safe locks and the one here on the right is used on all American Sentry's."

Katie picked it up and took a close look at it. The lock was surprisingly heavy and appeared to be very well made. Putting it down, she picked up the other two in turn and, although equally sturdy, seemed lighter than the first. She recognized the brand name on the third as being the one the Porters had at Rosegate.

"What can you tell me about the American Sentry lock as compared to the others?" she asked.

"Well, for one thing, the drive cam, fence, and spindle are made of a thicker metal, making it sturdier. That's also what makes this lock heavier than the others. But the dial still moves smoothly, and you couldn't pry it off with anything short of dynamite! The other two are also very well made but they use a lesser grade metal, making them somewhat lighter."

"Does weight make a difference in the lock's ability to secure the safe?" asked Katie.

"No. All of these locks will do the trick," Mark answered. "It's more a matter of cost. The American Sentry is twice the price of the others."

"Interesting," replied Katie thoughtfully. "One could imagine that a salesman for the American Sentry Safe company might use the lock's weight to give the customer the impression that it's better, so worth the price."

"Yes, one could very well imagine a salesman doing that," said Mark, chuckling. "But I can assure you that there is no difference as far as that goes. The only real advantage is that this lock might last longer than the others but the life of a safe is hundreds of years so the customer could very well have died long before the combination lock fails to work."

Katie picked up the American Sentry lock in her left hand and gently turned the dial clockwise with her right. She could easily hear the click as the wheel notch passed through the fence. She then turned the dial counterclockwise and heard the loud click again. She duplicated the action with the other two locks. The clicking noise in those was softer than in the first although the action of the wheel notch was the same.

"The heavier the metal in the internal mechanism, the louder the click," pointed out Mark, almost as if he was reading her mind. "It's got quite a nice sound to it, don't you agree?"

"Yes," replied Katie. "Especially if one is a safecracker."

"Oh, are you planning on becoming one?" joked Mark, spinning the combination dial on one of the locks.

"You never know," she replied with a smile as she thanked him and left the shop.

* * *

She stopped by the reception desk upon her return to the *Gazette*.

"Sorry Katie," said Nancy, shaking her head. "No messages."

"Thanks," replied Katie. "Perhaps he tried to call me at Rosegate."

Nancy raised her eyebrows. "Yes, perhaps," was all she said.

"I think I'll go home and work from there," smiled Katie, turning to leave. "It's so much quieter in my study. It's hard to concentrate here."

"Yes, indeed. Shall I call you at home should your important call come through here?" asked the receptionist.

"Yes," replied Katie brightly. "That would be helpful. Thank you, Nancy." And she made her way out of the newspaper office and headed for Rosegate.

Her grandmother was tending her roses when Katie arrived and wandered out to the sunporch.

"Hello dear," said Gran, glancing up from a sad looking rose bush. "You're home early. Are you not well?"

"I'm fine, Gran," replied Katie, walking over and giving her grandmother a kiss on the cheek. "I just thought it might be quieter to work from home. It's so noisy in the pressroom at the newspaper."

"Yes, I would imagine so," said Gran, frowning at the bush. She lopped off several buds.

"Did I happen to get any calls today?" Katie asked, as she watched her grandmother continue to massacre the sickly bush.

"No, none that I am aware of," replied Mrs. Porter. "Did you check the message pad by the hall telephone?"

"Yes," replied Katie, turning to leave the sunporch. "Well, I think I'll go into the library and try to crack our safe."

"Have a nice time," said her grandmother absentmindedly as she moved to another rose bush.

"Sorry Nugget," Katie said to the Yorkie as she entered the library. The dog had a bed in just about every room in the mansion and he now glared at his mistress for waking him by her arrival. "Go back to sleep. I'm just here to look at our safe."

Nugget, however, stepped out of his bed and, yawning, left the library in search of quieter quarters.

Katie walked to the bookcase and ran her fingers over the third shelf until she felt the lever. She pressed it, releasing the bookcase from the wall and allowing her to pull a section of it forward to reveal the Porter's wall safe. She noted the brand and saw that she had been correct. It was a Bakersfield not an American Sentry.

"Well, that's one positive thing I've found today," she sighed to herself. "Now let's see what I can hear." She leaned toward the safe and rested her ear on the door as close to the combination lock as she could. Carefully turning the dial, she concentrated on hearing the click when it reached the correct number which, fortunately, she knew. She heard nothing. Turning the dial in the other direction, she tried to pick up the second click. Again, she heard nothing.

"I should test the combination to make sure it still works," she said out loud and she turned the dial using the correct combination and the safe door swung open easily. "So, I had the numbers right," she mused. "But my hearing, although very good, isn't quite good enough to crack the safe."

She stood back and shut the safe door, spinning the dial to make sure it could not be pulled open without using the combination. Then she pushed the bookcase back in place.

"Well, I'm not too surprised that I couldn't hear the clicks on our Bakersfield. I wonder if I could have heard them on an American Sentry?" she wondered, sitting down on the couch. "Of course, it's possible that our safecracker might have a tool of some sort that helps him pick up the sound. Perhaps a tube or glass

She reached over and picked up the phone to call Jim, planning on discussing her theory with him. Halfway through dialing his number, she realized what she was doing. He wasn't home. Damn him! *Why didn't he call?* she wondered, hanging up the telephone. Perhaps she would hear from him tonight. They had made it somewhat of a habit to talk to each other nightly.

She returned to the sunporch just in time to join Gran for a glass of wine and they talked of roses, this year's garden club show, and the upcoming tennis tournament. All the while, Katie's mind mulled over combination locks and safecrackers. Soon, they were called in for dinner where Gran inquired after Jim as they were served porkchops smothered in baked apples.

"I hope that he's feeling better," Gran remarked, cutting into her chop. "How did he look when you saw him at lunch?"

"I'm afraid I haven't seen Jim since yesterday," Katie replied, looking down at her plate. "He had to leave town suddenly to tend to some business at home."

"Really?" said Gran, tilting her head a bit as she gazed at Katie. "I hope it's nothing serious."

"I wouldn't know, Gran," replied Katie softly. "He hasn't called me either."

"That's very strange," Gran responded, now studying her granddaughter more closely. "But I'm sure there is some reason that he'll be able to explain when he does."

"Yes, I'm sure you're right," muttered Katie, lifting her wine glass and taking a sip to avoid any more comment.

It was much later that evening, around dusk, when Katie looked out her bedroom window and saw the lights dancing through the trees along the back woods of Rosegate. She grabbed her binoculars from her desk drawer and peered out.

"Definitely torch lights!" she exclaimed. "Looks like our ghost is at it again!"

Sliding into her sturdy Oxfords and pulling on a sweater, she called for Nugget to follow her.

"We're going ghost hunting, Nugget, so be brave!"

The little dog danced up and down with excitement as he followed his mistress down the stairs and out the back door. They reached the edge of the woods within minutes and Katie paused to click on her flashlight before stepping onto the path and making her way in the direction of the creek. Soon they were within sight of it and she signaled Nugget to stop. Before her stood a lighted torch, jammed into the ground, about four feet from the stump, just as before. However, this time there was no sign of the young men who had previously waited there to meet the ghost.

"Perhaps we've beat them here and they're on their way," she thought, deciding to climb up the hill and wait in hiding like she and her friends had done before. Signaling Nugget to follow, they carefully scampered up the incline and hid behind the large rock. It was only moments before they heard the screech of Golden Joe and saw him glide down the path from the opposite direction. Just like before, the ghost floated a foot or two off the ground and the glow from his ghostly form nearly blinded Katie, who had to shield her eyes for a minute. Nugget let out a soft growl and, pinning his ears back and tucking his tail between his legs, flattened himself down on the ground.

"Holy smokes," muttered Katie softly. "This guy is even creepier than before."

Golden Joe floated over to the stump and, without waiting for his team of young thieves, leaned down and tucked a piece of paper into the hollow space. Then he turned and floated back up the path, disappearing within seconds.

"Just as the Badger Tribe described! There hadn't been any of the gang present then, either. Come on, Nugget. Let's see if we can do a little intercepting ourselves!" And she and the Yorkie scrambled back down the hill and over to the stump. Katie quickly reached in and removed the message. Unfolding it, she saw that, like the one before, the code was written out in pictures and numbers.

Suddenly Nugget began to growl and bark at something, or someone, coming down the same path in which the ghost had travelled.

"Hush, Nugget! Do you want to wake the dead?" Katie said as she tried to read the message under the light of the torch.

"Too late," she heard a deep raspy voice whisper and she look up and into the hideous ghostly face of Golden Joe.

Katie let out a scream and stepped back, knocking over the torch. Fortunately, the flame was not extinguished when it hit the ground, giving her and Nugget just enough light to make a run for it. But the ghost of Golden Joe wasn't giving up and he snatched up the torch and began chasing after them, his shrill screech echoing through the woods.

Although Katie knew the path well, it was still very dark, and she stumbled and tripped over tree limbs and rocks several times along the way. Once, she fell to the ground, and Nugget, who was in the lead, doubled back and stood over her, growling and barking at the approaching ghost who began swinging the flaming torch at them.

Katie quickly picked herself up off the ground and they continued their race through the woods and finally out into the clearing. Breathing heavily, Katie slowed and looked over her shoulder to discover that Golden Joe had vanished from sight.

She fell to her knees to catch her breath and called out to Nugget. The little dog turned and ran back, leaping into her arms. "Nugget, you brave little rascal. Why, you're shaking!"

Nugget was indeed terrified and tucked his nose under her chin, refusing to be placed back down on the ground. Katie stuffed the message that she had managed to hold onto into her pocket and carried the brave little dog home.

Gran was waiting for them on the back patio, a look of confusion on her face.

"What have you two been doing?" she asked, as Katie walked past her and placed Nugget down in the hallway. The poor animal gazed up at her, still shaking. "What was all that racket I heard coming from across the lawn?"

"We've been out ghost hunting, Gran," replied Katie, reaching into Nugget's treat jar sitting on a side table in the hallway. She tossed the treat to the little dog who snatched it up and ran away in the direction of the game room. "Then we stole one of Golden Joe's messages just as he was returning, and he chased us through the woods making the worst screeching noise one ever heard and waving a lighted torch at us."

Gran stood still for a moment and gazed at her granddaughter. "Katie, if you don't want to tell me what happened, you don't have to."

Katie started to laugh and pulling the message from her pocket, she held it up for her grandmother to see. "Gran, I'm telling you the truth! Nugget and I stole a message from Golden Joe's ghost and now I must decode it. Let's go into the library. I believe I have just interrupted the plan for the next robbery since the thieves never got a chance to read it!"

Katie took out a blank piece of paper and seated herself next to Gran who spread the message out on the table in front of them. It contained ten pictures of creatures along with corresponding numbers. Using the same method as before, they quickly began to decode it.

"The first picture is that of a seagull," said Gran. "It has the number 1 next to it."

Katie wrote down the letter "s".

"That looks like a monkey," said Katie, pointing at the second picture. "No wait, it's an Orangutan. With the number 6. That means our next letter is a "u". I'll add that next."

"This one is a Lion with the number 4," replied Gran. "And then a squirrel with the number 1."

Katie systematically wrote down each letter as Gran called out the identities of the creatures and their numbers. There followed an eagle with number 5, a parrot with number 6, a python with number 4, an armadillo with number 6, a sloth with number 2, and a chinchilla with the number 8.

Katie gasped as she finished writing down the message. The location of the next burglary was Sunset Hill.

"Oh, Gran," Katie exclaimed, jumping to her feet. "We must warn the Whites!" But before she could move the telephone rang. Running into the hallway, Katie picked it up and heard Ruth's frantic voice at the other end.

"Katie?" she cried. "We've been attacked by intruders. Can you come over, please? Poppy has been hurt and they've kidnapped Boots!"

CHAPTER 11
DELAYED LOVE AND ALARMS

Katie and Gran arrived at Sunset Hill is less than 5 minutes, nearly colliding with two police cars passing through the entrance gate. An ambulance, its sirens blaring, fell in behind Katie's roadster, adding to the parade of vehicles racing up the estate's driveway and coming to a screeching halt in front of the main house.

"Ruthie! My goodness! Are you OK?" exclaimed Katie, racing over to her friend who was standing just inside the door.

"Katie, thank goodness you're here," cried Ruth, falling into Katie's outstretched arms.

"Where is your mother?" demanded Gran, brushing past the young women.

"She's in the living room, Mrs. Porter," replied Ruth. "With Poppy."

"Can you tell me what happened?" Katie asked her friend.

"How about you tell both of us," they heard Detective Grant say as he walked up behind them. "Is there a quiet place we might talk?"

"Yes, over here in the library," replied Ruth, turning from Katie and leading them into the room just off the hallway.

They settled around a circular gaming table and Charlie Grant took out a notepad from the pocket of his overcoat.

"We had all retired for the evening and were up in our bedrooms preparing for bed when suddenly the electricity went out. I remember glancing out the window thinking that perhaps a storm had come but it was very quiet outside. I opened my bedroom door to investigate and met Poppy in the hallway. It was then that we heard what sounded like one of our windows being opened on the ground floor."

Katie leaned forward. "So the electricity goes out and you believe you hear a window opening."

"Yes, that's right," Ruth nodded.

"Interesting," muttered Katie under her breath.

"Go on, please," Detective Grant said to Ruth, shooting Katie a sideward glance.

"We started down the stairway with Tom, who had joined us, and paused at the bottom of the steps trying to determine exactly where the noise was coming from. That's when we heard what sounded like footsteps and the Connor Landscape being taken off the wall."

"Connor Landscape?" asked Charlie Grant.

"One of my editor's paintings. He's a wonderful artist and Ruth's mother fell in love with one of his landscapes," explained Katie. "It's of Cape Hatteras."

"My parents spent their honeymoon there," added Ruth, nodding.

"And this painting hangs over your safe to hide it?" asked the police detective, not really caring where the Whites spent their honeymoon.

"Yes," replied Ruth.

"Please continue," instructed Charlie, making a notation into his pad.

"Wait, Ruthie," interrupted Katie. "Don't you have an alarm system? I seem to recall setting it off late one evening when Ruddy and I were out past curfew and he had the bright idea to have us crawl through the window."

Detective Grant raised his eyebrows and looked over at her, a twinkle in his eyes.

"I was only 12 at the time and Ruddy was 14," added Katie, sensing that Charlie was about to ask something embarrassing. "Ruth's brother was a bad influence on me."

"I see," was all the detective said. He scribbled another note down in his pad.

"Yes, we do," nodded Ruth. "Only for the first floor. Poppy sets it when the family goes up to bed."

At that moment, two medics pushing a stretcher carrying Mr. White came down the hallway, passing by the library door. Poppy's head was wrapped in a towel and blood could be seen trickling down one cheek. Mrs. White, accompanied by Gran, was walking behind and Gran paused for a moment to stick her head into the library and address her granddaughter.

"Katie, we're going to the hospital," she stated calmly. "It looks like Ruth's father is going to need stitches and be checked for a concussion. Please meet me there in one hour."

"Yes, Gran," replied Katie, coming to stand by Detective Grant who had jumped to his feet when he saw Mrs. Porter. "Of course."

"And you, young man," remarked Gran, looking rather severely at Charlie Grant. "I don't know what this town is coming to when the Fairfield Police Department can't protect a state judge and his family."

"But, ma'am…" sputtered the embarrassed detective.

"And I suggest that you start looking for their youngest daughter, who is still missing by the way, instead of wasting time flirting with my granddaughter and her friend!" declared Mrs. Porter, giving Charlie Grant a final withering glare before turning back to Mrs. White and following her out the door.

"Oh dear," said Katie, smiling up at Charlie. "You're in for it now! You've angered Gran!"

The detective looked from Ruth to Katie and then back to Ruth again before saying, "Look here, Ruth," he said rather meekly. "I've got a team looking for your sister right now. We haven't forgotten her and if she's been snatched, we'll find the culprits pronto!"

"Yes, Charlie, I'm sure," replied Ruth graciously, although she was nearly out of her mind with worry.

"Perhaps you should check in with them for an update," suggested Katie. "We'll wait right here for you until you get back."

"Yes, good idea," replied the detective, pocketing his notepad and moving toward the door.

"Don't go anywhere," he warned Ruth, walking quickly from the room.

"OK, Ruthie," said Katie hastily. "Before he comes back. Did Poppy remember to turn on the alarm?"

"Yes, of course," replied her friend.

"So I suppose it doesn't work once the electricity is off?" asked Katie. "Or else the intruders would have set it off when they came through the window."

"Doesn't matter," said a voice from the door. Katie looked up to see Tom limping into the room. "It's on a backup battery."

"Are you sure you're all right, Thomas?" asked his concerned sister.

"Yes, I'm fine, Ruthie," replied Tom, sitting down in the chair next to her. "A bit sore is all. That gorilla nearly threw me clear through the wall!"

"Yes," nodded Ruth, taking his hand. "You were very brave to try and save Boots."

"Lots of good it did," he replied sadly. "They took her anyway."

"Wait a minute," Katie said suddenly, holding up her hand. She looked over at Tom thoughtfully. "You just said that the alarm system is on a backup battery. Why didn't it go off when the burglars opened the window even after they apparently flipped off your electricity? I didn't hear it over the telephone when Ruthie called."

"Well, that's because there is a delay from the time the system switches from the electrical current over to the battery," Tom explained.

"How long is the delay?" pressed Katie, becoming excited.

"I'm not sure, exactly. 5 or 10 minutes, maybe?" shrugged Tom.

"It must have come on while the intruders were in the house," Katie continued thoughtfully.

"Yes," replied Ruth. "It just about scared the daylights out of all of us, especially the intruders."

"You were in the same room with them at the time?" asked Katie, leaning towards her. "Please tell me exactly what you remember. It's extremely important."

"Well, as I was saying, Tom, Poppy, and I heard the painting being removed from the wall and we crept into the library to see who was there," Ruth recited. "When we entered the room, there was a man standing by the safe in the process of putting the painting on the floor. He was wearing a mask and knit hat. Just coming through the window was another man dressed the same way. Both were wearing dark clothing."

"Was the second man wearing anything on his legs?" asked Katie.

"Dark leather work boots, I think," replied Ruth. "Poppy yelled 'what do you think you're doing?' or something of the sort and this caused both men to look up."

"The one by the window said, 'open the safe, old man,' but Poppy just shook his head," Tom chimed in. "That's when the other guy pulled out a knife and pointed it at Ruthie. He said 'How 'bout we cut the doll and see if you'll change your mind?' That's when Poppy agreed to open the safe."

"Did either of the men call each other by name?" asked Katie hopefully.

"No, I don't think so," replied Ruth, shaking her head. "Poppy certainly took his time unlocking the safe, because I've seen him open it much quicker."

"Perhaps he was waiting for the alarm to switch to the battery and go off," suggested Katie.

"Yes. Now that you say it, Katie, I'm sure that's what he was doing," nodded Ruth. "I just remember that it seemed to take forever because Boots came into the room at that very moment. The man nearer the window rushed over and grabbed her before any of us knew what was happening. Poppy yelled something like 'let her go' but the men only laughed."

"That's when the one closest to Poppy hit him over the head with the butt of the knife and Poppy fell to the ground," said Tom. "That made the guy holding Boots mad and he yelled 'now look what you've done' to the guy at the safe. That gave me a chance to jump on his back and try to get him to let go of Boots, but he was stronger than I expected, and he tossed me against the wall. Knocked the wind clear out of me."

"It was then that the alarm finally went off," continued Ruth, still holding her brother's hand and looking at him fondly. "The two men nearly jumped out of their skins and ran to the window, dragging poor Boots with them. One threw her over his shoulder and both climbed through the window and were gone."

"It took me a minute or two to get my breath back and Ruthie was trying to take care of Poppy, so we let the alarm continue to go off," added Tom. "Then Ruthie worked the code and disabled it so that she could call the police and you."

"I hope the police find Boots soon," said Ruth hopefully. "I hope she's all right."

"She will be," replied Katie, standing and beginning to pace the floor, thinking to herself.

"How can you be so sure?" asked Ruth.

"Because I believe I know who these intruders are," replied Katie.

"And I don't think they'll want to harm her. They just needed her to secure their escape. My guess is that they'll let her go before they go much farther."

At that very moment, as if by magic, the front door swung open and in walked Margaret "Boots" White, dusty and dirty but unharmed.

"Is anybody home?" she called out.

"Boots!" cried her siblings, racing out of the library to embrace her. "What happened?"

"Those two lunatics carried me out the window, threw me into the back of their van, and then didn't have the wherewithal to lock it," explained Boots, brushing a hand over her nightgown. "I waited until we had gone about half a mile and then I opened the back door and jumped out. I wish I had thought to slip on some shoes when I came downstairs, because the worst part was hiking back in bare feet!"

Tom, Ruth, and Katie burst out laughing just as several police officers, who had been investigating the immediate surrounding area, entered the hallway. Detective Grant was among them. Their mouths dropped open at the sight of Boots.

"Here is your kidnapping victim, Charlie," exclaimed Katie, chuckling. "You can bring in the hounds now! Goodness, I must be on my way to pick up Gran!" she added, glancing at her wristwatch. And giving Ruthie a quick kiss, she flew out the door and was on her way.

The hospital was experiencing its usual atmosphere of chaos as Katie made her way through the emergency room and on to the back corner where a special room was located for patients considered VIPs by the hospital. That designation certainly included the Honorable Judge James "Poppy" White. Katie entered the room just as Robert, Poppy's doctor and future son-in-law, had finished stitching up the small gash in Poppy's forehead and a nurse was now applying some fresh bandages.

"Ah, Katie," said Gran, looking up from a chair in the corner. "Here you are. We're nearly ready to go."

"Wonderful, Gran," replied Katie, and then smiling at Ruth's parents said, "Hello Mrs. White, hello Poppy. Good news! Boots has returned safely! She was able to get away from the culprits before they got very far."

"Oh thank goodness!" replied Mrs. White with relief.

"I'm glad you weren't seriously injured, Poppy," continued Katie. "I've seen you hurt worse playing tennis with Tom."

"Indeed so, Katie," chuckled Poppy, pushing himself off the examination table and standing on his feet.

"Careful, Poppy," warned Robert, gently taking hold of his arm. "Let's make sure you can stand."

"I'm fine, Robert," huffed Poppy, swaying slightly before regaining his balance.

"Do what the doctor says, please darling," Mrs. White gently urged her husband. She had been in the bathtub as the run-in with the intruders was taking place, only jumping out and throwing on some clothing once the alarm went off. By the time she made her way downstairs, Ruth had handled everything and the police, the Porters, and an ambulance were on their way.

"Is Ambrose outside to pick us up?" the judge asked Katie.

"I'm afraid everyone in the household is still being questioned by the police," replied Katie, smiling. "I am the only one available to pick you up. You're at my mercy, unfortunately."

"Do you think we can all fit into the roadster?" asked Mrs. White, somewhat shocked and not looking forward at all to the ride home in Katie's little car.

"We drove over in my car, Mary," Gran assured her, as if reading her mind. "I don't like riding in that thing either."

"Is Poppy OK to be released, Robert?" Katie asked. "We don't have far to walk. I was lucky enough to find a parking space close to the emergency room entrance."

"Yes, he can go," nodded Robert, jotting down a few notes in the judge's medical record. "I'll come by tomorrow, Poppy, to see how you're doing."

"Good man," replied Poppy, sliding into his coat. "I may let you marry my daughter after all."

"Thank you, sir," smiled Robert. This was an ongoing joke between them as the matter had been settled long ago and by Ruth.

The group slowly made their way back through the hospital and out to Mrs. Porter's sedan parked a few yards away. The Whites slipped into the back seat as Gran climbed into the passenger seat next to Katie. She drove them all back to Sunset Hill, making sure to stay within the speed limit, delivering her charges in about 20 minutes safe and sound.

As he stepped out of the car, Poppy was enthusiastically greeted by his children, who ran out the front door and threw their arms around him, joined by Mrs. White. Katie and Gran sat in the car and watched the family safely enter their home before pulling away and heading back to Rosegate.

"Katie," asked her grandmother softly, as they walked arm and arm up their front steps. "Was this the work of our ghost?"

"Yes, Gran," replied Katie. "I believe it was. Not him, per say, but at his direction." And then a thought occurred to her. "Nugget and I were being chased by him through our woods at the same time the intruders were breaking into Sunset Hill. That's not their usual pattern. I wonder what it means?"

"It means that Golden Joe and his gang are keeping us on our toes," said Gran, smiling at her granddaughter. "And getting much more sleep than we are. Do you realize that it's nearly midnight, Katie?"

"It's been a very long day, Gran," replied Katie, kissing her grandmother goodnight. As she started up the staircase, she discreetly glanced over at the pad by the telephone and saw that there were no messages. Jim had not called. Sadly she made her way to her room and, after changing into her nightgown, climbed into bed. Just before closing her eyes, she murmured to herself, "I've figured out how they did it, Jim. I know how they bypassed the alarm system," and then she fell fast asleep.

* * *

"I need your help, Charlie," said Katie, arriving at the Fairfield Police Station shortly after noon the next day.

"I can't give you any information on the bank heist investigation or the Sunset Hill break-in," replied the flustered detective. "So it's no use asking me, Katie Porter."

"Good thing I'm several steps ahead of you, then," she teased him, plopping down in the chair across from his desk. "I'm here on other business."

"OK, shoot," said Charlie. "What do you need?"

"Well, for starters, I wonder if you would give this envelope of money to the Dempsey sisters?" she asked. "And tell them that the police found it in the woods at Rosegate."

"You want me to give the Dempseys an envelope of money and lie about it?" replied Charlie, taking the envelope from Katie and glancing in it. "Geez, Katie there must be…"

"$500 dollars," said Katie. "And yes, you would be lying about it but it's for a good cause. If you're uncomfortable about it, I could always throw it into the woods in front of you and have you pick it up."

Detective Grant chuckled. "OK, Katie. I get it. I'll give it to the sisters, but you didn't have to do this, you know."

"It was at my grandmother's insistence and you don't want to remain on her bad side after last night, do you?"

"No, indeed," replied Charlie, wincing slightly. "The police commissioner was none too pleased to hear that we had no leads when he called this morning. And he's instructed us to post two of our officers at Sunset Hill around the clock until the culprits are captured."

"Very prudent of him," smiled Katie. "He and my grandmother go way back."

"So I've been told," nodded Charlie, placing the envelope inside his vest pocket. "I'll go over to the Dempseys this afternoon."

"Wonderful. Thank you," replied Katie. "Now there is one more thing," she added, reaching into her purse and bringing out the note that was thrown through her window. "This arrived by way of our window the other night. I wonder if you could have the handwriting analyzed by one of your experts."

"Yes, that won't be a problem," Charlie replied, glancing at the note. "What exactly are you hoping to find."

"Well, first off, what kind of person would write such a note," she replied. "And secondly, if it might possibly be your esteemed colleague, Sergeant Smith."

"Katie! Aren't you going a little overboard with this?" replied Charlie. "I know she doesn't like you very much but throwing notes through windows is hardly the action of a police officer."

"Just bear with me, Detective?" asked Katie gently. "Let's just say I'm following a very important lead."

"OK, but don't we need a sample of the sergeant's handwriting for comparison?"

"Yes," replied Katie, glancing over at the desk that Sergeant Smith was using during her stay in Fairfield.

"Now Katie, really!" Charlie Grant protested. "I can't rummage through an officer's desk just because you're following a lead."

"I'm not asking you to rummage," replied Katie, in mock defense. "I have a question concerning one of the bank heists and I believe the information might be found in the same file that you read from when we talked over the phone."

Charlie leaned back and started laughing. "Boy, you don't miss a trick, do you Katie Porter?" He got to his feet and walked over to the sergeant's desk, returning a few minutes later with the file. Flipping it open, he handed it to Katie. "Will this do?"

Katie glanced down at the first page which contained a lengthy handwritten narrative of the heist as well as Sergeant Smith's signature attesting to her authorship.

"Yes, I believe that will work very nicely, Detective Grant," smiled Katie, handing the file back to Charlie and watching as he removed the page. "I'm grateful that Sergeant Smith prefers to write out her reports instead of using a typewriter.

Charlie smiled. "I'm just the opposite although I'm not very fast. Only use two fingers," he added, holding them up. Then, reaching inside a desk drawer, he took out a large manila envelope and slid both the note from Katie and the page from the police file into it and taped it shut.

"We've got a crackerjack handwriting expert that works for the state police. I believe she's currently in town visiting relatives. I'll give her a call and see if she's willing to take a look at these. I'll let you know."

"Thanks, Charlie! I owe you one," said Katie, jumping to her feet and rushing from the room before Charlie Grant could come up with a way for her to repay the favor.

As she drove back to the *Fairfield Gazette*, she passed by the library and decided to stop in and see if she could find a translation for "Cariad," the name that Jim had given her when introducing her to the Badger Tribe boys.

"It probably means dog-face or some such nonsense," she chuckled to herself, knowing Jim's propensity for teasing her.

Katie did not use the public library very often since Rosegate had a quite extensive collection of novels and reference books. However, the Porters did not possess a Welsh Dictionary, so she made her way over to a gray-haired librarian working behind the main counter and stated her request.

"A Welsh Dictionary?" repeated the librarian. "Well Miss Porter, we don't get many requests for it, but we do have one. It's over in the reference section, row 8, halfway down. Let me give you the number…" and she turned to the card catalog behind her and, flipping through the index cards in one of the drawers, found the book's Dewey Decimal number. She jotted it down on a scrap of paper and handed it to Katie. "Please let me know if you need my assistance."

Katie thanked her and proceeded to the back corner of the library and began searching the shelves until she found the volume. Taking it over to a nearby table, she sat down and turned to the pages containing words beginning with "c." It took her only a moment to find "cariad" and her heart did a flip flop when she read its English translation. It meant "sweetheart."

"Well now, Mr. Fielding," she murmured, smiling to herself. "So that's what's been on your mind."

She placed the book back on the shelf and thanking the librarian once again, left the library and drove on to the *Gazette*.

As she walked through the newspaper's lobby, she was flagged down by Nancy Applegate.

"I have a phone call for you, Katie," said the receptionist, pointing to the phone receiver in her hand. "I'll give you a minute to get to your desk and then transfer it."

"Thanks, Nancy," cried Katie, rushing through the pressroom and sliding into her desk chair. This had to be Jim, finally, she told herself. She didn't know whether to be angry with him or thankful that he had called. She didn't have to be either because it was Ruth who was on the other end of the line when Katie picked up the phone.

"Hello, Ruth," Katie said, trying not to sound disappointed. "What's up?"

"You don't sound very happy to hear from me," said her old friend over the phone line. Ruth knew Katie better than anyone, with the exception, perhaps, of Gran. She could hear the disappointment in Katie's voice immediately.

"That's not true, Ruth White," replied Katie. "I always enjoy hearing from you. I had something on my mind when the phone rang and was a bit distracted, that's all."

"Hm," responded Ruth, but she decided to let it go. "Listen, champ, the tennis tournament is in three days and we haven't practiced since over a week ago. You may not need it, but Robert and I certainly do. How about meeting tomorrow afternoon for a couple of games?"

"Yes, OK," replied Katie, wondering what she was going to do if she didn't hear from Jim soon. He was her doubles partner, after all, and she couldn't play against Robert and Ruth by herself. "Shall we say 2:00 at Rosegate?"

"Yes, that's fine," Ruth confirmed. "I've already spoken with Robert and he only has rounds at the hospital in the morning."

"Wonderful," replied Katie, thinking how she might change the subject. She usually told Ruth everything, but she just didn't feel up to telling her about Jim at the moment, especially from her desk at the *Gazette*. "By the way, Ruth, how is the family doing after the intruder episode last night. Any lasting trauma?" she finally asked.

"No, none at all," said Ruth, chuckling. "We're a pretty tough family, you know. A nighttime break-in, a kidnapping, and a few stitches hardly phase us. Besides, we discovered we now have police protection around the clock. Our gardener was nearly shot trying to water the flowerbeds this morning."

Katie smiled at the lightness of her friend's tone. Ruth was downplaying the entire incident although Katie knew that the Whites must have been terrified and probably had trouble going to sleep after all of it.

"By the way, Ruthie," began Katie. "I forgot to ask you last night but did either of the intruders try to open the safe themselves?"

"You mean, before they asked Poppy to do it?"

"Yes," Katie replied. "You mentioned that they demanded that Poppy open it as soon as you entered the room. Then, after he was knocked out, the one man said to the other, 'now look what you've done' or something like that."

"Yes, that's right. Why?" said Ruth, not sure where Katie was going with this.

"Ruth, in the bank heists, and even the Dempsey robbery, the safes were cracked," Katie explained. "The thieves didn't need anyone to open the safes for them."

"Perhaps we interrupted them before they could get started,"

Ruth suggested.

"Yes, that true. Much easier to have Poppy open it instead of having to go through the process of cracking the combination lock," replied Katie. "Although that meant that they were reliant on him doing it before the alarm went off."

"They may not have known that we have an alarm system," countered Ruth.

"Then why cut the electricity?" responded Katie. "No, something's up, Ruthie. For some reason the attempted robbery at Sunset Hill is different from the rest. I think that they may have been unsure as to whether they could crack your safe. They may have planned to give it a try and then, when Poppy appeared, making him do it seemed the better choice."

"That's what I would have done if I were in their shoes," replied Ruth. "Wouldn't it make more sense to have the person who knows the combination open it?"

"Not if you're trying to get in and out before the alarm resets to its battery backup," said Katie. "You see, in the other robberies, the safecracker was successful in opening the safe in under 5 minutes. I bet Poppy tried to drag that out much longer."

"Well yes," replied Ruth. "He fiddled with it for quite a few minutes until he was knocked out."

"My point exactly!" responded Katie, slapping her desk. "Of course, there is the chance that you have a safe that the intruders have never cracked before. What's the brand name, anyway?"

"Hm, well let's see," Ruth replied, thinking for a moment. "Yes, now I remember. It's an American Sentry, the best money can buy!"

"Oh dear," sighed Katie, shaking her head.

"Gosh! Look at the time!" exclaimed Ruth suddenly. "I'm supposed to meet Robert in 30 minutes, and I haven't begun to get ready. We're seeing a movie and then going to dinner. Call him, Katie..."

"Have a good time," said Katie, her mind still on safecracking. "Wait. What did you say, Ruthie?"

"I said, give him a call, Katie dear. It's been two days and you haven't heard from him. Quit being stubborn and pick up the phone, silly."

"How on earth did you know?" asked Katie, completely dumbfounded.

"Reporters aren't the only ones who have their sources," Ruth replied with a chuckle and she quickly hung up the phone.

Katie had, in fact, thought of calling Jim several times but each time she had put it off. However, later that evening, right after dinner, she finally convinced herself that waiting for him to call her was driving her crazy, so, after taking a deep breath, she picked up the telephone in her bedroom and made the long-distance call to the Fielding home in East Haddam, Connecticut.

"Mrs. Fielding?" she asked nervously into the telephone to the pleasant-sounding voice that answered the other end of the line.

"Yes? This is Mrs. Fielding."

"My name is Katie Porter. You don't know me but I'm a friend of your…"

"Yes, Katie," said Jim's mother. "I know who you are. My son has told me quite a lot about you. How are you dear?"

"He has?" stammered Katie, startled. "I mean…I'm fine, ma'am, and you?" She knew that she must be sounding like a complete dimwit. "Pull yourself together, Porter, before this woman hangs up on you," she warned herself, trying to collect her composure.

"I'm very well, thank you," replied Mrs. Fielding. "Although the weather could be better. It's raining here in Connecticut and ruined my plans to garden today. James has most likely told you that I have quite a nice rose garden, although it's nothing that compares to your grandmother's."

Jim never told me about his mother growing roses or much about his family at all, Katie thought to herself. But, then again, they never talked much about his home.

"I imagine Jim…er…James, gets his love of roses from you?" she asked instead.

"Yes, I suppose that's true," Jim's mother replied, chuckling. "Although he's much better at growing them than I am."

Mrs. Fielding voice had a faint Welsh lilt to it and her soft, gentle, lighthearted tone over the telephone reminded Katie of Jim.

"Mrs. Fielding, the reason for my call is, well, I wonder if Jim is there? He left Fairfield rather hastily and I…um, I suppose I'm a little worried about him and wanted to call and make sure everything's all right. May I speak to him, please?"

"I'm afraid he's not here at the moment, Katie. He has taken his sister to the movies and I believe they won't be home until very late."

"Oh, I see," replied Katie, discouraged but breathing a sigh of relief. He was well and had not been killed at least. "Would you please let him know I called?"

"Yes, dear, of course."

"It's been nice talking to you, Mrs. Fielding," Katie said, somewhat reluctant to hang up.

"Yes, and to you as well," replied Jim's mother. "Goodbye."

"Goodbye," replied Katie, holding the phone to her chest for several minutes after the line went dead. It didn't make sense. None of it. The ghost, the break-in at Sunset Hill, and Jim. Especially Jim. Things were not connecting, and it was because she was missing something. But what could it be?

Why did Jim leave so suddenly, and without telling her, when there didn't appear to be an emergency at home? Surely his mother would have mentioned it if there had been. And, why would the ghost of Golden Joe give her a clue but only as the break-in was in progress? Was it a trap? No, it appeared to be more of a taunt. Some very sick individual was taunting her but why?

She placed the phone receiver back into its cradle and walked over to her desk to retrieve her notes. Returning to her bed, and propping herself up on her pillows, she spread the pages across her bed covers where she studied them for several hours before finally turning off her light. Completely exhausted, she quickly drifted off into a fitful sleep, the mantra of taunt, taunt, taunt, echoing in her mind.

The ringing of the telephone woke her hours later and glancing at the clock beside her bed, she saw that it was midnight.

"Hello?" she answered, groggy from sleep.

"Katie?" she heard Jim's voice say. "I'm sorry. I didn't mean to wake you, but my mother told me that you called and that it sounded urgent. Is everything OK? Are you all right?"

"Jim!" Katie replied, relief washing over her. She sat up in bed, now completely awake. "I could ask the same of you. What's happened? Why did you leave Fairfield so suddenly and without telling me?"

"I had a few things to take care of," he replied nonchalantly.

"In the middle of the night?" she shot back at him.

"It was 8:00, Katie, not the middle of the night," he replied.

"And you asked E.M. to take you to the train station," she countered. "When you had just left Rosegate without giving any indication that you were leaving. You told me that you had a headache!"

"I made the decision to come to East Haddam only after I left you…"

"And you couldn't call me…" she interrupted angerly.

"Should I have?" he countered.

"You're asking me if…" she paused as her throat tightened and her voice cracked. She was determined not to cry but she could feel the tears already beginning to roll down her cheeks.

"Katie," Jim replied softly after a moment. He took a deep breath before continuing. "Listen, I don't mean to upset you, but I thought perhaps that I'd been mistaken about…well, maybe I've been rushing things along…you see…damn, I'm not explaining this very well."

"No, you're not. I'm not understanding any of this," Katie replied, dabbing her eyes with a tissue.

"No, I guess not," sighed Jim. "You see, I'm crazy about you, Katie Porter. I want to be with you all the time. I look forward to meeting you for lunch and listening to you tell me what you're working on. I like coming to dinner and talking about your day. I love making you blush when I flirt with you. I love holding you in my arms when we dance. Katie, I've been on cloud nine ever since we've started dating. And, well, you didn't seem to mind so I thought that perhaps you felt the same way. But then we had that discussion about Charlie Grant taking you out and I admitted to being jealous and you…"

"Oh gosh!" she exclaimed, suddenly remembering the conversation. So there is was. Finally. She hadn't realized.

She had never taken Charlie Grant seriously so, when Jim admitted to some jealously, she had intended to reassure him by downplaying the whole situation. And, if she was being completely honest, she was still struggling with her deep and growing feelings for him.

"You told me that we were dating now but if that changed, I'd be the first to know," he explained. She could hear the heartbreak in his voice.

"Giving you the impression…" she began.

"That you're just interested in a casual, most likely temporary, relationship," he replied, finishing her sentence. "I've been needing to sign some papers here at home but have been putting it off because I didn't want to miss spending time with you. But now, well, it seemed as good a time as any to finally take care of things and, at the same time, give you a chance to follow your news story without me tagging along. Since this is casual for you, I assumed that you won't need or want me to call to let you know. Besides, I'd probably be back before you even knew I was gone."

Katie remained silent. She realized that her own emotional struggles had inadvertently caused her to hurt him. She had really blown it.

"I'm terribly sorry," Jim continued sadly. "I must have driven you crazy. All this time I've apparently been misreading all the signals..."

"Jim," Katie interrupted softly. "You haven't."

"What?"

"Misread any signals," she replied. "I'm the one who should be apologizing. I made light of a serious conversation, unintentionally giving you the impression that I didn't care. That's wrong. I do. Very much. I've been worried sick about you, Jim Fielding. I miss you. Please come home."

Jim was silent for several seconds and Katie held her breath. She couldn't begin to guess what he must be thinking.

"So, this whole thing has been one big misunderstanding?" he asked finally, his heart pounding in his chest.

"Yes, it looks that way," she replied. "Which is very odd for us since we usually tend to read each other's mind."

"And you do care for me?" he asked hopefully.

"Yes," she replied. "I'm afraid so."

"Then what in god's name am I doing up here in Connecticut? I'll be on the early morning train," he said decisively. "I should arrive in Fairfield around 10:00 am.

"I'll be waiting for you on the platform," she replied, breathing a sigh of relief. And then joked, "I'll be the one wearing a red rose in my lapel."

"And I'll be the one with the foolish grin on my face," he joked back. "See you in a few hours. Goodnight, Katie."

"Goodnight, Jim," she replied, smiling as she hung up the phone. She flopped back down on her pillows and was soon fast asleep, this time thinking about his wonderfully foolish grin spread across his handsome face.

CHAPTER 12
THE HANDWRITING ANALYSIS

"You seem very happy this morning, dear," observed Gran, looking up from her newspaper as Katie, humming to herself, broke open her hardboiled egg. "You must have slept well."

"Yes, Gran, I did," Katie replied, smiling at her grandmother. "And you?"

"Yes, very well, thank you," replied Gran, returning Katie's smile. "It says here in the paper that the police believe the bank robberies, the Dempsey robbery, and the attempted one at Sunset Hill are connected. Do they know about our ghost?"

"No," replied Katie. "I haven't said anything about that yet. I've been waiting to gather more proof of a connection before going to the police and getting laughed out of the station."

"But you can show them the coded messages."

"We only have the one showing the Savings and Loan," pointed out Katie. "And it could have been created after the actual break-in."

"How about Sunset Hill," countered Gran. "You retrieved that one during the break-in itself."

"Which is one of several things that makes that incident very different from the others," shrugged Katie. "Someone may have been playing a trick on me, Gran."

"Yes, I see," agreed her grandmother, taking a sip of her coffee before returning to her paper.

"But that gives me an idea," said Katie, suddenly standing and turning towards the hallway. "I'm going to call Mr. Martin and Mr. Watkins, of the two banks that were robbed, and ask them to time the delay in their alarm system battery backups."

Gran, not having any idea what Katie was talking about, just nodded her head and said, "Well, can your calls wait until after you've eaten your breakfast, at least?"

But Katie was already picking up the telephone and placing her first call before Mrs. Porter had a chance to finish her sentence.

Both bankers agreed to time the minutes between the alarm system's transfer from electrical power to the battery.

"Don't be surprised if it's more than 5 minutes," Katie warned Mr. Watkins.

"That would not be acceptable, Miss Porter," responded the banker. "A lot can happen in 5 minutes."

"Yes, exactly, Mr. Watkins," agreed Katie. "And that, in a nutshell, may be the key to this entire story."

She was returning to the breakfast table when the phone rang. Picking it up, she heard Detective Grant on the line.

"Katie? This is Charlie. Listen, Grace has finished analyzing those handwriting samples. She's available to explain everything to you this morning. Can you swing by the station say around 10:30?"

"Yes," replied Katie with excitement. "I'm picking Jim up from the train station at 10:00 and we'll come straight over from there."

"Perfect," he responded. "See you soon."

"So Jim is returning home today," said Gran, when Katie returned to the breakfast table. "He must be finished with his out of town business. How nice."

"Yes, Gran," replied her granddaughter softly. "Very."

* * *

To Katie, it seemed forever before the train arrived at the Fairfield station but, in fact, it was right on time. She strained to catch a glimpse of Jim as the passengers on the crowded train disembarked. He finally stepped from one of the middle compartments and, looking anxiously around, spotted her standing several feet down the platform. His face broke out into a wide grin and he waved his hat at her as he danced and dodged his way around fellow passengers all moving towards the same exit.

Katie was so excited to see him that she could barely breath. Finally, he was there in front of her and they stood very still for a moment, just looking at each other, before he dropped his suitcase and took her into his arms, lifting her off the ground in a tight hug.

"Katie," was all he said, breathing her in.

"Jim," was her only response, pressing her cheek against his.

"Katie Porter!" they heard the voice calling. "Boy am I glad to see you!"

It took a second before the couple realized that they were being interrupted by Eloise Dempsey as she strolled up alongside them.

"My goodness, what a trip!" Eloise continued, without skipping a beat. "I nearly missed getting on in North Central because the ticket line was so long. They really should do something about that. More ticket windows would be helpful..."

Jim gently put Katie back down onto the platform and gave her a wink. She looked up at him ardently and then turned to address Eloise.

"Hello, Eloise," Katie responded. "How are you?"

"Terrible," replied Eloise. "My feet are killing me. I should have worn better shoes, I know, and Margaret is always telling me so, but these are my favorite and I just had to show them off to Cousin Mary."

Jim picked up his suitcase and followed the two women down the platform towards Katie's roadster.

"...so I said to Margaret," continued Eloise. "Next time hide the money behind Daddy's picture above the fireplace. But you won't believe it! The police found the money and now we've got it all back. Isn't that simply wonderful! Oh, yes, I was wondering if you could give me a lift home. I usually take a cab but since you're here, well, it's on your way isn't it?"

"Well, um..." Katie began. "We're are our way to an appointment and..."

"Wonderful!" replied Eloise, opening the door of Katie's car and sliding in the passenger seat. "That's so nice of you."

Jim chuckled and crawled into the rumble seat, pulling his suitcase in behind him.

"Watch out for the baby," said Eloise, holding onto her hat as Katie backed away from the curb and turn out of the parking lot. A young woman pushing a baby stroller was walking down the sidewalk toward the train station several yards away. "Just like the cab I was in on 5th Avenue. The driver was going too fast and I thought for sure that he was going to run over a woman pushing a baby carriage across the street. Just imagine! But of course they drive fast in New York City, weaving in and out of traffic. But I do like the shops. Have you ever been to New York, Mr. er...?" she asked, looking back at Jim.

"Yes, several times," he replied, nodding.

"I try and go as much as possible although my sister loathes the trip but, then, Margaret doesn't like to travel far from...," Eloise rambled on as Katie drove through the streets of Fairfield to Miller's Landing and then took a right onto Brownstone Avenue, finally pulling up to the curb in front of the Dempsey home.

"Well, here we are! Thank you so much, dear. You saved me cab fare," Eloise remarked, stepping from Katie's roadster and moving up her front steps where she paused to look through her handbag. "I know my keys are in here somewhere. Oh, there you are Margaret! I'm afraid I've left my keys..."

Margaret Dempsey glanced up at Katie and Jim from her open front door and waved to them as she held out her hand to her sister. "Come in, Eloise. You're letting the bugs in."

Jim climbed out of the rumble seat and slid into the passenger seat beside Katie as she shifted gears, putting the car into reverse.

"I don't think that woman drew breath the entire time," Katie replied, turning toward the police station. "I was hoping to update you on everything that's happened since you've been gone before we got to the police station, but now we'll have to wait until lunch."

"Oh, we're going to the police station?" asked Jim, stretching an arm across the back of the seats and placing a hand on Katie's shoulder.

"Yes," she replied, giving him a warm smile. "We're meeting a handwriting specialist who I hope will be able to tell me if our friend,

Sergeant Smith, threw a large rock through my window with a threatening note attached."

"It's sure nice to be home," chuckled Jim, glancing over at Katie.

"Yes, it certainly is," she replied seriously.

They pulled into the parking lot at the Fairfield Police Station and hurried into the building.

"There you are, Katie!" said Detective Grant, standing and taking her outstretched hand, "I'd like you to meet one of the best graphologists in the country!"

The young woman seated in the corner stood to shake Katie's hand. She was about 28 years old, with a professional demeanor and confident air about her. Katie liked her immediately.

"Hi, Miss Porter, I'm Grace Waters. It's so nice to finally meet you. Charlie's told me a lot about you."

"Well, then, don't believe a word of it," replied Katie, smiling and giving Charlie a wink.

After introducing Jim to Grace, the graphologist pulled out the handwriting samples and laid them across the detective's desk. Then she turned and, bringing out a folder from her briefcase, handed it to Katie.

"It's all in here," she said. "But I will give you a summary of what I found."

They looked over her shoulder as Grace Waters started her explanation. "The samples clearly show the psychological make-up of the writer, even though the individual tried to disguise their handwriting in the Rosegate note."

Katie nodded and leaned forward. "First note the size of each letter. They are very large in size and include quite large angular loops," the graphologist continued. "Now, note the gap around the bottom of the lowercase "d's", and the lack of closure with the "s" and "a" letters."

Jim and Katie looked closer at the notes, intently studying each of them.

"The most interesting detail is the inconsistency of the writing throughout," continued Miss Waters. "If you look very closely, you will see that some of the letters are written over or, in some cases, corrections attempted. Finally, the writer appears to be playing with their handwriting. In a manner of speaking, this is a person who has no clear handwriting style themselves and is practicing or attempting to create one. Unfortunately, this individual will never be satisfied with their results so attempts to establish their own style will never be successful."

"What does this all mean?" asked Jim, feeling completely lost.

"It means that the author of these samples is a sociopath," answered Miss Waters. "Without a doubt."

"A person without real human emotion," said Katie, softly and thoughtfully. "Could this person be very dangerous if provoked?"

"They're not necessarily killers, if that's what you mean," answered Miss Waters, shaking her head. "However, I wouldn't rule it out. Sociopaths have no remorse about what they do in order to save themselves. They would have no qualms about killing if they felt it was necessary."

"Do you believe that the samples are written by only one individual?" Katie asked.

"Yes," answered Miss Waters, nodding. "All of these were definitely written by the same person."

Katie glanced over at Charlie Grant and he returned her look with raised eyebrows.

"I think you'd better call the stations in Wakefield or Cumberland, whichever place she's from, and get some information on our friend, don't you think, Charlie?" said Katie.

"Indeed," replied the detective, nodding his head. He had a worried expression on his face.

"Thank you. You've been extremely helpful," Katie said to Miss Waters. "And very generous with your time. We really appreciate it since I know that we have interrupted a visit with your family."

"Just my father," smiled Grace. "And you have saved me from losing quite a bit of money playing poker with him and his buddies."

Jim and Katie chuckled and, bidding Miss Waters and Detective Grant goodbye, left the police station. Soon they were back in Katie's car and on their way.

"Polly's?" asked Jim, stifling a yawn. He had gotten up very early to catch the first train back to Fairfield.

"Yes, and then to Rosegate to play some tennis with Ruth and Robert," replied Katie, smiling at him. "We'll have to swing by your place first so that you can pick up a change of clothes and your tennis racket."

"You're killing me, woman," teased Jim, but he was so happy to be with her that he would have done anything she asked.

* * *

"A magnet?" asked Jim, biting into his ham sandwich at Polly's. A large slice of apple pie sat to the left of his plate, courtesy of their waitress who seemed as happy to see Jim as Katie was, and he kept eyeing it as he listened.

"Yes, I believe that the thieves used a strong magnet to shift the metal sash locks on the windows over to the open position," she responded. "I tested out my theory on our own windows at Rosegate and was able to do it."

"Very interesting," Jim replied. "So that's why you were so interested in the magnet taken from the crime scene at the Savings and Loan."

"Yes, and not placed in the evidence bag by Sergeant Smith," added Katie. "Go ahead and eat your pie, Jim. I know that it's driving you crazy. You're allowed to eat your dessert first if you wish," she added, chuckling.

"No, sandwich first, pie after," he remarked stubbornly. "It's a test of wills, you see."

Katie raised her eyebrows at him but chuckled. "I am puzzled as to Sergeant's Smith role in all of this, though. She's hiding evidence and throwing notes through my window to warn me off. Either she's trying to help the thieves or perhaps slow down the investigation for some reason."

"Or both," added Jim, stealing a bite of pie before returning to his sandwich. "Maybe she's doing neither and just wants to be the one to arrest the culprits and get all the credit. You are definitely getting in her way, Miss Porter."

"Yes, perhaps," Katie pondered. "And then there's the safecracking situation. Did you know that E.M. wrote the *Stars and*

Stripes article that you remembered?" She then related what she had learned about Harry C. Miller's method and her visit to Dickson's Locksmith and Keys shop. "Apparently the American Sentry Safes use a combination lock that is built with very thick metal and the clicking noise is quite a bit louder than the others. I heard it myself. Of course, I held the lock in my hand, so it was easy, but I believe a skilled safecracker, perhaps using a stethoscope, would have little trouble unlocking it."

"Do you have any idea how long it would take someone like that to crack the safe?" asked Jim.

"I'm not positive but I believe our guy is doing it in less than five minutes."

"Wow," replied Jim, moving the pie in front of him although he had only eaten half of his sandwich. "I seem to recall that it took Mr. Miller at least 20.

"Yes," said Katie, nodding her head. "But I would place money that he hasn't tried an American Sentry yet. We have a Bakersfield at Rosegate, which appears to be much harder to crack. It most likely would take both Mr. Miller and our safecracker much longer than 5 minutes."

"Good point," nodded Jim.

"Which makes the delay in the alarm system very important," continued Katie.

"Delay in the alarm system?" asked Jim, taking the last bite of pie and returning to the remains of his sandwich.

"Yes," she nodded. She proceeded to tell him about retrieving the message in the stump, being chased by Golden Joe, and the break-in at Sunset Hill.

"It was happening while you were being chased?" asked Jim.

"Yes."

"And they wanted Poppy to open the safe?"

"Yes," Katie answered. "Which, scary as it was, gives us our first real lucky break. You see, if the alarm systems in the banks have an extended period of time switching from electrical power to battery backup, then all our thieves need to do is make sure they are in and out of the building during that delay. That's why Poppy was trying to take as much time as needed to set off the alarm and he succeeded in doing that."

"So, I bet by now you have a theory about all of this," Jim remarked, his eyes twinkling.

"Yes," replied Katie, wrinkling her nose at him. She set her napkin on her empty plate and leaned forward on her elbows. "Here is how I think they do it. The guy on the ground turns off the electricity and then climbs up on the guy with the stilts, who is waiting nearby. They walk over to the second story window and one of them uses the magnet to unlock it. The guy being carried climbs through and cracks the safe, carrying bags of money to the guy on stilts who, presumably, is timing the whole thing. When their 5 minutes is nearly up, our safecracker climbs aboard the other and they walk away on the stilts, leaving behind the tell-tale marks."

"Leaving the police to set off the now activated alarm when they arrive to investigate the break-in," Jim added, finishing the scenario.

"Exactly," nodded Katie.

"Quite ingenious, really," replied Jim thoughtfully. "With a successful plan such as that, I wonder why they risked breaking into homes."

"Yes, I wondered about that myself," Katie agreed. "They had more time at the Dempseys because there was no alarm system. But Sunset Hill was very different. They broke in through a ground floor window so didn't use the stilts. And they were reluctant to crack the safe themselves, opting instead to try and get Poppy to do it."

"Yes, that is strange," replied Jim. "Why not hold the family at bay, perhaps by knife point, and take care of business themselves?"

"My thoughts, exactly," replied Katie. "So, thinking this might be due to the brand of the safe, I checked with Ruth. The Whites have the same safe as the banks, an American Sentry, so the thieves should have had no trouble cracking it. In fact, it would have been to their advantage given that the alarm system could go off at any minute."

"Which means?" asked Jim.

"That there has been a change in personnel," replied Katie. "Golden Joe may no longer have the talents of the first safecracker, a young man very adept at doing the job in a very short period of time."

"Hm," responded Jim with a smile. "I have a feeling you have an idea who this very adept young man might be?"

"Yes, unfortunately I believe I do," replied Katie softly. "It's Walter Issacs."

CHAPTER 13
A TRAP IS SET

"Walter! Oh Katie are you sure?" exclaimed Jim.

"Yes," she replied. "You see, while you were around the corner giving Frankie a lesson in how to behave in front of women, I happened to pop in and meet Walter as he was repairing Mrs. Winfield's mantel clock. He used a stethoscope to listen to the gears turning in the timepiece. Clock gears click, or in their case, tick. Essentially the sound is the same. You mentioned that Frankie had a close friend named Walter Issacs and we already suspect that Frankie may be one of the young men picking up the messages from Golden Joe. It fits together, Jim. Young Walter could very well be our safecracker."

"He is on the small side," nodded Jim sadly. "If Frankie is our stilt walker, which we don't know for sure, at the moment, then it's quite conceivable that he could lift Walter up to the window and then carry him away."

"Yes," replied Katie thoughtfully. "So our next move should be..."

"to drive over to the boys club and have a talk with Walter," Jim interjected, standing and sliding out of the booth. "Do we have time before tennis?" he added.

"Of course," nodded Katie, glancing down at her watch before joining him. "Even if we didn't, this is more important. Ruth and

Robert can wait. Besides, they are probably at Rosegate now getting in some extra practice so that they can beat us," she joked.

"I'll need to stop off at the *Times* and check in with my editor," remarked Jim, holding the café door open for Katie. "He still thinks I'm up in East Haddam."

It only took a few minutes for Jim to speak with his editor and he returned soon to Katie's car.

"He's got an assignment for me," said Jim, stepping back into the passenger's seat. "But since I wasn't due back yet, it can wait a few more days."

"Wonderful!" exclaimed Katie. "Now to the Boys Club!"

They arrived at the club minutes later and found Mr. Decker, the organization's director, in the office speaking with Allen Thompson. They both looked up as Jim and Katie entered the lobby.

"Ah, there she is now," exclaimed Allen. "We were just talking about you!"

"Oh, yes?" smiled Katie, walking over to them.

"Mr. Decker and I were discussing the camping trip on your property," explained Mr. Thompson. "And wondered when we might be able to ride over and talk to you about it."

"How does next week sound?" asked Katie. "Say Wednesday at around 3:00?"

"Yes, perfect," replied Mr. Decker. "Thank you."

"We'd like to speak with Walter Issacs," Jim spoke up. "Is he here in class today?"

"No, we haven't seen him in several days," replied Allen Thompson, shaking his head.

"Perhaps he's ill," replied Katie. "May we have his home address so that we might swing by his house and check on him?"

"Yes, certainly," replied Mr. Decker. "And please let us know how he is. We are very fond of Walter and would like to help him if needed."

"And we'd like to have Frankie Cooper's address as well," said Jim, smiling over at Katie.

"Oh?" responded Mr. Decker. "Well, OK. Since it's you who's asking..." he added, walking back into his office.

Bidding the men goodbye, Katie and Jim were soon on their way to the worst part of town in Fairfield. It lay over the train tracks on the south side's outer limits.

"Gosh I don't think I've ever been in this part of town," admitted Katie, searching the street signs.

"I have once or twice," replied Jim grimly. "Following news leads. Take this right."

Walter's home was located three doors down from the corner. The tiny house looked dilapidated and the yard completely overtaken by tall grass and weeds. The picket fence surrounding the property was broken in several places, including the gate which hung by only one hinge.

"Stay here, Katie," Jim warned, stepping from the roadster. "I'll go knock on the door to see if anyone's home."

"No, I'm coming with you," Katie insisted, sliding out of the car and joining him as he struggled to swing open the gate. It came off in his hands, instead, and he laid it on the ground. Taking Katie's arm in his, they walked up and onto the front porch and knocked. No one answered.

"You won't find anyone home," said a voice behind them.

They spun around and saw a young woman standing in the yard. Her face and hair were dirty, and she wore a torn dress with dirty knee socks that sagged around her calves. She held a small child in her arms and another, slightly older child, hid behind her leg, clutching tightly to the hem of her skirt.

"Are you with the government?" the woman continued, suspiciously looking them up and down.

"No, we're looking for Walter," said Jim, giving her a warm smile. "Do you know when he'll be back?"

"What do you want with Walter?" asked the woman. "He hasn't done anything wrong. He's a hard-working young man."

"Yes," Katie remarked, stepping off the porch and coming over to her. "I need his services. You see, I have a broken clock and he's the only one who can repair it."

"Ah, well," nodded the woman, finally giving them a smile that revealed several missing teeth. "Yes, he's good at that. He can fix any clock that's given to him.

"Excuse me," said Katie suddenly. "You look very familiar. Do I know you? Have we met before?"

The woman took a few steps back and shook her head. "No."

Katie studied her for a moment and then caught her breath. "Maxine. Maxine Wells! It's you, isn't it?"

The woman let out a sigh and looking down at her feet, shook her head once more before looking back up at Katie.

"Yes, Katie," she said softly. "It's me. I didn't know it was you until I came into the yard and then it was too late. I was hoping you wouldn't recognize me."

"Maxine how are you?" said Katie, stepping forward to give the woman a hug. Maxine, however, stepped back, remaining out of Katie's reach.

"I'm fine, Katie," replied Maxine. Suddenly a youngster's voice called out from the house next door. "Ma! Come fix dinner. I'm hungry."

Katie looked over to see a boy of about 5 years of age, leaning out a window. He wore no shirt despite the cool temperature of the day.

"Henry, close that window. I'll be there in a minute!" Maxine hollered back him, and the boy ducked his head back inside and disappeared.

"Jim," said Katie, turning to him as he stepped from the porch and came up beside her. "This is an old classmate of mine. Maxine Wells, er, I mean Gibson. Maxine Gibson. I remember now that you're married."

"A widow, now," replied Maxine soberly.

"Oh, I am so sorry," said Katie, remembering Harold Gibson, another classmate of theirs. He was a tall handsome boy, with flowing blond hair and an easy smile. He was the captain of the basketball team and quite popular with the girls. He and Maxine had gotten married quite suddenly, when she was only sixteen, and the rumors spread quickly throughout the high school. Katie had to admit that she barely recognized the woman standing before her, so drastic was the change in Maxine's appearance from that of the beautiful young girl in school.

"Harold was killed in France, just like thousands of other guys," stated Maxine bluntly. "You married Ruddy White, didn't you?"

"No, he was killed before the wedding," replied Katie. "In the war. Three years ago."

"Oh, I'm sorry," said Maxine, giving Katie a compassionate look. "I guess the war didn't spare many, did it?"

"No," nodded Katie. "But some did come home, Maxine. This is Jim Fielding. He was seriously wounded on Omaha Beach and survived."

"Nice to meet you, Mrs. Gibson," said Jim cordially.

Maxine Gibson gave him a nod as she mumbled, "How do you do."

"I'm helping Jim track down Walter," explained Katie as calmly as she could.

"You see, I volunteer at the Fairfield Boys Club where Walter comes to get job training," added Jim. "He hasn't been to the club for several days and we were worried that he might be ill."

Maxine shook her head sadly. "He's taken his sisters and left town. You see, his mother died on Saturday and there was nothing he could do but try and get to his aunt who lives in Chicago. He was thinking that he might pick up some work there so that he could help take care of Mary and Thelma. He told me he had done some jobs fixing clocks and had earned just enough bus fare and food money to make the trip. They left on Monday."

"Well that explains it," Katie whispered to herself. Then, addressing her former schoolmate, she said, "well it's been lovely seeing you again, Maxine. Please promise to come by and see me soon. I'm still at Rosegate and would love to have you and the children."

"Thanks, Katie," replied Maxine, but she shook her head. "I don't think so. I don't get to that side of town very often."

Not quite knowing how to respond, Katie just gave her a warm smile and, waving to the children, she and Jim walked toward the roadster. Suddenly Jim stopped and bending down, picked something up from behind a massive weed stock.

"I believe you dropped this when you came into the yard, Mrs. Gibson," he exclaimed, walking back to her and pressing it into her hand.

She waited until the couple drove away before opening her palm to see what it was.

"Jim Fielding!" chuckled Katie, gazing into her rearview mirror at the shrinking image of Maxine standing stunned in the yard and looking up at the retreating car. "You know very well that Maxine Gibson did not drop a $10 bill in those weeds."

"She could have," replied Jim, smiling over at her.

Katie shook her head at him. "You have a soft heart you know that Jim Fielding?"

"As do you, Katie Porter," he countered.

"Oh yes?"

"Yes. The police didn't find the Dempsey's cash in the woods, now did they?"

"I refuse to answer on the grounds that it might incriminate me," chuckled Katie. "To Frankie's now?"

"Yes, turn at the next corner," he replied, pointing ahead. "It should be about half a mile down the road.

* * *

"I'm terribly sorry," said Frankie's mother, as she poured Katie a cup of Earl Grey tea. "I haven't seen Frankie in several days. I just haven't been able to manage him lately."

They were seated in the living room of a modest well-kept home, surrounded by several pieces of very nice furniture. It was apparent that Frankie's mother had fine taste as well as a sense of fashion. She was dressed in a popular skirt and blouse ensemble accented by an expensive sweater. Her shoulder length hair was pulled back and held by a lovely hair pin that could very well have been an old family heirloom.

She handed Katie the cup and then turned to Jim. "I'm very grateful for the work you do with the boys at the Boys Club, Mr. Fielding. Frankie has told me a lot about you. He has great respect for you."

"Thank you, Mrs. Cooper," replied Jim, stirring his tea as he eyed the plate of cookies on the table in front of him. "I'm pleased to hear it although I'm just one of several men who volunteer their time trying to help the boys."

"Yes, good male role models are very important to growing boys," nodded Mrs. Cooper. "Especially these days. That's what so tragic about Frankie's situation. You see, my husband didn't have to go."

"Didn't have to go?" asked Katie, raising her eyebrows. "I'm not sure I understand."

"My Gerald, Frankie's father, was a chemist," Mrs. Cooper explained. "We left England years ago so that he could work on a special program here in the U.S. His work exempted him from active duty, but he felt strongly about defending his home country, so he went back to Kent and enlisted. Since I'm an American and so is Frankie, having been born here, we decided it was safer for us to wait out the war here in the States."

"So Frankie's father was a British citizen?" Katie asked, lifting the plate of cookies from the table and handing it to Jim.

"Yes," replied Mrs. Cooper. "From a very old established family. Those are two photographs of Gerald over there on the mantel. The one on the left is of him as a boy on their small country estate and on the right, him in his British Army uniform."

Katie walked over to the fireplace mantel and looked at the photographs. It was the picture on the left that mostly caught her attention. She carried it over to Jim and pointed down at it.

"Jim, look at this picture of Frankie's father as a boy. See anything?"

"I see a nice-looking young man who resembles Frankie quite a bit," replied Jim, studying the photo.

"Yes, one could say that Frankie is the spitting image of his dad," smiled Mrs. Cooper fondly.

"Look closer. Look at the two men seen in the distance just behind Mr. Cooper's right shoulder," said Katie.

Jim put down his teacup and half eaten cookie and took the picture from Katie. He tilted it toward the light and then shook his head.

"Is something wrong?" Mrs. Cooper asked with confused concern.

"No, not at all. We've just discovered something very interesting," Katie replied. "You see, there are two men in the background who are wearing stilts. Did Mr. Cooper's family grow Hops by any chance?"

"Why yes," answered Mrs. Cooper. "They had one of the largest Hop farms in Kent. And every year a group of townspeople from the lower classes would come down and earn extra money picking the crop. The Coopers did that for years before the war and it worked out well for everyone. The family got the crop picked and those in need earned some money."

"Did Frankie's father ever learn how to walk on those stilts?" asked Jim, leaning forward.

"Yes he did," replied Mrs. Cooper, somewhat puzzled at her guest's interest in Hop picking. "He even made a pair when Frankie was about 6 and taught him how to use them. Not to pick Hops, of course, but because my husband thought it was a good way to strengthen one's sense of balance. He even tried to teach me, but I never got the hang of it."

"Does Frankie still use the stilts?" asked Katie, now very excited.

"Yes, on occasion when he's hired for parties or for parades," replied Frankie's mother. "He was Uncle Sam at last year's July 4th parade celebration. Why do you ask?"

Katie and Jim looked at each other and decided to tell the woman the truth.

"We're not quite sure, yet," Jim told her. "But Frankie may be mixed up with some very bad people who are responsible for the recent break-ins of several Fairfield banks."

Mrs. Cooper gasped and brought her hands up to her face. "No!" she exclaimed, shaking her head forlornly. "I was afraid something like this might happen. How could he!"

"We hope we're mistaken, Mrs. Cooper," said Katie, placing her hand on the woman's shoulder. "I'm terribly sorry, but I have to ask. May we please see Frankie's stilts?"

"Yes, of course," replied Mrs. Cooper, pulling herself together with resolve. "They're in the shed in the back yard. Here, I'll get the key and unlock it for you."

Katie and Jim stepped outside and walked around to the backyard. "I really hope we're wrong, Jim," said Katie reluctantly. "But I don't think so."

Jim nodded his head, his jaw tight and his face drawn. It only took Frankie's mother a minute to join them with the key. She quickly stepped forward and unlocked the shed door, swinging it open. They anxiously peered inside but the stilts were gone.

"That's strange," said Mrs. Cooper, shaking her head as she looked around. "They've always been stored here, and I know of no engagement where Frankie would need them. I can't imagine what's happened to them."

"We can," Jim replied grimly. "We most certainly can."

* * *

"It's time to set a trap for our thieves and catch them at their own game," Katie said with determination as she and Jim walked across the back lawn of Rosegate toward the tennis courts. After leaving the Cooper home they had swung by Jim's place where he dropped off his suitcase and grabbed his tennis gear.

"I agree, but we'll have to be very careful," he replied. "If we're not successful, it could go one of two ways. Either the thieves leave town because things have gotten too hot for them, just as they did in Wakefield and Cumberland, or they decide to do something to scare us off so that they can continue their criminal activities."

"Yes," Katie nodded, waving to Ruth and Robert who were already on the courts. "Another question is how much to involve the police. I'm not sure that Charlie Grant won't be compelled to include Sergeant Smith and, as you know, I don't trust her. Especially after what we learned from Miss Waters. It's clear that the sergeant doesn't want me working on this story, but we're not sure why."

"She may be concerned that you'll steal her "collar" even though you're not a police officer," Jim suggested.

"I suppose it would look bad to be outdone by a mere newspaper reporter especially if you've been sent to Fairfield by your superior officers to solve the case," sighed Katie.

"Her actions do suggest that she has something to prove," agreed Jim. "Perhaps we can come up with a plan where we don't need the police? You know, like in the movies where the good guys squash the bad guys and have everything wrapped up just before the cops arrive. They'll have their hands full trying to outdo the team of Fielding and Porter!"

Katie chuckled and then grew serious. "Jim?" she said, stopping for a moment to look up at him.

"Yes?"

"I'm awfully glad that you survived the war and came home."

"I am, too, Katie," he replied softly. "I am, too." And he reached over and took her hand in his as they proceeded to the courts and their tennis challengers.

The rest of the afternoon was spent enjoying the company of good friends; a welcome distraction from the topics of thievery, poverty, and the fate of old schoolmates. In the end, after fierce competition, it was Ruth and Robert who managed to squeak out a win, aided by the exhaustion of Jim who missed several shots.

"Sorry, Katie," he remarked, apologizing to his tennis partner. "I'm afraid I was off my game today."

"Please don't apologize, Jim," she responded, handing him a cold glass of lemonade, as the four of them sat around a small table in the sunporch. "I'm the one who plucked you off an early morning train, ran you all over town barely stopping long enough to eat, and then dragged you to the tennis courts to be walloped by our two friends here."

"In other words," interjected Ruth. "A normal Katie Porter day."

"Hey!" exclaimed Katie, but she joined in the laughter. "Which reminds me...."

"Here we go," said Robert, winking at Ruth.

"I think it's time to confront our thieves," said Katie. "The police aren't getting anywhere and, although Jim and I have uncovered several clues, it appears that neither are we. I have reason to believe that the gang has replaced some of its members and they're not quite as adept at carrying out Golden Joe's instructions. We need to push things along before someone gets seriously hurt."

"I'm not sure I like this, Katie," responded Ruth, shaking her head. "What exactly is it that you have in mind?"

"A trap," Katie replied. "We need to come up with a way to catch the culprits in the act."

"Perhaps a fake robbery location," suggested Jim. "We could leave Golden Joe a note suggesting his gang rob the gas station downtown and then lay in wait for them."

"Won't he figure out that's what we're doing?" replied Robert. "Surely he's smart enough not to take the bait."

They sat quietly for several minutes sipping their lemonade and pondering the situation. Suddenly Katie snapped her fingers.

"He might believe it if the suggestion came from one of their former gang members," she explained, looking around at each of them. "Perhaps Walter Issacs should be the one to suggest the next robbery location!"

"But Walter's left town," countered Jim.

"All the more reason to have him write the note," replied Katie, her eyes twinkling. "Or at least sign his name to it."

Jim smiled at the plan. "Yes, that just might work. And since we suspect Frankie of being one of the gang members, we could place the note on the bulletin board at the Boys Club with his name on it. There's still a chance that he'll stop by and see it there."

"Yes, that's true," agreed Katie, rubbing her hands together in excitement. "Even if he doesn't, someone from the gang will notice it and pick it up. You see, I suspect that the Boys Club may be a recruiting ground for new gang members and our ghost is either one of the older boys or a man who volunteers there."

Jim sat bolt upright. "If I find out that it's one of the men, I'll…" he sputtered.

"But didn't you say that Frankie and Walter were close friends at one time?" Ruth interrupted. "Frankie would be the one person who would most likely know that Walter is not in town. Won't he become suspicious? And that applies to other Boys Club gang members, as well?"

"Not if we pretend that the note was sent through the mail," replied Jim, regaining his composure. "All we have to do is put it in an envelope addressed to Frankie Cooper. We'll add a stamp and then run a fake postmark over it. I'll pin it to the bulletin board along with the other letters the boys often receive at the Club."

"That's downright diabolical," said Katie with a grin. "Remind me to stay on your good side, Fielding."

He just smiled and winked at her.

"Yes, that might just work," replied Robert thoughtfully. "Now for the location. Whose place gets robbed?"

"I don't recommend another residence," replied Katie, shaking her head. "Too dangerous, even if the homeowner agrees to it."

"How about another bank?" suggested Ruth.

"No, that would raise suspicion," responded Katie. "I think it should be someplace that the thieves haven't tried before. A place that would tempt them."

After several suggestions, they finally agreed to approach Keith Early of Early's Drugstore. Keith and Ruth were old friends and had, in fact, dated throughout her junior year of high school. It was agreed, then, that she should be the one to ask Keith's permission to use his store.

"I'll come with you," volunteered Robert, looking at her anxiously.

"There's no need, Robert," replied Ruth. "Besides, you may be on shift at the hospital when I go to speak to him."

"Well, just schedule a time when I'm free," he insisted. "Or I could get someone to cover…"

"Robert Reed!" chuckled Ruth, leaning over and wrapping her arms around his neck. "I dated Keith a long time ago and then we broke up. He's now happily married to a lovely woman named Elizabeth and I will soon be the wife of a wonderful man with whom I am deeply and passionately in love."

Robert started to speak and then smiled sheepishly and pulled his fiancée onto his lap. "I was acting like a fool just now, wasn't I?"

"Yes, you adorable man," replied Ruth. "Now kiss me and then let me get off your lap before Mrs. Porter catches us."

Jim glanced over at Katie and saw that she was looking back at him. He said nothing but held out his hand toward her. She slipped her hand into his, blushing slightly, and both couples sat quietly for several minutes until the sound of Gertie, approaching with a tray of finger sandwiches, broke their combined reverie.

It was Katie who accompanied Ruth to Early's the next morning to handle the first stage of setting their trap.

"Hello Ruth, hello Katie," said Keith, greeting each woman with a friendly kiss on the cheek. "I see the team of Porter and White is still together."

"Yes, of course," replied Ruth, linking her arm through Katie's.

"And still up to trouble," added Katie, smiling.

"Which is why we're here," explained Ruth.

"We need you to allow a group of ruthless thieves to break into your shop and rob your safe," remarked Katie nonchalantly.

"This will be after you close for the night so no one will be hurt," Ruth assured him.

"Do you have an alarm system?" Katie asked.

"And you should empty out your safe in advance so nothing's actually taken," suggested Ruth.

"Is your alarm system backed up with a battery?" asked Katie.

"We'll be here watching to make sure nothing is ruined," said Ruth.

"Ladies, ladies!" exclaimed Keith, holding up his hands in a sign of surrender and looking from one to the other. "What on earth are you two talking about?"

Ruth and Katie stopped and looked at each other before bursting out laughing.

"I guess we should slow down and give you all the details," said Katie, catching her breath. "Ruthie, why don't you explain our plan to Keith while I shop for a pair of nylons and pick up a bottle of aspirin for my grandmother. I'll meet you at the cash register in 10 minutes."

It took less time than that when Ruth joined her in aisle 6 as Katie was trying to decide whether Nugget needed another chew toy when he already had over a dozen.

"He's agreed," said Ruth, smiling. "He'll wait for our call and then let us in the back door before he closes up for the night. He'll pretend to set the alarm in case the gang is watching but he won't actually do it so that we can leave whenever we need to. We don't want to set it off ourselves."

"Good idea," replied Katie, nodding as they walked to the checkout counter. "If the thieves follow the same MO by flipping off the electricity, they won't know any difference."

Katie paid for her items and she and Ruth left the drugstore and headed for Ruth's car.

"The Ruth White charm still works, I see," teased Katie, sliding in next to her friend.

Ruth smiled and started the ignition. "Anything for you, dear," she replied, pulling away from the curb and heading in the direction of Sunset Hill.

They arrived just in time to see Tom White walking up the long driveway toward the house. He turned and, seeing his sister's car approaching, stuck out his thumb like a hitch hiker and signaled for a ride.

"Excuse me, sir," said Ruth, rolling down her window. "But my mother taught me never to pick up strange hitch hikers," she teased him.

"But I'm not a strange hitch hiker, ma'am," said Tom, tipping his hat and doing his best imitation of an old sailor. "I'm your long-lost brother returned from the sea!" he joked.

"Really?" replied Ruth, allowing the car to slowly progress forward as Tom walked briskly alongside. "I don't recall having a long-lost brother but, all right, you appear to be a decent enough looking fellow. Hop in beside my friend and behave yourself."

"Thank you, ma'am," said Tom, hurrying around the car and sliding in next to Katie. "It is an honor to be in the company of such fine-looking ladies."

"Oh, for goodness sake, you two," Katie chuckled. "Will you cut it out? We have serious business to discuss and, unfortunately Thomas White, we're going to need your help."

"Of course, my dear future wife," replied Tom, his eyes twinkling. "I'll do anything for you, but it'll cost you one kiss."

"I seem to recall that you collapsed to the ground the last time I kissed you," Katie retorted, rolling her eyes.

"You kissed my brother?" Ruth asked, surprised, as she parked the car and they stepped out.

"She certainly did," replied Tom, taking both their arms in his. "It was when I burned down her shed."

"It's a long story, Ruthie," replied Katie, waving away any further discussion. "I'll explain later. Right now I need your worthless brother here to copy down the note we need to send to Frankie. It will look better in a male handwriting than in mine."

Fortunately she had the foresight to purchase some cheap stationary at the drug store and now placed it in front of Tom. She dictated while he carefully wrote and soon the note was completed. *"Hey Frankie,"* it began. *"Stopped by Early's drugstore on my way out of town. Noticed they have an American Sentry. Just so happens that Brinks did a pick-up while I was there. That would be Monday so they should be loaded again by Thursday. Might pass this along to the ghost so that you guys can make a hit. Just my way of giving back to the gang. Say hi to the boys for me. Walter."*

"That should do it," said Katie, folding the letter and placing it into one of the envelopes that came with the paper. She glanced down at her watch. "I've got to go meet Jim at the *Times* so that he can press on the fake postmark. Then we'll deliver it to the Boys Club."

"I hope this works," remarked Ruth, walking her friend to her roadster, which Katie had left at Sunset Hill that morning.

"It's got to, Ruthie," Katie replied, waving goodbye as she pulled away and started toward town.

She arrived at the *Middleton Times* and saw that Jim was waiting outside the building for her. He looked well-rested and as handsome as ever.

"Good morning, Ace," he greeted her cheerily, bending down to give her a kiss on the cheek. "Let us go into the building together to begin our life of crime."

"Good morning to you too, competitor," Katie chuckled, walking beside him through the front door. "My *Gazette* colleagues might say that entering the lobby of a competing newspaper is a crime in and of itself."

Jim chuckled as he led the way to his desk. "That's probably true but I was referring to placing a United States postmark on a letter, which is actually illegal. I'll be using this instead." And he opened a drawer and pulled out a rubber stamp and an ink pad.

"And this is?" Katie asked, dropping into a chair on the opposite side of the desk.

"A stamp that makes little lines on small sheets of music. It was made by a friend of mine who makes tiny things for doll houses," he explained, tapping it on the ink pad and then pressing it onto a blank sheet of paper. He held up the pattern for Katie to see.

"Not bad, Fielding," she replied, looking at the small parallel lines. "Do you think it'll work?"

"Not if someone studies it closely," shrugged Jim. "But no one really notices postmarks when they receive a letter, especially our youngsters at the Boys Club. I think it will work."

"You know the most interesting people," remarked Kate, smiling over at him.

"Yes, I know," he replied. He carefully addressed the envelope and placed a postal stamp on it before pressing the rubber stamp over it. "I don't think it matters that the address is written in a different hand than the letter itself. It would not be unusual for Walter to get the assistance of the postmaster in looking up the address of the Boys Club and writing it down on the envelope."

"Time to set our plan in motion, Mr. Fielding," said Katie, jumping to her feet and turning toward the door.

"Right beside you, Miss Porter," he replied, placing his hat on his head and following her out the door and over to her parked car.

The Boys Club was several miles from the *Times* so Katie had time to update Jim on what had occurred at Early's Drugstore that morning.

"So we're all set to stake out the store. I put in the letter that the next hit should be Thursday, which is tomorrow, so hopefully the letter will be picked up before then," explained Katie, making the turn onto Maple Avenue. "As soon as it's been taken, we'll call Keith and let him know that we're ready to spring our trap."

"Sounds good, Katie," replied Jim. "Let's hope it goes like clockwork."

They needn't have worried because the letter disappeared within an hour of being placed on the board by Jim. He and Katie had run over to Polly's for a quick lunch and returned to the Boys Club to find it already gone.

"That was quick!" replied Jim, returning to the car where Katie sat waiting.

"Yes," she answered thoughtfully.

"What's wrong?" he asked, sensing her mood as she started the roadster. "What are you thinking?"

"I'm wondering if this is indeed proof that one of the male volunteers is our ghost. Few boys were around this morning when we planted the letter. Unless Frankie or another of the gang happened to come by just at the right moment, the only people regularly at the club would be the instructors and Mr. Decker."

"Then I'll be knocking someone into next week," growled Jim, holding up a fist.

"Save it for tomorrow night, hero," smiled Katie, shifting gears in her little car as she picked up speed. "We might need that fist of yours when we apprehend our thieves at Early's Drugstore!"

CHAPTER 14
OUTSMARTED!

"Jim, wake up! You're snoring," whispered Katie, poking him in the ribs. She and Jim were sitting on the floor behind the pharmacy counter, their backs propped up against several cabinets. They were lying in wait for the thieves to break into Early's Drugstore and Jim had fallen asleep. Katie couldn't blame him, really. They had been there since midnight and it was now 3:00 in the morning. She had struggled to keep awake herself.

Across the store, Ruth and Robert were hiding behind a second counter, and Tom was behind a cosmetics display in the middle of the showroom. Andrews, the Porter's butler, was also there, though, at Katie's request, without his father's saber. He had stationed himself near the office door behind which the safe was located.

Although Katie expected no more than two members of the gang to show up, they hadn't wanted to take any chances.

"What? Where?" responded Jim, waking up startled and automatically reaching for a military sidearm that he no longer possessed. He came up with a pen, instead, that he had stuck in his trouser pocket.

"You were snoring," Katie repeated. "And please give me that before it goes off," she teased, taking the writing utensil from his hand.

"What time is it?" he asked, yawning.

"3:00," she replied, glancing once again at her watch. "We'll wait one more hour before we call it quits."

"Right you are, Captain," Jim responded, leaning back on the cabinet door and falling quickly back to sleep.

It seemed forever before the hour of 4:00 am finally came and Katie stood up from her cramped position behind the counter and called out to her team. She had to shake her legs to get the feeling back in them, before she could walk out into the middle of the store. Her tired friends, some of whom she suspected, like Jim, had been asleep for some of the time, joined her.

"I'm sorry, everyone, but it looks like we've been stood up. I don't know quite what happened but perhaps the gang discovered our plan, so I see no reason to stay here any longer. It will be dawn in a few hours so let's go home and try to get some sleep."

Mumbling in agreement, they left by the backdoor with Katie locking it firmly behind her. After saying their goodnights, Ruth and Tom left in her car, while Jim climbed into his Renault. Robert followed close behind in his car, leaving Katie and Andrews to bring up the rear in her MG roadster.

"All buckled in, Andrews?" she asked the butler sitting beside her.

"Yes, Miss Katie," he replied, grasping the passenger side door handle and holding his breath.

Katie pulled out onto the main street and headed in the direction of Rosegate. "You'll have to breathe eventually, Andrews," she teased him. "You can't hold your breath all the way home."

"I was a deep-sea diver during the war, Miss Katie," was his reply. "I'll make it."

Hours later, having slept through breakfast, Katie joined Gran for lunch at noon. She was weary and disappointed that they had not been able to nab the thieves.

"You must have known that might happen, granddaughter," said Mrs. Porter. "You couldn't be certain that they would attempt a break-in last night."

"That's true, Gran," nodded Katie, taking a sip of coffee. "But I had hoped. We have an abundance of clues but no real idea when they might strike next. Or where, for that matter."

"Can you be sure that the gang received the letter?" prodded Gran. "Anyone could have removed it from the bulletin board."

"That's possible, of course," replied Katie, tears coming to her eyes. It had been a completely wasted night. Why was capturing these crooks so difficult?

Her grandmother must have sensed her frustration because she reached over and patted Katie's hand.

"No use worrying about it, dear," she said softly. "You are a very smart young woman. I have no doubt that you'll figure it out."

Katie smiled weakly at her grandmother. "I hope you're right, Gran," she said. "Because right now I'm being outsmarted by a very clever ghost!"

The phone call from Mr. Martin of the First National Bank came about an hour later just as Katie was finishing her meal.

"Miss Porter, you were right," he exclaimed over the telephone. "We tested the delay in our alarm system, and it is 6 minutes, exactly. I called Mr. Watkins over at the Banking and Trust and his came out about the same, which is not surprising since we have the same system."

"Oh, Mr. Martin," exclaimed Katie. "This is good news! I mean, not for you, of course, but it does explain how the thieves were able to commit the crime without setting off the alarm, and why the police triggered it when they came to investigate."

"Yes, well," bristled the bank president. "I'll be making a call to the alarm company as will Mr. Watkins. They'll have to come out and adjust the timing so that there isn't such a long delay. Thank you for letting us know! Without your help we would have never discovered the vulnerability in our security." And with that, he said goodbye and hung up the phone.

The phone receiver still in her hand, Katie dialed Jim's number at home and then, when he did not answer, she tried the *Middleton Times*.

"Hello beautiful," he said softly into the telephone causing her to blush deeply.

"Hello Jim," she replied. "You took an awful chance that it would be me on the phone or do you always answer it that way."

"Well, it is easier than having to remember the names of all my women," he teased. "Although my editor didn't appreciate it when he called."

"I can imagine," replied Katie. "If you will give me the number to your direct line, I won't have to go through the *Times* switchboard. I suppose the young lady told you who was calling, which is odd since I didn't give my name."

"Ah, you caught me," Jim chuckled. "Mabel recognized your voice. You and my mother are the only women who ever call me."

"Poor man," she teased. "Are we done yet because I've heard from our bankers."

"Of course. What'd you find out?" he asked, becoming serious.

"There is a 6-minute delay from the time the alarm system is cut from electricity to when it transfers to battery backup," Katie informed him. "Plenty of time to pull off a heist if you're good at it."

"Doesn't sound like a very good security system," observed Jim. "So, what's our next move?"

"Well, I think I'll write a follow up to my original article and include some of the new details that we've found," she replied. "Hopefully that will rattle some cages and cause the gang to trip up."

"You mean do something during their next robbery to give us a chance to catch them," stated Jim.

"Yes, starting with letting us know the location of their next hit," Katie mused.

"A thought just occurred to me, Katie," said Jim. "We may be using the wrong mailbox."

"But the gang is at the Boys Club," Katie pointed out.

"But the ghost of Golden Joe is in the Rosegate Woods," replied Jim.

"And the mailbox is the stump by the creek!" exclaimed Katie. "Jim, you're a genius! Why didn't I think of that?"

"You would have, Ace," assured Jim. "If you had gotten as must sleep as I did last night."

"So our next move should be to check the stump to see if our ghost has left another message for his gang. How about tonight? We'll go right after dusk and intercept the message before the gang comes to collect it. Can you break a few dates with these beautiful women you speak of and come to dinner?"

"I would be honored," he replied. "See you at 7:00."

* * *

A crescent moon was just peeking through a layer of clouds in the night sky when Katie and Jim, flashlights in hand, quietly made their way across the back lawn of Rosegate and into the woods. With Katie in the lead, they crept along the path in the direction of the stump by the creek. Their plan was to check for a message first and then, if none was there, to hide and wait to see if Golden Joe would appear and leave one.

When they arrived at their destination, Jim checked and, finding no message, he signaled to Katie. They climbed up the small hill and, just as they had done before, hid behind a cluster of large tree trunks overlooking the clearing below and watched.

They expected to remain there for quite some time but, within minutes, they heard the now familiar wail of the ghost and saw its glowing form float down the path toward the clearing. Then it stopped and, glancing around in either direction, paused by the stump.

"Eeeeeeeeeeee!" it suddenly screeched, throwing back its head and sending chills down Katie's spine.

Gosh, I'll never get used to that! she thought to herself. She glanced over at Jim who gave her a meaningful look, his eyebrows raised. Perhaps this was a signal to the gang that another message had been delivered. Katie nodded. They were about to find out.

The ghost of Golden Joe then leaned forward and placed a message into the hollowed-out space in the stump. It then turned and, taking only a few steps this time, quickly vanished from sight.

Pausing for a several seconds to make sure the ghost was indeed gone, Jim and Katie scampered down the hill and over to the stump. Katie reached in and grabbed the message and, grasping it tightly, they made their way down the path until they were a safe distance away.

"Let's see what it says," she suggested, unfolding the message as Jim flicked on his flashlight and held it over the paper. As expected, the message was made up of pictures and numbers.

"The 5th letter in the word Tiger is an "r", and the 1st in Owl is an "o" so that gives us R-O," said Jim.

"The 2nd letter in Ostrich is "s"," said Katie, and suddenly she held her breath.

"And next is the "e" in Monkey," continued Jim.

"Oh no!" exclaimed Katie, her hands shaking. "We've got to run, Jim!"

It took him only a second to realize what she was saying. The remainder of the message spelled out the name Rosegate.

They dashed through the woods and out into the clearing, Jim pausing only momentarily to give Katie a chance to catch up. Then they sprinted to the mansion. They arrived to find the patio doors smashed to bits with shards of glass strewn throughout the hallway.

"Gran! Gran!" shouted Katie, carefully making her way across the glass and toward the library. "Where are you? Are you all right?"

Stepping inside the room, she heard a moan and quickly found her grandmother lying on the floor behind the sofa.

"Gran!" Katie cried, tears streaming down her face as she dropped to her knees next to the elderly woman and gently placed her head in her lap.

"Katie, I smell gas," said Jim, stepping in behind her. "Which way to your kitchen?"

"Straight down the hall and through the dining room," sobbed Katie, waving her hand in the direction of the hallway.

Jim ran from the room just as Gran slowly opened her eyes.

"What happened?" she asked, reaching up and placing a hand on her forehead. "Have I had a heart attack?"

"I don't think so, Gran," Katie replied, tears still running down her cheeks. "We've had a break-in and..." she stopped, noticing for the first time a small rag laying under her right foot. She had stepped on it in her haste to get to her grandmother. Picking it up, she examined it and then quickly tossed it several feet away. "Chloroform," she muttered. "Gran, you've been knocked out. Did you sense someone sneaking up behind you and holding this rag over your nose and mouth?"

"No, dear," replied Gran, pushing herself up to a seated position. "All I can remember is Nugget barking fiercely and then waking up to your worried face. You can stop crying now, little one," said Gran gently, reaching over to wipe away Katie's tears with her hand. "Your old grandmother is going to be all right."

There was the sound of footsteps upon glass and then Jim's head peered around the library door. "Are you all right, Mrs. Porter?" he asked in a worried tone.

"Yes. Katie help me to the couch," she instructed, as Jim stepped in to help Katie gently lift the woman onto the sofa.

"I've got to call for an ambulance and the police," he said softly. "We've had a close call, I'm afraid. I found Gertie and Andrews on the floor of the kitchen. Someone had knocked them out and then turned on the gas oven, locking the door behind them. Fortunately, the key was still in the lock, so I had no trouble getting in. I've managed to drag both outside and turn off the gas but everyone, including you, Mrs. Porter, should be taken to the hospital to be checked out."

"No, I'm not going anywhere," said Gran firmly. "They can take Gertie and Andrews, of course, but I'm fine. All I need is a few minutes until my head clears."

Katie looked over at Jim and gave him a slight shake of her head.

"Let's call Robert," she suggested instead. "He can examine Gran, Andrews, and Gertie and make the decision as to whether to call an ambulance. We will, however, have to call the police. The library is in shambles although it doesn't look like they got into the safe."

True enough, as they looked around the room, they saw dozens of books shelves cleared and their contents thrown to the floor. Two large urns, Porter family heirlooms, had been bashed to pieces and the mirror on the far wall smashed. The bookcase that hid the safe was also emptied of books but had not been pulled from the wall to reveal the safe behind it.

After making sure, one final time, that Gran was all right, Katie ventured through the kitchen and into the side yard to check on Gertie and Andrews while Jim made the calls to Robert and the police. The two staff members, more like family than employees, were sitting in the grass by a large oak tree.

"I tried to stop them, Miss Katie," said Andrews sadly. "But they overpowered me and clamped this rag over my face!"

"Are you both OK? Katie asked, bending down to take Gertie's hand. The housekeeper nodded her head but the look on her face told Katie that she had been frightened out of her wits. "Can either of you tell me what happened?"

"Yes," Gertie replied, glancing at Andrews. "I was at the stove just getting ready to lift the hot water kettle off the burner. Andrews was at the kitchen table reading me the news of the day from the *Gazette* while I made us some tea. We do that every evening about this time, after we get your grandmother settled in the library."

Katie nodded and smiled. She remembered sitting as a young child with Gertie and their former butler, Mr. Milton, in the kitchen as the elderly gentleman read the newspaper to them. Perhaps that's where she got her love for the news, she now reflected. It appeared that Gertie had kept up the tradition with Andrews.

"Suddenly two men, dressed in all black and wearing masks, burst in and grabbed me," said Andrews, adding his part to the story. "I tried to fight them off best I could, but they had the upper hand by surprising us. Before I knew it, they had forced a rag over my face and that's all I can remember until I woke up just now."

"When I saw what was happening to Andrews, I reached for one of my frying pans to use as a weapon to try and stop them, but a hand came around my face and out I went."

"Wait a minute," said Katie. "You saw two men struggling with Andrews and, at the same time, were knocked out yourself?"

"Yes, Miss," nodded Gertie. "That's right."

"Then there must have been at least three people who broke into the house," she said thoughtfully. "And that makes our break-in different from the others."

At that moment, they heard the sirens of approaching police cars. Telling Andrews and Gertie to stay put until the doctor could examine them, Katie walked back through the mansion to meet the police. As she passed through the hallway, she noticed evidence of more damage. Two side tables had been turned over and a landscape painting of Rosegate, done by Mr. Connor, had been slashed by a knife. Katie had bought the painting from her editor a few months ago as a gift for Gran on her birthday. Another mirror had been smashed and several holes punched in the wall in various places. Ironically, the front door was intact and untouched.

"They came and went from the back of the house," said Katie under her breath as she opened the door to Detective Grant, standing on the mat with a worried expression on his face. Just behind him was Sergeant Smith along with several other officers.

"Are you all right?" asked the detective, walking inside as Katie stepped back to allow them entrance. "Anyone hurt?"

"Everyone seems to be OK, Charlie, although we've called for a doctor. There has been quite a lot of damage, though."

"How much did they get?" asked Sergeant Smith. "From the safe, I mean."

"Nothing," replied Katie, looking steadily into the sergeant's eyes. "It doesn't look like they found the safe, but I suppose I ought to check." She led the way to the library and pulled away the bookcase. Sure enough, the safe was found locked and, after Katie opened it, they saw that its contents were untouched.

"Katie," said Jim, suddenly appearing by the library door. His face was pale and his expression grim. "Oh hi, Charlie. Sergeant. I've got something to show you all." And he stepped back into the hallway and headed to the Porter's game room, with Katie and the police following close behind. When they entered the room, Katie let out a gasp. Scrawled across the wall in large red painted letters were the words, *"you're next, Katie Porter!"*

"Looks like someone's out to get you," said Sergeant Smith, dropping her head over her notepad to hide the fact that she was smiling.

"Yes, I have to agree with the sergeant," Charlie nodded. "It looks like robbery wasn't the motive here. The intruders wanted to warn you off your story, Katie, by breaking up the place and roughing up your grandmother."

Jim came up behind Katie and placed his hands on her shoulders. "I think it would be prudent to assign some of your officers to Rosegate for the next couple of days, don't you think, Detective?"

"Yes, of course," replied Charlie. "I'll see to it personally. And you'll be working from home for the next few days, Katie, where we can keep tabs on you, just in case."

"No, I don't think so, Detective," said Katie rather loudly. "You see, tomorrow is Friday, and the country club is holding its big dinner dance as a prelude to the tennis tournament on Saturday. All competitors are expected to attend, isn't that right Jim?" she added, reaching up and patting his hand. "So, you can plan on us being there!"

Something in her tone told Jim Fielding that this woman, whom he loved more than life itself, was up to something. Most likely something dangerous. He vaguely remembered the dance and they had only tentatively discussed attending. She was setting the stage for a showdown.

"Yes, Katie's right, Charlie," he said, giving her shoulders a gentle squeeze. "We're required to attend."

"Well, I don't know," Charlie Grant mused, scratching his chin. "But since there will be lots of people there, I suppose it will be all right. Besides, you'll be right there with her."

"I'll never leave her side," smiled Jim.

At that very moment, Robert Reed, with Ruth at his heels, burst into the hallway and started for the library. Katie and Jim excused themselves and stepped from the game room to greet them.

"Oh Katie! Are you all right? How is your grandmother?" cried Ruth, taking Katie's hands in hers.

"She's all right, I think, but I would appreciate if Robert would examine her as well as Gertie and Andrews."

"How about you and Jim?" asked Robert, starting to pull his stethoscope from his medical bag.

"We weren't in the house at the time of the attack," explained Katie chagrinned. "We were in the woods wasting our time waiting on a ghost! I believe the entire thing was a trick!"

* * *

It was an hour later, as her friends and the police were leaving, that it occurred to Katie that she hadn't seen Nugget. He would have been following Jim all over the mansion.

She searched for him in the house but when he couldn't be found, she stepped outside and circled the building, calling his name.

Just as a feeling of panic began to overtake her, she finally found him sitting near a large flower bed by the front drive. He was covered in mud and held up one of his front paws.

"Nugget! My goodness, where have you been?" she exclaimed, scooping him up and carrying him inside. "You're a mess. What have you been chasing?"

The poor little dog whimpered as Katie shifted him in her arms. "Are you hurt?" she asked, examining his paw. She couldn't tell but, from Nugget's cries, she suspected that it might be broken. Trying to decide whether to give him a bath first, Katie picked up the telephone and dialed the number of Nugget's veterinarian.

"Hello Katie," said the kind voice of Dr. Spencer. "Is it one of the horses or that little rascal of yours, again?"

"It's Nugget, Doctor," replied Katie, trying to sound calm. "We've had a break-in at Rosegate and I'm afraid that Nugget's been hurt in the scuffle. His paw may be broken."

"Bring him in immediately, Katie," said the veterinarian firmly. "I'll ready our machine for X-rays."

With Nugget still in her arms, Katie slid into her car and quickly drove down the long driveway, giving a wave to the policeman guarding the front gate. She arrived at Dr. Spencer's office in under 10 minutes.

Dr. Harriet Spencer was quite fond of the little terrier and took the whimpering Nugget gently in her arms and over to the exam table.

"Nugget, you rascal," said the doctor softly, as she examined him. "You look as though you've been in quite a fight."

Nugget gave a yelp when she gently touched his right side. "Katie," said the vet. "I believe that Nugget's been kicked. I can't be sure until I take a few X-rays but, at the very least, there's bruising on several of his ribs."

Katie was shocked. She remembered Gran telling her that Nugget had been barking just before the attack. "I think that he was trying to protect my grandmother," explained Katie, her heart hurting for her pet. "She told me that he was barking at something. Or someone. The intruders must have kicked him to get him out of the way, although that wouldn't have stopped him."

"No, he's a brave little fellow, aren't you Nugget?" said Dr. Spencer, giving him a gentle pat on the head.

"He most likely chased them from the house. I found him outside by the flowerbed near our front drive," Katie confirmed, leaning closer.

"Well, several of his toenails have been chipped or broken off," replied the doctor. "That could make him a bit uncomfortable. I'll go ahead and do an X-ray, but I don't believe his paw is broken."

Twenty minutes later, Dr. Spencer had taken several X-rays and was able to report that Nugget had no broken bones, but his ribs were badly bruised as if someone had given him a hard kick and his painful paw showed indications of having been stepped on.

"This little guy is very lucky," said Dr. Spencer as she gently placed Nugget back in Katie's arms. "But he's going to be very sore for several days. Try to keep him as quiet as possible and give him these pills, twice a day, to help ease the pain. Please call me immediately if his condition worsens."

Katie nodded and, after thanking the kind veterinarian, climbed back into her car and gently settled Nugget in the passenger seat beside her. As she drove home, her anger rose. Golden Joe had led her on a wild goose chase through the woods while his gang broke into her home, attacked her grandmother and the staff, and hurt Nugget. She was furious. Someone was going to be held accountable for all of this. And soon!

CHAPTER 15
THE SHOWDOWN

"Katie, her name is Dorothy Smith," said Charlie Grant over the phone the next morning.

"Lovely name. How nice," replied Katie, rather sarcastically.

She could hear Charlie chuckle. "No, it's not that, friend. But I suppose I should start at the beginning."

"Always a good place, Charlie" replied Katie, propping the telephone receiver on her shoulder so that she could pull open the doors to her bedroom closet.

"I followed your suggestion and called over to the police department in Cumberland. The chief there had never heard of her, so I tried Wakefield. There I got an earful from the sergeant on duty."

"Really?" replied Katie, suddenly very interested. She stopped what she was doing and, coming over to sit at her desk, placed the receiver back in her hand and listened intently.

"Miss Dorothy Smith came to work for the Wakefield police station from a station over in Summerset. She had good references and, since she had worked for the police before, they hired her immediately."

"As a police officer?" asked Katie.

"No. As a secretary," replied Charlie. "She's not a police officer. Never has been.

"Interesting," murmured Katie.

"Yes, I thought you might find it so," continued Charlie Grant.

"About two weeks into her job at Wakefield, she started flirting with one of the officers. A young sergeant named Daniel Smith. Dorothy told people that she and the sergeant should get married because they had the same last name and she wouldn't have to change hers."

"Charming," Katie remarked.

"Yes. Except that Daniel wasn't interested. You see, he was already engaged to someone else, a nice local girl named Marie Stoddard. They had already set the wedding date and reserved the reception hall. So, everyone was quite shocked when Miss Smith and Sergeant Smith ran off together early one evening, leaving the future Mrs. Smith in the lurch. Folks there say she still can't believe it."

"Oh my!" exclaimed Katie.

"Wakefield lost track of Dorothy, but they were very surprised when I told them that Sergeant Smith was here in Fairfield, on temporary transfer, to investigate the bank heists…"

"Wait, don't tell me…" interrupted Katie, sitting bolt upright. "And that he is now a she."

"Exactly."

"Charlie, when she wears her uniform, which I must admit is rare," Katie asked. "What does her nametag say."

"D. Smith," replied Charlie.

"And her badge and identification card?"

"The same. D. Smith," he replied. "Although the picture on the card is definitely hers. Wakefield sent over Daniel's picture. He's a dark-haired young man with a beard. She couldn't pretend that was her picture."

"Easy enough to stick one of hers over his," responded Katie.

"Yes, that's true," replied Charlie. "The real question is why? Why would she want to impersonate a police officer and try to catch a gang of thieves? That's illegal. It would be better to have the real Sergeant Smith help her. Why isn't he?"

"Perhaps he's come to his senses and left her," suggested Katie. "And is now too embarrassed to return home."

"Perhaps. That would certainly explain it," he agreed. "If she's trying to protect a son or brother, who is part of the gang, she sure is going through great lengths to do the investigation herself. It would be much easier to ask each police department for help."

"Yes, the one here in Fairfield has been great," Katie quipped before she could stop herself.

"OK, I suppose we deserve that," replied the good-natured detective. "But we're not finished yet and we always get our man."

"Or woman, in this case," added Katie. "Charlie, do you dance?"

"Yes, why?" asked the surprised police officer.

"Because I think you should be at the country club dance tonight. I have a theory and, if I'm right, you'll need to be there to make the arrest."

* * *

The Fairfield Country Club was lit up with rows of flaming torches and colorful festival lights. The sounds of big band music filled the air and Katie smiled up at her handsome dance partner as he held her in his arms. Jim Fielding had bought a new suit for the occasion and he looked smashing. "I have to look nice for my girl," he had told her when he picked her up that evening. Now he was turning heads as they danced.

She, herself, had taken great pains to look extra nice for him. *Funny,* she thought to herself. *I've always dressed nicely for occasions but never specifically to impress someone. Must be...nope, I'm not going to think about that,* she added, stopping herself in mid thought.

She was wearing flats and hadn't counted on Jim being so much taller than she was used to, making it harder for her to gaze over his shoulder and keep track of everyone's movements. It was also easy to get carried away by the music and the delight of being in his arms and she had to remind herself to be ever vigilant. After all, it was she who had set the trap.

However, the evening proceeded at an uneventful pace and between dance numbers, Katie visited with several friends, took the ribbing of her tennis challengers, and traded gossip with Ruth and Robert.

Jim was also enjoying the evening. He found himself accepted into her circle of friends, a reflection of the changing times perhaps, as men from all segments of life had, just a few years earlier, found themselves fighting alongside each other in war against a common enemy and for a common cause.

"Having a good time?" Katie whispered, placing a hand on his arm.

"Yes, a wonderful time," he responded, giving her a warm smile.

"Mostly because I'm here with you."

She smiled up at him fondly. "Well, if you could stand to be away from me for just a minute, I need to go over and say hello to the Summers, but I'm parched. Would you mind grabbing a glass of lemonade for me if one's close by?"

"Sure thing," Jim replied. "There's a table on the patio. I'll be right back."

"Thanks, Jim," she said, turning to walk over to her friends.

Jim whistled as he climbed the steps to the patio. It covered the top area of a slight incline in the lawn and overlooked the dance floor at the bottom that had been installed for the occasion. The floor, itself, would disappear during the night and be replaced by concession stands for tomorrow's tournament.

"What a beautiful place," he was saying to himself when he spotted the car moving up the street. It slowed and then stopped a few feet from the party. At first, he thought that another party guest was being dropped off and he started to look away. But then, suddenly, he saw the light from the festival lights reflect off something metallic as Frankie Cooper stepped quickly out of the vehicle and silently approached. Call it intuition or a heightened sense of awareness, but Jim knew that it was a knife even before he could clearly see it. It was clutched tightly in Frankie's hand and he was creeping up behind Katie.

Without hesitation, Jim jumped over the patio railing and took two running steps across the lawn in Katie's direction.

The first swing of the blade just missed her, whizzing by her ear and blowing through her hair. Katie thought that a bug was buzzing her, and she was lifting her hand to swat it away when she suddenly felt herself being thrown to the ground.

Jim had taken a flying leap and tackled her and, as they fell, he felt the knife blade tear through his shoulder.

Within a split second, another blow struck him in the back and through his rib cage, driving deep to a point just below his heart.

Then there was the sound of someone running followed by the screeching of tires as the car sped away. Katie was aware of screams from those around them, the sound of running footsteps, and the heavy weight of Jim's body on top of her.

She slid out from under him, rolling him over and onto her lap. He looked up into her eyes and struggled to say something, but no sound came from his mouth. Suddenly, his head flopped to one side and he lost consciousness. She could feel his life beginning to slip away.

It was then that she noticed the blood. They were both covered in it. Rolling him slightly onto his side she saw the two wounds and she placed her hand over the one in his back trying to stem the flow of blood. She sensed someone coming up alongside her and she looked up to see Robert. He quickly knelt and, placing his medical bag beside them, started his examination of Jim.

All that Katie could do was to wrap her arms around Jim's shoulders and cradle him as he lay across her lap.

"No!" she heard a voice saying, realizing after a moment that it was her own. She was rocking slightly. "No, no, no!"

Someone must have called for an ambulance because the night was suddenly filled with the sounds of sirens. Robert looked over at Katie and whispered, "he's still alive but barely. His pulse is very faint and he's losing quite a lot of blood. I'm not sure he's going to make it, Katie. I'm terribly sorry."

Katie could only nod, tears streaming down her face. This is what she had feared most. This was why she had tried her best not to fall in love with him and now it had happened.

As Robert turned to signal the ambulance, Katie clung tighter to Jim and whispered, "Please Jim, please! Hang on! Don't leave me! Please don't leave me. Please!"

Suddenly the ambulance was there, and Jim was being pulled off her lap and onto a stretcher. The medics cut away his shirt and applied pressure to his wounds to stop the bleeding. He was then lifted into the back of the ambulance and an oxygen mask was placed over his face. One of the medics reached for a bag of blood and, strapping Jim's arm down, started the transfusion.

"That should help hold him over until they get him to the hospital," said Robert. "I'll ride along with him."

He stepped up into the back of the ambulance as one of the medics hopped down and quickly shut the doors, double checking to make sure the latch was closed. He then ran to the front of the vehicle and jumped into the driver's seat. Within minutes, they were speeding away with sirens blaring.

Her dress completely covered in Jim's blood, Katie, still sitting on the ground, looked up to see Dorothy Smith standing on the patio a few feet away. She was surprisingly lovely, dressed in a beautiful gold Lamay gown with gold slippers, her shoulder length hair flowing.

She was laughing.

"You may have succeeded in killing Jim but you're not going to get away with it!" exclaimed Katie loudly and, pushing off the ground, she started to sprint toward the woman. When Dorothy saw her coming, she turned and took off in the opposite direction, down a cobbled walkway, and into the dark woods that surrounded the country club.

"Dorothy!" yelled Katie, chasing after her. "It's no use! I know all about you!"

Dorothy let out a shriek that sounded like something between a cackle and a laugh. It sent a shiver down Katie's spine as she raced to catch up with the young woman.

The woods were dark and the narrow path not easy to navigate. Katie was thankful that she had worn shoes with low heels. Still, she tripped over hidden roots that slowed her progress and pulled at brambles that tore her gown.

A few yards in front of her, Dorothy was having the same difficulty and Katie had no trouble keeping her in sight. In her golden gown with its flowing sleeves, she resembled a ghostly apparition as she ran through the woods.

"This is not exactly how I had hoped to take her down," thought Katie. "But she WILL pay for what she's done, if it's the last thing I do!" and, with determination, she increased her speed and started to gain on Dorothy.

Suddenly, the two women ran into a large clearing along the edge of a cliff. Katie had Dorothy cornered.

"Time to give up," she said, standing with her hands on her hips.

Dorothy moved to the edge of the cliff. "Oh, you think so, do you, Katie Porter?" she responded.

"Yes," replied Katie, "as you can see, you've run out of ground. You have no choice but to give up!"

Dorothy dangled one foot over the edge and started to laugh. "You thought you were so smart, didn't you? But I was smarter!" she smirked. "You were all puppets and I pulled the strings!"

"Dorothy," said Katie, fighting to control her voice and keep it level and calm. "The police know about you and Sergeant Smith. They just want to talk to you about it. They'd like to help you. Come, let's walk back to the club," she urged, extending her hand out to Dorothy.

"You know," said Dorothy, giving Katie a sinister grin. "Jim Fielding is quite handsome and very fond of me. Asked to see me nearly every day. He's been playing you for a fool, Katie Porter. He pretends to like you, but he really wants to be with me. You're nothing to him."

Katie knew this game. Dorothy was trying to make her lose her temper and put her off her guard. She decided to turn the tables.

"Is that why Frankie stabbed him, Dorothy?" asked Katie.

"Frankie's an idiot!" snarled the woman. "He was supposed to kill you! How were we to know that Fielding would jump in and play the hero!"

"And now Jim will die," said Katie. "That's a murder rap, Dorothy, for you and Frankie."

Dorothy just shrugged her shoulders. "It's not like this would be the first time I've killed someone, Katie Porter," she said, turning back toward the cliff's edge, slipping her hands into the hidden pockets of her gown.

"What do you mean," asked Katie, newly alarmed.

Dorothy raised her chin, looked up at the sky, and let out a loud laugh.

"You really aren't very smart, are you?" she scoffed, "not the bright young ace reporter everyone thinks you are!"

Katie stared at the woman for a moment and then said, "I think you're bluffing. You haven't killed anyone."

"Oh, please," yawned Dorothy. "This is getting ridiculous!" And then leaning toward Katie, she said, "can't you guess who it is I've killed?"

Katie went over in her mind all the possible victims. The bank robberies and home burglaries had not resulted in anyone getting killed. Then it came to her.

"Sergeant Smith!" she said to Dorothy. "You killed him so that you could take his place!"

Dorothy laughed, "Good guess! Perhaps you're not that dumb after all!"

Katie was horrified but she tried not to show it. "Why? So that you could lead the gang of thieves and then interfere with the police investigation?" she asked.

"Of course!" Dorothy snarled. "It was so easy! I got Daniel away from his girlfriend, just like I was doing with your Jim Fielding. Silly men. They'll do anything for an attractive woman if you flirt with them even a little."

"How did you…" began Katie but Dorothy interrupted her.

"Kill him?" replied the deranged woman. "I poisoned him, of course. Slipped it right into his coffee and watched him die. I had no choice. He was going to turn me in to the Wakefield cops and then marry that girl. I killed him and then drove his body out into the woods and buried him."

"But not before stripping off his uniform shirt," interjected Katie. "You needed his identity to help you get out of town."

"Yes, of course," replied Dorothy. "It was all so easy! D. Smith became D. Smith! Then I bought a new uniform that fit better and buried Daniel's out in your woods. But your stupid dog dug it up. I should have shot the mutt when I had the chance."

Katie paused for a moment and studied the young women. "Isn't it time to stop all this, Golden Joe?" she said softly.

Dorothy looked startled and then started to laugh. "So you've figured that out as well, have you?"

"You came to town and started to put together your gang of thieves. You hired Frankie and Walter from the Boys Club because of Frankie's ability to walk on stilts and Walter's unusual talent for cracking safes," continued Katie. "You must have heard about our local legend of Golden Joe and so you decided to impersonate the ghost. The perfect way to scare the boys and keep them in line."

Katie thought she heard some rustling among the trees. Were the police finally coming? She had to keep Dorothy talking!

"Yes, it also helped to hide my true identity!" Dorothy smirked and then, rubbing her hands together, she added, "I had them all scared stiff! What a gimmick! First, I would put on my uniform and become Police Officer Smith," she said, giving Katie a lazy salute. "I'd case our next hit by pretending I was conducting the investigation on the bank heists. God, it was hilarious. I could hardly keep from laughing sometimes!"

"Then you would go into the woods and dress like Golden Joe," Katie continued for her. "And give the instructions to the boys, creating a code to make it mysterious."

"Yes," said Dorothy gleefully. "The real challenge was to make it believable but easy enough for them to figure out. Those kids are not the brightest bulbs in the box. Then they'd make the hit and bring the money to the ghost. I'd give them some and then take the rest for myself. And why not? I'm the brains of the outfit, after all!"

"Who dropped the empty money bag?" asked Katie.

"Frankie. He accidently lost it in your woods after taking the money out. I was pretty mad at him but then I realized that it could place the guilt on you," chuckled Dorothy. "The whole thing was a perfect set-up until you came along, Katie Porter!"

Now Dorothy, too, heard the rustling and she suddenly pulled something from her pocket. It was the size of a large flashlight and resembled a retractable antenna of sorts. She pressed a small button, extending it to its full length. Katie could now see that it was fencing foil that had been adapted to reduce small enough in size to fit into a small bag or a coat pocket. It had been filed down to razor sharp.

"One of my own designs," explained Dorothy proudly. "Light and compact but very sharp and lethal. Beautiful, don't you think?" And suddenly she lunged the foil at Katie, missing her by a fraction of an inch.

Katie stepped back and, glancing around quickly, grabbed a large stick and held it across her body in preparation of another attack.

"I'm going to finish you off," snarled Dorothy, stepping back and positioning her body in a menacing crouch. She tightened her grip on the handle of the foil. "And I must warn you, I'm pretty good with this thing!"

A twig snapped somewhere among the trees causing Dorothy to look away for a split second, and Katie saw her chance. She lunged forward, throwing herself against Dorothy, and grabbed for the weapon. Although she managed to get both her hands on it, she could not release it from the other woman's grip.

Dorothy was surprisingly strong and the struggle that ensued was fierce. Katie knew that she was fighting for her life and she used all her strength to keep Dorothy from gaining the upper hand. As they struggled, Dorothy, looking over her shoulder, realized that they had moved very close to the edge of the cliff. She suddenly stopped fighting and let go of the foil. Then, clutching Katie's wrists, she stood still and smiled at her. Katie, caught by surprise, also stopped fighting and, in that moment, Dorothy Smith flung herself over the edge of the cliff taking Katie Porter with her.

The two police officers running into the clearing heard a scream and then a thud.

"Katie!" shouted Charlie Grant, running forward.

"I guess we're too late!" exclaimed the second officer, following close behind.

They carefully made their way over to the edge of the cliff and looked down.

"Well, I'll be!" Detective Grant exclaimed. He quickly dropped to his belly and stretched his arm down the side.

A foot below hung Katie, hands grasping a tree root, her legs dangling in the air.

"Hi Charlie!" she smiled upward. "A little help, please?"

Katie finally reached the hospital 6 hours after Jim had been taken there by ambulance. She was still wearing her blood covered dress, but she was unmindful of the stares as she walked down the corridors on her way to his room. She was frantic to know his condition, so hadn't even considered stopping to change. When the hospital's receptionist told her that Jim was no longer in surgery and had been moved to room 306, on the third floor, she started breathing again.

His room was dark and, at first, she didn't see Ruth sitting by his bedside. Ruth quietly got up from her chair and greeted Katie as she entered.

"There you are," she whispered. "I'm glad you made it. We nearly lost him several times but he's going to be all right," she added. "He's sleeping now."

Katie crept quietly toward the bed and looked down at the man she loved.

"Oh," was all she could say, the realization of what could have happened causing her knees to weaken. Ruth quickly put her arms around her friend and lowered her into a chair.

"He's going to be all right," Ruth repeated. "Fortunately the ambulance medics started an immediate transfusion, so Jim was receiving blood even before he got to the hospital. They tell me that's what most likely saved him."

"Ruthie, I..." Katie couldn't finish. The day had been too much. The story, Frankie trying to kill her, holding the dying Jim in her arms, struggling to get the fencing sword away from Dorothy, falling over the edge of the cliff, Dorothy's crumpled dead body at the bottom, the lateness of the hour, and now facing Jim's narrow escape from death. Katie was exhausted. It really, *really*, had been too much.

Thankfully, Ruth White didn't expect an explanation, or any conversation, from her. Seeing Jim's blood covering her friend's torn dress, the scrapes and bruises on her arms and hands, and the relieved but exhausted look in her eyes, Ruth said nothing more and leaned forward to hold Katie's hand as she fell soundly asleep in the chair.

Katie dreamed that she was running through the woods at Rosegate with Nugget. They were chasing the ghost of Golden Joe but every time they closed in on him, he just evaporated into thin air. "He's not real. There's no reason to be afraid. He's not real," Katie was telling the dog in her dream.

Then Nugget turned to her and said, "Katie," in a soft lovely baritone voice. "Wake up, Katie Porter."

She awoke and lifted her head to see Jim looking at her fondly. It was morning, and she had apparently slept slumped over in her chair, with her arms and head resting on his bed. He had awakened to find her there and had reached out to stroke her hair. Although still very pale, he looked wonderful. She, however, knew she looked awful and she ran her fingers through her hair and tried to brush off her dress.

"No need to worry, Miss Porter," Jim said, smiling. "You always look gorgeous to me!"

"Jim," she whispered, looking at him with relief. "I'm so glad your..." but her words caught in her throat and, overcome with emotion, all she could manage to do was reach over and rest her hand on his cheek.

He brought up his own hand and laid it over hers. "Do you have any idea how much I love you?" he asked softly, gazing into her beautiful blue eyes. "I know I'm probably not supposed to say it, but I do love you, Katie, with all my heart."

She said nothing for a moment as she looked back at him. Then, quite suddenly, everything became very clear to her. She was no longer afraid. She was no longer reluctant. She knew exactly what she wanted, and she knew exactly what she was going to do. She leaned over and kissed him deeply, sending a shock wave through them both and leaving them breathless.

"Wow," was his reply when they finally separated, his handsome face breaking into a wide grin.

"Wow," she nodded with a shy smile. "I love you, too. When I thought I had lost you..." She shook her head and couldn't finish.

He had risked his life to save hers. He had jumped in without hesitation or thought for his own safety. Her greatest fear had always been that she would lose him just like she had Ruddy. But she also realized that this hadn't prevented her from falling in love with him. Love, it seemed, had a will all its own.

"So, are you really all right?" she asked, regaining her composure.

"Well, the knife wound that hit my shoulder didn't do much damage. I'll have to wear a sling for a while, though, so that it heals properly," Jim replied, looking toward his shoulder. "Robert tells me that the knife wound in my rib cage was a bit dicey, but I should be back on my feet again in a few days. The bandage wrapped around my chest hurts almost worse than being stabbed," he added, smiling.

"Everyone awake?" came a voice from the door. Katie and Jim looked up to see Robert entering the room carrying a large cardboard container. "Katie, I thought you might be hungry, so I brought you some breakfast from the cafeteria. It's not Camilles but at least it will tide you over for a while."

"Oh Robert, how wonderful!" exclaimed Katie, realizing that she was indeed very hungry. "It smells delicious!"

"I didn't know what you wanted so I got a little of everything," remarked the doctor. "Sorry, I can't stay and visit. I've been so busy wrestling our friend here from the clutches of the Grim Reaper that I've fallen completely behind in my rounds."

"Robert, I don't know how I'll ever be able to thank you for saving my life," said Jim, looking up as a nurse entered the room with his hospital food tray.

"Don't thank me yet until you've tasted the food," joked Robert, turning to leave.

"Robert," Katie said, stopping him before he could go. She stood and walked over to him. "I don't know how I'll ever be able to thank you either." And she threw her arms around his neck and hugged him tightly.

Robert held her for a moment, rubbing her back. "There, there, Katie," he said gently. "No need to thank me. I'm just lucky that Jim is too stubborn to die. Besides, I owed you one."

"You did?" Katie asked, releasing him and stepping back. "For what?"

"You were the one who introduced me to my Ruth," replied

Robert. "The least I could do was to keep Jim alive for you." And, with that, he left the room, whistling his way down the corridor.

Jim looked from his food tray to Katie's container and sighed. She chuckled and shook her head.

"I'm sure this is against doctor's orders," she teased, slipping him two pieces of bacon as the nurse left the room, closing the door behind her.

As they ate their meal, Jim finally noticed Katie's dress.

"My blood?" he asked.

"Afraid so, Fielding," she replied, glancing down at the garment. "As soon as I get home, it's for the trash heap."

"I suppose I owe you a new one," Jim replied.

"I suppose I owe you my life," responded Katie softly, and she leaned over once again and kissed him.

CHAPTER 16
THE GHOST OF GOLDEN JOE

The night sky was clear, and the stars shown bright, as Jim and Katie walked slowly through the woods at Rosegate. They had brought several packets of hot dogs out to the Badger Tribe and their chaperones to roast over their campfire.

"I'm sorry you couldn't camp out with them and sleep under the stars, Jim," said Katie, as she illuminated the path in front of them with her flashlight. It had only been three days since his release from the hospital and his arm was still in a sling. His ribs were free though of their constrictive wrapping leaving the wound covered only by a large bandage.

"That's OK," he replied, smiling. "I wasn't looking forward to the hard ground anyway."

Katie chuckled. "Poor Mr. Decker. He had to take your place although the boys would have much preferred you."

"We must all make sacrifices, sometimes," teased Jim with an exaggerated sigh. "Which reminds me. You took yourself out of the tennis tournament. Why? You were the leading contender in all of the matches."

"Except in mixed doubles," replied Katie, gazing up at him. "You may recall that I lost my partner."

"But Katie," Jim countered. He stopped and looked intently at her. "There are at least a dozen men who would have stepped in and taken my place."

"No deal, Fielding," she replied, squeezing his hand. "No one is taking your place. And as for the other matches, well," she added after a while, "it seemed rather silly for me to be playing in a tennis tournament while you were laid up in the hospital."

Jim smiled warmly at her. "Well, Robert and Ruth did well, at least. I believe Ruth took first in every category she played with the exception of mixed doubles where she and Robert came in second."

"Yes," nodded Katie, and then added with a chuckle, "Mark Dickson and his wife won again but he refused to take my money for losing the bet. He told me that he wanted to hold it over until they have a chance to play against us. We'll beat them next year!"

"Well, then," replied Jim, his eyes twinkling. "I guess we'll have to start getting in plenty of practice!"

"Indeed," smiled Katie. "And now that we're not running through the woods chasing ghosts, we might just have the time."

"Which reminds me," Jim remarked. "You never got a chance to finish telling me how you figured out it was Dorothy Smith behind this entire scheme."

"Hm," Katie said, pausing for a moment to collect her thoughts. "Well, you may remember that I was always bothered by Dorothy not turning in evidence. But I may not have even noticed that she had slipped the magnet into her pocket had she not first made such a fuss about Nugget finding the police sergeant's uniform shirt. Not turning in either piece made me suspicious so, after I had Dorothy's confession, Charlie and a team of police officers searched her motel room and her car and eventually found the shirt stuffed under the driver's seat. He sent an officer over to Wakefield and the folks there confirmed that the shirt belonged to Daniel Smith."

"Have the Wakefield police found his body yet?" Jim asked.

"No, not yet," Katie replied solemnly. "But his fiancée, although grief stricken, at least knows now that Daniel did not run away with Dorothy and had actually planned on arresting her and turning her in."

"What a dangerous woman!" exclaimed Jim, shaking his head.

"Interestingly enough," Katie continued, nodding. "If the Wakefield police had bothered to check on their new employee's references, they would have found out that they were fake and that our dear Miss Smith had a rap sheet a mile long."

"She may have realized that the Fairfield's police station *would* check, so she became an officer "on loan" from another department," Jim guessed. "Since she had already taken on the identity of Sergeant Smith to help her get out of town. Her behavior certainly fits with Miss Water's analysis of her handwriting…lack of remorse, thoughts of entitlement, and justifying her actions in order to get what she wanted."

"Yes," replied Katie. "And, in a practical sense, working as a police officer gave her the opportunity to case banks and homes as potential hits as well as interfere with the investigation. She's been robbing banks for years and almost always recruited poor or neglected boys in need of money. That's why she sought out the Boys Club. According to Frankie, there was a flyer placed on the bulletin board looking for boys willing to do odd jobs, which is how she got hold of Walter. You were the one, Jim, who told me that he worked to put food on the table. It was Walter who recruited Frankie. After a few weeks, they were instructed to meet a ghost in these woods to get their instructions. It was their fear of Golden Joe and his possible retribution that kept them in line. Besides, Dorothy made sure that they were paid for their trouble by giving them a small cut of the loot."

"Who was it that took our fake letter off the bulletin board?" asked Jim.

"I can't be sure, but it was most likely Dorothy herself," Katie answered. "Charlie told me that she had given herself the assignment of tailing me all over town. He actually shuddered when he told me. She must have seen us plant it there."

"And the magnet trick and figuring out the alarm delays?"

"Tricks of the trade she picked up during her years of committing such crimes," explained Katie, shrugging her shoulders. "The one thing she never mastered, though, was safe cracking which is why Walter was so useful to her. She must have been very angry when he skipped town and she had to deal with using other boys."

"Have the police caught Walter yet?" Jim asked somewhat sadly.

"No. Frankie's been arrested along with two other boys. The stilts were found in the trunk of Frankie's car, by the way. But Walter is still on the run."

"This may sound awful, Katie, but I hope they never catch him," remarked Jim. "I don't condone what he's done, of course, but I do understand what it's like to support one's family."

They walked hand in hand in silence for a while, thinking about

Walter's fate. Jim didn't know it, but Charlie had told Katie that the Fairfield Police were not rushing to find the youngster. And Katie had replied that if they ever did, she would personally pay for the best lawyer in town to defend him.

"How on earth did Dorothy manage to become a ghost?" Jim asked suddenly, breaking into Katie's thoughts. "We all saw it. She was quite convincing."

"Phosphorescent paint, black clothing, a mask, and a flowing hooded cape," chuckled Katie. "I found several cans of it along with the mask and cape in a wooden box stashed in a small shed just on the other side of the creek. It occurred to me to look there when I was taking down Mr. Connor's damaged landscape from the wall in our hallway. The shed appears in the painting."

They paused for a moment so that Jim could catch his breath.

"For her nocturnal meetings," continued Katie, looking up at him. "Dorothy would wear black trousers and shoes, put on the mask which resembles an old miner, and then wrap herself in the cape. She had painted one side of it with gold phosphorescent paint but left the other side black. In the darkness of the woods, her legs and feet virtually disappeared making it look like she was floating. And when our ghost wanted to vanish, all she had to do was flip the cape over her head and body, revealing the black side. Because our eyes couldn't see her in the darkness, we were tricked into thinking she had disappeared when, all along, she was crouched on the path under the cape where she waited until the coast was clear. Add a bit of great acting and, poof, you have the ghost of Golden Joe."

"I imagine the old legend helped as well," added Jim. "It's funny how people believe what they want to believe or, perhaps, are frightened into believing."

"Yes," replied Katie. "They refuse to accept the truth even when they may know it deep in their heart," she added sheepishly. "But I'm glad I was finally able to accept mine, *cariad.*"

Jim stopped and looked at her in surprise. "So, you've uncovered that, as well," he remarked, grinning widely.

He was leaning over to kiss her when Katie caught glimpse of something a short distance away on the path in front of them. She gasped, and Jim, turning, saw what looked like a glowing orb spinning slowly. It was floating several feet above the ground and, as they watched, it slowly began to unravel, morphing into a shape, not quite human and not quite ghostly. More like a rippling mass of yellow glowing light. After a few seconds, the shape stopped spinning and Katie and Jim could just make out the whiskered face of an old man. He floated over the path for a few moments smiling at them. Then, giving a nod, he suddenly flew up through the treetops, disappearing into a burst of light that joined the stars.

Their jaws hanging open, Jim and Katie turned to look at each other.

"Did you see...?" Jim started to ask.

"Nope, didn't see a thing," Katie answered, shaking her head. She clasped his hand tightly.

"Yeah, you're probably right," Jim answered.

They continued along the path and into the clearing, slowly making their way home.

* * *

"Dear mother," began Katie in her journal late that evening. She always addressed every entry that way. It was a type of mother-daughter discussion that she had adopted long ago as Mrs. Porter, although still very much alive, was not available to her only child.

I've been terribly afraid for a very long time and didn't know it. Perhaps it was because my fear didn't lie on the surface, not even when being chased by a ghost or attacked by a dangerous gang. Those things didn't frighten me. No, my fear resided deep within my own heart. But I suppose that's where most people hide their fears.

What a mighty emotion it is! It's a primal instinct that has kept our human species alive. Sadly, it's also what can influence the choices we make. And, if we're not careful, it can be used against us by evil people to manipulate our thoughts and actions.

Someone once said that the definition of courage was not that one wasn't afraid; it was that one did what needed to be done despite it.

For me, well, I am glad that I have finally found the courage to love again and that has made all the difference in the world.

Katie

~ THE END ~

ABOUT THE AUTHOR

K.T. McGivens is best known as a poet and her poems have been published in newspapers, community publications, and anthologies. She has written six books of poetry and recently published an anthology of her best works.

She has now ventured into the world of mystery novels and has begun writing a series of short mystery novels featuring her character Katie Porter. The novels are geared toward young adults and focus on strong female characters, problem solving, trusted friendships, and tenacity; a formula she learned from growing up reading the Nancy Drew Mysteries.

Ms. McGivens grew up in Maryland and earned both a Bachelor's Degree and a Master's Degree from the University of Maryland. She now lives in the panhandle of Florida.

Made in the USA
San Bernardino, CA
27 May 2020